"Kudos to one of television's best producers for writing the thriller of the year."
Sam Donaldson, White House reporter

"If the phrase 'a crackling good yarn' evokes an era before Twitter, Facebook, cell phones, videotape, DVD's or cable television, welcome to Terry Irving's fast-paced thriller."
Ted Koppel, anchor for NBC Nightline

"Terry Irving was one of the most imaginative and enterprising television producers I ever worked with. It's not surprising then that Courier' is a terrific page-turner with a clever backdrop and compelling characters."
Erik Sorenson, President of MSNBC

"In his debut thriller, Terry Irving masterfully re-creates early 1970s Washington, and then proceeds to race the reader through his world at breakneck speed. True to its title, Courier delivers!"
Erik Daniel Boudreau, author of Tidal Force

"If you can remember the Sixties, you never lived through them. If you lived through the Seventies, you'll never forget. Irving masterfully brings back the cold-eyed conspiracy lurking behind the smiley face."
Marshall Arbitman, senior writer, Anderson 360 on CNN

"I am a former rider myself, and I was instantly transported back to that feeling of tremendous power between my knees and feeling my hand twist the throttle just a little bit more – pushing my personal limits to balance the fear with the utter exhilaration I felt."

Loriann Murray, Scribbles & Sensibilities

TERRY IRVING

Courier

ANGRY ROBOT
An Angry Robot imprint
and a member of the Osprey Group

Lace Market House,
54-56 High Pavement,
Nottingham,
NG1 1HW,
UK

Angry Robot/Osprey Publishing,
PO Box 3985,
New York,
NY 10185-3985,
USA

www.exhibitabooks.com

An Exhibit A paperback original 2014

Cover by Nick Castle Design
Set in Meridien and Franklin Gothic by ePub Services

Distributed in the United States by Random House, Inc., New York

ISBN 978 1 909223 79 0
Ebook ISBN 978 1 909223 80 6

Printed in the United States of America

9 8 7 6 5 4 3 2 1

To Ann, for everything.

CHAPTER 1

Tuesday, December 19, 1972

It felt like the motorcycle had become a part of his body – a part that made him whole. The back tire of the BMW R50/2 had started to lose traction on the crusted ice – ice that had hung around for months in the shadowed parts of the alley, where the sun never reached. The wheel was spinning now and drifting left, the back end approaching a ninety-degree angle to the front, but Rick Putnam realized, with a bit of surprise, that he wasn't concerned.

He saw the patch of dry concrete coming up and blipped the throttle just a bit as he crossed it. Dropping his weight back on the bench seat made the rear wheel grab on the concrete and pop back into alignment. It was all reflex action – as automatic as walking.

At the end of the alley he flicked his eyes to the right, saw an opening in the traffic, downshifted, and slammed across the sidewalk. Entering 19th Street, he locked the rear wheel, threw his body to break the big bike to the right, and skidded smoothly into the moving line of cars. He heard the screech of brakes, and an angry horn went off behind him, but the bike was already picking up speed, flicking past the two- and three-story brick-row houses.

He liked Washington. It was as if the city had exploded during World War Two and then stopped, exhausted from the effort. The town houses were modest and usually a bit crooked, the brick painted every color imaginable, and the stores, restaurants, and bars on the ground floor varied and eccentric.

The relatively few large office buildings stood out like Stalinist mistakes – square and featureless, built to the exact millimeter of the height limitations. Alleys cut through the center of most blocks, often just cobblestones or an uneven mixture of asphalt and concrete patches.

A century ago, these alleys had held a separate city of poor whites and freed slaves. Rick had learned that from the same rider who'd showed him how they were the secret to the city – a way to evade traffic lights and bypass commuters. The alleys may not have held another city these days, but they were still more than just urban driveways. Hidden from view were bars, restaurants, nightclubs, and little food stores – a Washington that tourists would never see.

He took the right onto K Street and all thoughts of the city – and everything else – were lost in the crystalline concentration of the dance.

Fifteen miles ahead of the courier, a specialist in the restoration of silence began his latest assignment.

In a quiet Virginia suburb, his black Chevy Impala was parked against the curb on Fairfield Street some fifty feet from where Fairfield met Fairmount in a T intersection. Taking off his hat to lower his profile, he sat perfectly still and watched the single-story brick Colonial straight ahead of him – the perfectly white shutters and clipped shrubbery indicating a precise, even obsessive, owner. A white AMC Jeep Wagoneer with a strip of simulated wood running down the side sat at the curb, partially blocking his view of the lawn but still revealing a carefully placed wooden Santa and a pair of wicker reindeers.

Looking through the Wagoneer's windows, he could see large, heavy-looking equipment cases that had obviously been pulled from the Jeep's cargo area. One case was open, revealing shiny metal rods and bits of colored cellophane. He assumed it was lighting gear for the television crew now inside the house. They were probably filming their interview and almost certainly did not know they were being observed.

He scanned the street in front of him, then, without moving his head, methodically checked behind him in the rearview mirror. Catching a glimpse of himself – something unusual since he never sought out mirrors – his startling blue eyes under deep brows stared back. Women might find them mesmerizing, but he regretted how they made him so easy to remember. Usually he wore dark sunglasses, but in today's gray afternoon light, sunglasses might result in one of those curious second looks that sometimes proved so inconvenient.

He had spent many years making sure he was neither noticed nor remembered. His name – which a long time ago had been Ed Jarvis – had faded under a succession of false identities, leaving him defined by his occupation: an operative, an agent, a useful tool to get things done, a restorer of silence. Stroking his mustache down, making it just a bit less noticeable, he resumed his watch.

Fairfield Street was tree-lined, quiet. No one was walking a dog or scraping the last bits of ice off their driveways. It had begun to warm in the past few days, and there wasn't much ice left, anyway. That was good; he'd seen enough ice for a lifetime. When he thought about it, which was far too often, he could feel the searing cold of a Korean winter still sleeping deep inside him.

His careful scrutiny went on for a full fifteen minutes. Nothing set off his internal alarms. He got out of the car, took a beige parka from the backseat, and put it on over his gray suit. Then he began to walk down Fairfield Street, away from the T intersection. There were no sidewalks, so he walked in the road – just far enough away from the curb to stay out of the puddles of snowmelt. Keeping a steady pace gave him the appearance of a man out for a little exercise to break up an afternoon cooped up at home.

He made three left turns, circling the block, and approached the Colonial from the opposite direction, his deliberate pace giving him time to verify that no one was in any of the backyards. Without changing his pace, he walked past the left side of the Wagoneer, reaching down slightly and placing a small box into the top of both wheel wells. He could hear the faint *chunks* as their magnets pulled them tight against the metal.

He continued back to his car, feeling confident that – even if anyone were watching – no one would have noticed such a minor change in his stride. Back in his car, he sat for a long moment to be certain that no one had appeared on the street or come to look out of any nearby windows. Then he put the car in drive.

Moving at a smooth, unhurried speed, he turned to the left on Fairmount, away from the house, and made three right turns to circle around the block behind the house. Now he was certain that there were no other surveillance teams watching the Colonial. He didn't think any other team – even from the FBI or CIA – would be a problem, but it was always satisfying to know that he could work free of distractions.

He came slowly down Fairmount from the same direction he had just approached on foot and stopped as soon as he had a good view of the Wagoneer. He was safely hidden behind a Dodge station wagon, and after looking up, he reversed a couple of feet into the deep shade of an oak tree. He knew the shadows would only deepen as the short December day waned.

Then he sat and waited.

Waited to do his work.

To stop the voices.

To restore silence.

To kill.

The left lane was clear, and Rick came up through the gears, hearing the solid *ka-chunk* each time the transmission engaged. The BMW might not be slick, but it was steady, dependable, and fast enough if you gave the engine the time and torque to reach full power. It didn't have a tachometer, so he listened to the exhaust sound and shifted a couple of seconds after the engine's normal throaty putter rose to a shout.

By the time he hit the elevated freeway that cut past Georgetown, he was in top gear and running fast. The wide handlebars felt solid and secure under his thick gloves. Even the winter wind, which was numbing his face and slicing through the zipper of his leather jacket, felt good – a sharp, cold bite after the steam of the overheated news bureau.

That would change in just a few miles, the zipper stream becoming a shard of ice impaling his heart, his face stiffening, hands cramping into claws, only his eyes behind the heavy glasses safe from the wind's sharp whip.

There were cars lined up at M Street, but hell, why ride a motorcycle if you couldn't dance? He kicked down to second, slid between cars on the centerline, cut in front of a Dodge waiting patiently for the light to turn, and swung up onto Key Bridge.

Halfway across the Potomac River, he was back in top gear, and he cut the corner hard when he reached the Virginia side – almost grinding the big side-mounted cylinder on the asphalt – and let the bike fly down the entrance ramp to the George Washington Parkway.

Traffic clotted the parkway – commuters and, undoubtedly, police cars up ahead. None of that mattered. He was dancing now, carving graceful curves right down the centerline in top gear with the throttle nailed. Cars flashed by as he wove between them.

He couldn't look at the speedometer, couldn't take his eyes off the road, couldn't spare a second of concentration from the delicate ballet of shifting weight, tire grip, and wide-open throttle, rejoicing in each deep dip into a turn and the swooping acceleration coming out.

He jolted back to reality when the exit to Chain Bridge Road came up on the right. Unable to bleed off enough speed before the exit, he took the curve way too fast, jamming the bike down on its side, twisting the handgrips against the turn – fighting to keep his wheels from drifting into the treacherous gravel on the outside. He knew that if he touched the brakes, the tires would lose all adhesion and fly out from under him.

He kept his gaze straight ahead – searching for the end of the turn – and the BMW held like it was locked on rails as it carved a perfect line through the curve. The rear end had just begun to drift slightly when he spotted the stop sign and straightened up. Now he could use the brakes, and he quickly wrestled the bike under control.

As he stopped, he felt the strange upward lift that the old-fashioned Earles front suspension always gave when he put on the front brake. Any other bike would plunge the front down into the telescoping front forks; the triangular links of the BMW floated the stress up and forwards.

For just a second, he kept the clean clarity of the dance in his mind, and then it was gone. Memories came flooding back. Blood, and stench, and screaming, the terrible beauty as napalm set the tall grass on fire and flowers of light burst from snipers in the trees. Only the dance could fill up his mind – speed and real danger frightening him enough to keep the phantom terrors away, if only for a few precious moments.

Rick sighed, then kicked the gearshift down into first and turned right – heading for his next film pickup.

CHAPTER 2

Rick spotted the Wagoneer as he came up Fairmount, and swung the bike in a semicircle right in front of it. Then he stopped, released the brakes, and let it slide backward until it bumped against the curb just in front of the Jeep. He pushed forward just a bit and then yanked the heavy machine up onto the center stand. He took off the scratched helmet with the tattered ABN News stickers and set it on the adjustment knob that sat in the center post of the handlebars.

It was about fifty degrees but dropping fast into the forties. Rick felt a bit of the loopy fog in his head that meant his core temperature had dropped, but it wasn't too bad – certainly not severe enough to slow him down on the way back. He took off the heavy riding gloves and bent down to cup his hands over the twin opposed cylinders – the "jugs" that gave a BMW its perversely old-fashioned look. He took care not to touch the hot metal but got his hands close enough to absorb some of the intense radiant heat.

He could feel sensation trickle back into his fingers, numbed even through the gloves' triple layers of leather. As he waited, he looked at the scarred and twisted palms of the gloves and remembered the time in the snow when he was so cold that he'd put his hands right on the red-hot exhaust pipes. At least the heat had permanently seared the gloves into the right shape for holding handlebar grips – if for nothing else. He didn't even want to think of what his bare palms would have looked like.

As soon as his hands had warmed up enough to regain flexibility, he unzipped the chest pocket on the worn and cracked leather jacket, pulled out a pack of Winstons, and then dug into his jeans for a battered steel Zippo. It was so worn that the engraving on the front and back was almost invisible. He snapped the lighter down and then back up against his thigh, flipping back the top on the downstroke and spinning the wheel to light the wick on the way up. It was a trick that showed years of practice.

Lighting his cigarette, he inhaled deeply, almost hungrily, and then pulled a paperback copy of *Fear and Loathing in Las Vegas* out of the back pocket of his jeans. Settling backwards on the motorcycle seat with his back resting against his helmet and his Frye boots up on the metal radio bolted over the rear wheel, he began to read.

Rick had only finished a couple of pages before the front door opened, and Joe Hadley came out and stood silhouetted in the light fanning out from the living room behind him. A small, neat man in a dark suit with a fat polyester tie and carefully combed hair, Hadley was the Associated Broadcast Network's best investigative reporter. He was the best because he was always on the move, walking at a pace that kept taller men almost jogging to keep up, breaking off conversations to make a phone call whenever he passed a pay phone, or to consult the narrow reporter's notebooks he carried in his coat pockets.

Now, Hadley was writing furiously in one of those notebooks, face impassive as he worked. Suddenly, he jumped and spun around with a curse.

"Damn it. I hate when you do that, Ed!"

"Well, if you'd get out of the damn way, it wouldn't happen." Ed Farr, the cameraman who had just goosed him, was a tall, thin, balding man in slacks and a dark blazer. He moved smoothly past Hadley and headed for the courier, carrying an enormous film magazine that looked like a pair of steel Mickey Mouse ears. Rick reluctantly turned over a corner of a page in his book to keep his place, returned it to his pocket, and swung his long legs off the bike.

"That had better not be a twelve-hundred-foot mag," he said as the cameraman approached. "You know we're not supposed to carry them anymore after Art got one caught in his rear wheel and damn near killed himself on the Beltway."

"It's twelve hundred feet of pure artistry, and if you think I'm going to get out the damn light bag and spend thirty minutes canning it for you, you're dumber than the rest of the cycle monkeys." Trying not to show the effort, Farr tossed the magazine to Rick, who caught it with one hand as if it were made of plastic instead of at least thirty pounds of metal. Farr looked impressed.

"Looks like you're keeping up with the weights, kid."

"Yeah, well, it's that or let the North Vietnamese win. The doctors in Japan said I'd never use this arm again." As he spoke, Rick put his right hand at the center point between the magazine's two round drums, balanced it, and then lifted it up and down in slow, lazy bicep curls. "But I'm still not sticking this monster in my bag. Are you trying to kill me?"

"Fucking right I am, and even if I wasn't, we don't have the time. This guy wouldn't stop talking, and you'll have to hustle to hit the soup by the deadline."

Tempting as it was to get into an argument with a cameraman, Rick knew Farr was right. One of the fixed facts about television news was that it took forty-two minutes for sixteen-millimeter color positive film to pass through "the soup" – the automatic film processor back at the bureau that developed, fixed, rinsed, dried, and spun the film onto edit reels.

Checking his watch, Rick realized that he was indeed going to have to hurry if this story was going to make the first network broadcast at 6 o'clock. That was OK, since pushing his bike to the limits for a legitimate reason was even better than just dancing for fun.

"All right, I'll do it this time because I like you. Remember what happened to Walt last week? Next time it could be you."

Ed's face flushed with anger. "Listen, you stupid bastard. I find that you've ever screwed with one of my magazines, I'll kick your ass! Simmons should have had that courier fired for that stunt."

Rick reflected that the courier actually had been fired, but that it didn't seem to bother him much.

Evidently, taping the end of the raw, unexposed film to a stop sign and letting all twelve hundred feet spill out behind him to be irretrievably ruined by sunlight as he drove away was a sufficiently satisfying statement of how he felt about cameramen and their bullying ways. Good couriers could always get another job, anyway.

Rick smiled at the memory of Walt Simmons's reaction – he'd screamed and smashed things in the crew room for over an hour.

Then, Rick nodded agreement to the cameraman and turned to pack the magazine securely into the battered canvas bag strung alongside the right rear wheel in an improvised web of bungee cords. The tough newspaper delivery bags a couple of the other couriers had swiped a few weeks ago would do the job, even if the bright red *Washington Star* logo looked a bit tacky.

"Take good care of this." Hadley was scurrying over from the front porch. "This is a goddamn big story. It'll make those jerks at the *Post* look like idiots and Watergate look like a cop taking an apple off a fruit stand."

"Well, I was planning to drop it in the Potomac, but now that you've told me how important it is, I'll try to restrain myself." Rick finished strapping the magazine down tight. "Now, if you gentlemen will stop bothering me, I'll be on my way."

"Wait!"

Pete Moten, a young black man who was the sound tech and apprentice cameraman on the crew, ran out of the house carrying a small camera and a metal film canister with red adhesive tape around the edge.

"Take the 'B-roll' with you. There's some still in the camera, so take the Bolex, too." The Bolex was a small hand-wound camera used to record "B-roll", silent cutaway shots and exteriors that would be combined in the edit room with the "A-roll", the film with an optical audio track, which had been shot with the primary camera.

"Shit," said the reporter, "I almost forgot about that. I don't know if we need to send it in. This guy gave us the whole story in the interview."

"Are you kidding? Talking is one thing." Pete patted the Bolex. "I got the real deal right in here. When you see what I shot while you were trying to get a straight answer out of that number cruncher, you're going to make me a real shooter. I'm telling you, man, I've saved your ass. Remember how Smithson caved to the White House on your last piece? Well, this time we've got the goods."

Paul Smithson was ABN's Washington bureau chief and – like many other senior press executives in this "company town" – had first worked in politics. He had risen to senior counselor to the Vice-President and then capped it off with a stint as White House Press Secretary before cashing in with a well-paid job with the networks. He didn't have to do much work, and the network got better access to the administration. It was a good deal for all concerned.

Usually, he had almost nothing to do with actual news – leaving it to the producers and desk editors – but two weeks ago, he'd ripped into Hadley over a report on questionable campaign contributions. The

reporter hadn't been able to document everything –
too many anonymous sources – and, eventually, he'd
had to make a painful public apology.

Investigative reporters were always caught between
stories that weren't big enough to be interesting and
stories that – like the money story – weren't solid
enough to stand up to the inevitable attack from those
accused of wrongdoing. Hadley knew his days as a
network correspondent were numbered if he blew
another story.

It didn't mean he was grateful for Moten's careless
reminder.

"Listen, *boy*. You're only here because someone
decided we had to hire some tokens after '68. It sure as
hell doesn't give you the right to tell me how to do my–"

Rick cut the reporter off. "Give it to me, Pete."

He liked Pete. As a group, network cameramen
were nasty to everyone, but they really took their
venom out on the one black guy with the audacity to
try being a shooter. It took guts to put up with it, and,
anyway, Hadley reminded him a little too much of
some jumped-up lieutenants he'd had to serve under
in the army.

He took the can, stashed it deep into the bag
underneath the heavy film magazine, and grabbed the
camera. He unzipped his jacket, tucked the camera on
his chest, pulled the zipper back up, and patted the
bulge.

"OK, safe as a baby. Now, can I please get out of
here?"

The reporter swore again and walked stiffly back
toward the house. Rick pushed the bike off the stand,

jumped on the kick-starter with all his weight, waited an instant, and then smiled as the twin cylinders caught with a rumble. He glanced both ways, waved over his shoulder, and headed off the way he'd come in.

Concentrating on building up speed, Rick didn't notice as the black Chevy pulled out and drove at a conservative pace down the street behind him. Passing the crew, now stacking camera cases into the rear of the Jeep, the driver pressed a button on a remote control on the seat next to him, saw the glow of the remote's green light reflect off the dashboard, and followed the taillight of the motorcycle into the dusk.

Rick took a different route back to the bureau – crossing Chain Bridge and pushing hard down the long curves of Canal Road. He was caught up once again in the dance, but this time, it wasn't just speed that occupied his mind. Increasing darkness and a slight mist were making it difficult to tell if the road ahead of him was wet or just shadowed. After months of driving the massive bike at its limits, he'd developed a visceral reaction to the parts of a road with poor traction. They would literally make his stomach hurt.

Since he was moving against the outward flow of commuter traffic, he still made good time as he cut back over Whitehurst and ripped down K Street. He was certain to beat the deadline with ten minutes to spare – time for the editor to make at least a couple of quick cuts before it was raced down the hall to the projectors. Hadley would have to read into the live microphone in the studio and match the pictures by watching his edited film roll on a monitor in the control room, but it would come together.

It always did.

As he picked up speed on the downhill slope of 18th Street – a block from ABN – Rick smiled as he remembered his early days at the bureau. Practical jokes were a constant. The assistant directors in particular had lots of free time and inventive minds. Several times, they'd told him to deliver the film to Joe Telecine – at least until Rick worked out that the room with the "Telecine" sign was just the transfer room where television was made from cinema.

Suddenly, the part of his mind that never stopped screening traffic demanded all his attention. He had long ago realized that the only way to stay alive on a motorcycle was to make it a rule that any accident would be his fault, because he'd sure as hell pay the penalty. That way he was always ready for drivers who would squeeze him into a line of parked cars without a glance or decide to make a left turn directly in front of him.

A black car coming along L Street on his left wasn't slowing as it neared the intersection at 18th. Rick rechecked – the light was still showing him a clear green. His eyes switched back to the car and saw that the driver's head – outlined in the store lights behind him – was turned so that he stared directly at the big motorcycle.

The black car blew the red and entered the intersection only yards ahead of Rick.

Time slowed.

Rick slammed down on both brakes, and both front and rear wheels began to skid. It felt like the side of the car in front of him was crawling by, stretching out longer and longer to fill all possible avenues of escape.

As his wheels screamed on the pavement, Rick knew that he was losing steering control and forced his right hand to loosen up on the front brake lever while keeping a full lock on the foot pedal that controlled the rear brake. He was bringing his speed down fast, but that damn black car was still blocking the road in front of him.

That son of a bitch must have slowed in the intersection!

He could feel the rear tire begin to skip and knew he was losing precious traction every microsecond that it spent in the air. He needed to get the back wheel down and in solid contact with the road – fast. He slammed his body back and actually came right off the seat to sit on top of the radio, throwing all his weight directly over the rear tire.

He felt the tire grab the road as the tread caught, and the stuttering of the rubber treads became a steady scream. He was still going too fast to go anywhere but straight ahead and that damn car was simply not moving fast enough to get out of his way, so he tensed for a jump. Getting his body up in the air and flying over the car's trunk would mean some nasty scrapes on the other side, but it was either that or turn into a red smear on the rear fender.

He fingered just a bit of tension back into the front brake, and that made the difference. He flashed past the car, and time jerked back to normal. His right leg couldn't have been more than a half-inch from the wicked-looking steel bar that topped the rear bumper.

He unlocked the rear wheel and slowly, carefully, pulled over to the curb and stopped. His hands were so clenched that he had to force them to relax finger by finger. After he released his death-grip on the handlebars, he held his gloved hands out in front of him and just watched them shake for a long moment.

The right hand – the brake hand – felt strained as if it were still grabbing for more stopping power. He looked down the right side of the BMW. The rear brake pedal was bent, almost broken. Calmly, he thought: going, *Going* to have to stop by the garage and get that fixed.

He looked back, expecting to see that the Chevy had stopped, and the driver was coming over to see if he was OK. More likely, he'd come over and yell at him for getting in his way.

The black car was gone.

As he sat there, he saw the light finally turn red.

Rick blew out a deep breath and drove the half-block to the bureau – slowly and carefully.

CHAPTER 3

The GW Parkway southbound was almost empty, so Ed Farr had the big Jeep way up over eighty miles per hour. He knew that they had to get to the bureau in time for Hadley to write and voice his story, and he was confident that they could fast-talk their way out of a traffic stop. After all, they were legitimate members of the national press corps on an important story, right?

Hadley was in the backseat, alternately looking off into the middle distance and furiously scribbling in his notebook. Pete Moten was in the front passenger seat. He lit a cigarette, leaned forward, and turned on the radio before remembering that he'd left it set to a soul station before they picked up Hadley.

The fast funk of "Whole Lot of BS" filled the car.

The reporter shouted without looking up, "Turn that crap off!"

"Cool out, man," Moten responded. "Just relax and feel the beat."

In the left-side wheel wells, two timers finished their countdowns, and the explosive devices clamped over the tires detonated almost simultaneously. Custom-made, they were essentially the reverse of a claymore mine. The standard US Army claymore was a convex metal plate covered on one side with C-4 explosive and ball bearings – built to spray death outward in a wide swath. These devices were built on a concave steel plate so that the relatively small explosion drove tiny ball bearings inward like a spear, shredding the tires instantly, but leaving little evidence of an explosion on the body of the car. The small metal boxes fell to the side of the road as the blast destroyed the batteries and released the electromagnets that held the devices to the vehicle.

The heavy Jeep swerved violently to the left, throwing the soundman and the reporter against the doors and wrenching the steering wheel out of the cameraman's hands. None of them were wearing seatbelts.

At this point in the parkway, right after the first scenic overlook, the grass median was wide and dropped down to a V-shaped point in the middle.

After lifting up onto its two right wheels and almost rolling sideways, the Wagoneer smashed back down just as it hit the median's lowest point, bottoming out the heavyweight springs and sending a spray of mud and frozen grass out to both sides. When the two-and-a-half-ton vehicle hit the opposite slope, it was still moving at over sixty miles per hour and the release of the massively compressed springs and its own momentum launched it into the air as it tore up the slope. It soared over the northbound lane, slowly rolling over to the right in midair and passing directly over a VW bug. It just clipped the low stone wall at the opposite shoulder with the right rear tire and began to roll forward as it disappeared.

The VW pulled into the parking lot of the scenic overview and jerked to a stop. The driver, a pale and shaken college student, opened his door, threw up, and then just sat and shook. His girlfriend got out of the passenger side and approached the stone wall at the edge of the drop. To her right, she could see the line of smashed trees and torn bushes that marked the path of the Jeep, but she couldn't see where it had landed. She climbed the stone wall and, clutching the sturdiest branches she could find, leaned out over the precipice.

At that point, the George Washington Parkway climbed high on the rocky shelf above where the Potomac River, driven by its rush down the six-hundred-foot-high fall line between the Appalachians and the coastal plain, had cut a deep wedge in the land. The Jeep had dropped about a hundred yards and smashed into one of the rocks that emerged from the rushing brown water.

The Jeep lay upside down, and the girl almost didn't recognize it as a vehicle. Then she realized that the roof had not only been flattened on the rock but actually driven inward, giving the tall truck-like vehicle the squashed look of a stepped-on cardboard box. As she watched, Pete Moten's cigarette ignited the fumes from the ruptured gas tank and a fireball erupted – painting orange shadows on the trees on the opposite bank and brushing her face with a gentle rush of warm air even far above where she stood.

She worked her way back to the parking lot, got in the car, told her boyfriend to pull himself together, start the car, and get her to the closest phone booth – even though it didn't look as if there could be any survivors. Since the closest phone was several miles away at a gas station on Chain Bridge Road, it was over a half hour before the DC police riverboats fought their way upriver from their base near the Tidal Basin to the crash site.

The bodies weren't identified until long after midnight.

CHAPTER 4

Rick strode up the short walk to the back door of the news bureau without taking off his battered helmet; radio and gloves clipped to his belt, boots tapping on the concrete, wearing the black T-shirt, worn blue jeans, and leather bomber jacket that made up his everyday wardrobe. His long, unruly hair came out in a spray from under the helmet, and his heavy black-framed glasses – essential for cutting windblast on the bike – gave him a studious look at odds with the tough image most couriers cultivated. To an observer, only the tightness around Rick's blue eyes – normally calm and somewhat bemused – would have revealed his anger over the close call with the black Chevy.

He had, of course, already lit up a cigarette. He held it in his left hand as he balanced the massive film magazine upside down over his shoulder with his right. Ridged pink scars webbed the back of the right hand, only a preview of the chaotic moments in battle and the long months of painful recovery that had been written in blood down the right side of his body.

Pushing through the two doors at the entrance, he started down the main hallway. Even after several months working for the news network, Rick still felt a thrill when he came into the bureau as the approaching deadline for the evening news stirred the place into an organized frenzy. Looking left, the newsroom was a sea of battered metal desks pushed into groups of two or three under harsh fluorescent lights. The room looked chaotic, with a lot of people moving quickly and talking loudly, but Rick knew the underlying choreography that welded them into a team.

In the far corner, a half-dozen wire machines the size of suburban mailboxes were hammering against long rolls of yellow multicopy paper. Two desk assistants tended the bulky machines, listening through the continuous jangles of single and double bells, which meant updates and new slugs, for the sequence of seven bells that signaled a significant news event. Every few minutes, they would rip the top four layers of paper against the sharp faceplate on the front of a wire machine, leaving the bottom copies to continue falling into serpentine piles in the back. The other copies were rolled, marked, and taped, then quickly brought to the senior producer, both writers, and the anchor.

The writers, quiet, older men who looked like they came straight out of the cast of *The Front Page*, scrolled through their rolls of wire copy. One would stop and rip out a particularly interesting story against the edge of the desk, spiking the ragged pieces on a small metal rod. The other – who wore a green plastic eyeshade – would meticulously clip items by holding down the scroll and slicing them off with a metal ruler and then fold them, mark them with a story title, and spread them in neat rows down the side of his desk.

Either way, by the end of the day, both of their desks would be covered with a slurry of wire stories, newspapers, and notepads. Periodically, they would turn to the solid upright typewriters that sat at a right angle to their desks, insert a thick script pack of ten interleaved colored pages and carbon sheets, and hammer out a few seconds of the anchor's script.

Over on the right side, the production assistant was discussing graphics with one of the artists, and as usual, it was escalating into a loud argument. The artist was defending the creative merit of her four-by-six gel, while the PA patiently tried to explain that, while it was indeed beautiful, it simply didn't have anything to do with the story it was meant to illustrate. In Rick's experience, graphic artists were eternally unhappy – torn between genuine artistic talent and the demands of producers with all the aesthetic vision of a plundering Visigoth.

The senior producer and the DC anchor were sitting at side-by-side desks near the front of the room. As usual, they were on the phone, probably talking to New York, their faces tilted down and their eyes glazed – their attention totally devoted to the conversation. The producer, a chunky middle-aged man named Tom Evans who somehow managed to keep a lit Lucky Strike between his lips even while talking, glanced up and saw Rick and raised his eyebrows in a mute question.

"It's Hadley's," Rick called, lifting up the film as he walked past. Evans nodded and gave him a thumbs-up before turning his attention back to the phone wedged between his shoulder and his ear.

"Jeez, hurry up and get that in the soup," said a voice to his right. Rick had to rotate his whole body to see around the bulky film magazine and find film editor Don Moretti standing in the door of his edit room.

"I've got to cut that for the six and I'll only have…" Moretti checked the large clock that hung over his edit table just as similar clocks hung in every room in the building. "Twelve minutes as it is."

"Darn, and here I thought I could take a cigarette break before I brought it in."

"You would, you son of a bitch." Moretti grinned and spun back to the big Steenbeck flatbed screener where other elements of the story were already loaded through the intricate maze of sprockets and audio heads.

Rick liked the brash editor. He was always moving, talking, and joking – leaping from subject to subject. Still, he was one of the fastest and most accurate editors in the place, and when it came down to those final minutes before air, Rick had often heard from the reporters that they wanted Moretti working their piece. After all, Moretti was the best damn editor in town. At least, that's what he would tell anyone who would bother to listen.

On the other hand, he also claimed that he'd played rhythm guitar and sung backup on Crazy Elephant's classic bubblegum song "Gimme Gimme Good Lovin'", but the song had come out while Rick was in Vietnam and he hadn't heard it enough to be sure it was Moretti's voice.

When he didn't have a run, Rick would spend hours in Moretti's edit room, absorbing the flow of the newsroom: the desk assistants running the scripts to the technicians, who typed them on to the paper cue rolls that would appear in a mirror in front of the anchor; the intense conversations between reporters and producers as they mapped out a story; directors race-walking down the hall to the control room to polish the final product. He enjoyed the atmosphere of rough camaraderie and black humor combined with serious conversations about oil shortages, election strategies, and distant wars.

Then there were the editors in their white cotton gloves, furiously spinning the film reels on either side of their edit bench. They would grab shots they had chosen earlier from where they were hanging above a cloth-lined cart – held by pins through their sprocket holes – whip them down onto the sync block to match them up with the rest of the edits, and then pull them off and onto the splicer. Two flashing cuts with the splicer's diagonal blades, a strip of tape to hold the ends together, and a final double slam of the side blades to trim the clear editing tape so that it was just slightly bowed in and wouldn't jam when it went through the projector. Don had told him that real film editors only used tape splices on a working copy and sent the original film out for professional processing for a smooth final cut. There was no time for that in a newsroom.

Rick continued down the narrow hall, past the audio booth where the recording engineer sat studying for his law degree – a clear indication that the reporters weren't ready to lay down a track yet –

and then made a right turn into the back hall. On the left were the double doors with the sign that labeled them as belonging to the office of the mythical Joe Telecine. Through the small window on each door, Rick caught a glimpse of the "two-inch" videotape machines in the back – the engineers who operated them bellied up as if they were playing six-foot-tall pinball machines. That was unfamiliar territory: union engineers had no time for scruffy couriers.

Straight ahead was the film crew's ready room, with battered lockers, equipment cages made of chain-link fencing, and at the end, his destination – film processing.

As usual, the place amazed him. A catwalk across the entire rear of the room held enormous white plastic tanks of chemicals. Alternating stacks of silvered aluminum and bright red plastic film cans covered the walls on either side, and on top were piles of shipping bags made out of a rough twine netting stamped with "Urgent Shipment Newsfilm" and the bright blue ABN logo.

Power lines and plastic pipes of all sizes ran in racks overhead and converged in the center of the room at two large machines. These were the automatic processors, which never stopped grinding away. When there was no new film to develop, yards and yards of clear junk film would be running up and down between spindles and in and out of chemical baths – the first baths covered with lightproof seals, and the later ones open.

The smaller unit to the left was for when the film needed to be darkened or lightened or have the color balance adjusted. The massive main unit on the right took up most of the room, churning out thousands of feet of sixteen-millimeter color-positive film a day. Rick could see the flickering images of developed film rolling toward the final take-up reels. The rest was clear. He knew that this meant Hadley's story wouldn't have to wait for another story to finish.

Two men in white jackets, looking like doctors or mad scientists, tended to the machines – checking temperatures, tapping meters, running tests on the chemical baths. One of them, a slight man with a receding hairline named George, looked up as Rick walked in.

"That's Farr's material?" he asked, and when Rick nodded, he sighed and said to the other technician, "Damn it, you know that Farr will have the aperture wrong."

In a thick German accent, the reply was, "Well, then run it through the B unit and correct it." Rick had never learned the other film tech's name. The man was taciturn and forbidding when he was working and not there at all when he wasn't.

With a dramatic sigh, George took the heavy magazine and headed toward the tiny darkroom where he would transfer the film to a lightproof covered reel that fitted to the input end of the processor. The film would then be rough-spliced into the endless reel of junk film and start its journey.

Rick pulled the Bolex out of his coat and said, "Hey, I got Moten's 'B-Roll' as well."

George didn't even turn around. "I'm not wasting my time with that goddamn windup toy; it takes forever to unload. Moten can pull the film out himself when he gets back. It'll be good practice." He closed the door, and the red Do Not Enter sign lit up.

The other technician said, "And don't even think of leaving that damn camera in here. Nothing gets dumped in here unless it's going straight into the soup."

Rick shrugged and put the camera back inside his jacket. He glanced up at the inevitable clock on the wall. It was 5.10, which meant there was plenty of time for the film to make air, even if it was the lead of the broadcast. As he turned to leave, he wondered if it would make the show at all. The collapse of the Paris peace talks and the massive B-52 raids on Hanoi would probably take up most of the precious few minutes of airtime.

Hadley would be lucky if he got his story in before the second commercial and the turn to incredible medical discoveries, "slice of life" tales of everyday nobility, and perhaps a water-skiing squirrel.

CHAPTER 5

The black Chevy pulled up in front of the house in Virginia. The driver was concerned that he had missed the courier but knew he had been successful with the reporter and the news crew.

He'd just spent thirty minutes in a traffic jam on the Parkway as cars crawled past a mass of police cars and tow trucks, and drivers had craned their necks out of their windows to catch a glimpse of the circling police helicopters.

Yes, he had failed to dispose of the courier, but he'd stopped at a pay phone, made a call, and requested that the film the biker had been carrying be taken care of. He didn't particularly like having others involved, but he knew he should use his contacts when necessary, and this would be as effective as calling in an artillery strike. The film would simply disappear.

Now it was time to deal with the talkative bookkeeper. He was certain the man was still home – lights were on in the first-floor windows and a car still sat in the driveway.

Again, he sat patiently for exactly fifteen minutes as he checked for lights in neighboring windows, evening strollers, or anyone else who might notice anything unusual happening in the small Colonial. Once, he slid down a few inches when headlights came up from behind, but the car passed and turned left without a pause.

Finally, he took off his hat, placed it on the seat next to him, and leaned back to pick up a white towel from the backseat. As a rule, he made a habit of staying at YMCAs in major cities whenever possible. They were cheap, anonymous, and no one counted the towels in the swimming pool area. He smiled briefly, thinking how odd it was that the Washington Y banned all bathing suits from the swimming pool – everyone went swimming naked. After that scandal with the old man in Eisenhower's administration, you'd think they'd have learned.

He slid out of the car, careful to close the door slowly, and only released the latch after it was shut, so that it engaged with an almost inaudible *chunk*.

At the front door, he placed the towel over the porch railing, out of sight of the door, then patted his front pants pockets and, satisfied, rang the bell.

Marshall Reese opened the door. He was only in his early thirties, but already his hair had retreated from the crown of his head to the sides and back with only a few carefully arranged strands pasted over the top. His eyes looked weak and nervous behind a pair of thick steel-framed glasses. He was still fully dressed with his necktie snugged up tight, and his collar buttoned.

"Hello, I'm John Snyder with ABN. I'm working with Hadley. Can I come in?"

Reese didn't reply, simply turned and walked away, leaving the door open. The agent picked up the towel, followed him in, then turned and carefully closed the door. For a moment, he continued to stand facing the door as he pulled a pair of yellow dishwashing gloves from his pocket and pulled them on.

Reese hadn't noticed – he was walking into the kitchen. "You're welcome to come on back and have a drink, but I can't imagine what you could possibly want. I told that guy everything." Then he added, softly, almost to himself, "And now, I've got nothing. If I don't get out of here, I'm going to lose my job or go to jail."

There was a third alternative that he clearly had never considered.

The white towel flipped over Reese's head and pulled tight against his face, completely covering his mouth and nose. A quick shove and the bookkeeper was face down on the floor with his visitor straddling his torso and pulling back hard with the towel, the ends wound around his fists.

After a moment of stunned surprise, Reese began to struggle to get free and fought to draw a breath. But the pressure never ceased, and the towel remained cruelly tight. After a few moments, his body went limp.

His attacker kept the pressure on for a full five minutes longer, then released the towel. He stood up and carefully inspected the body. There were no bruises on the back, Reese's heavy wingtip shoes had protected his furiously kicking feet from injury, and he had given the man no chance to reach back and grab or scrape him. He was pleased to see that Reese hadn't lost control of his bladder or bowels, because cleaning that up was always the worst part of this sort of work.

He was satisfied that this had gone just as he planned. There would be no signs of an unnatural death and no evidence of a struggle.

Turning, he walked into the kitchen, cheerily decorated with avocado-green appliances and country-style curtains. From Sears, he thought, probably all bought in a single trip. He stepped to the gas stove, pulled up the knees of his trousers, and, crouching down, opened the broiler, and peered inside.

He nodded as he confirmed that the main gas line to the stove came through the rear of the broiler in a flexible metal tube and not a solid steel pipe. In the end, it wouldn't make any difference, but it would mean a bit less work.

Straightening up, he went back to the body in the living room and, without any obvious strain, picked it up in his arms. Walking back into the kitchen, he placed it in one of the kitchen chairs, carefully crossing the arms on the table and resting the head on them. Stepping back, he checked the position from several angles and felt satisfied that it would look like Reese had fallen asleep. Noticing an open bottle of bourbon on the counter near the sink, he opened cupboards until he found glasses, and arranged the bottle and a glass in front of Reese's hands. Paying close attention to details was a habit that had kept him out of trouble for a long time.

He returned to the living room and carefully searched for any scuffs or scrapes left by the struggle on the hardwood floor or the imitation Persian rug. Then he picked up the towel, folded it carefully, and returned to the kitchen. Pulling a jackknife from his pocket, he put the towel on the floor in front of the stove, kneeled down again, and carefully pulled out the entire broiler drawer. He placed it on the towel to avoid getting grease on the floor.

Reaching into the open space, he located the metal gas hose. With his left hand, he pressed it firmly against the rear of the stove and shoved the knife he held in his right hand against one of the flexible joints until there was a small slit in the hose and he could smell the artificial odor they added to the normally-odorless gas to warn people of leaks.

He replaced the drawer with the smell of gas fumes already wafting over him. Standing again, he reached inside his pants pocket and pulled out a device similar to the one he'd used on the reporter's car. This one, however, was simply a small amount of C-4 explosive and a remote-control detonator. He placed it carefully on the top of one of the black metal rings on the stove where it was unlikely to leave identifying marks.

Again, not that it mattered much.

He had taken care of some problems after Dealey Plaza, and had become convinced that, even if police investigators suspected something wasn't right, so long as they thought there was any kind of official involvement, their reports tended to attribute the incident to either accidents or natural causes. Hell, if cops could accept that a mobster with terminal cancer just happened to shoot the prime suspect, they could swallow anything.

He picked up the towel and left the house, wiping down surfaces and turning off the lights as he went. Outside, he closed the door firmly – listening for the *snick* of the lock as it engaged – then took off his gloves, wiped the doorbell with the towel, and walked without haste back to his car.

CHAPTER 6

The courier desk was a bad joke.

A cubicle in the back hall, barely large enough to hold a single desk and three chairs, it was usually jammed with two or three couriers and all their helmets, jackets, dripping rain gear, radios, paperbacks, and biker magazines. Cigarette smoke had painted the walls a smudged greenish-yellow – the tar so thick in places that it had begun to drip – and the floor was cracked linoleum turned the color of ground-in dirt, and littered with ground-out butts. The battered phone in the center of the desk had no dial – it was a direct connection to the Assignment Desk and only rang when there was work to be done.

Luckily, Rick had it all to himself for now and sat happily in the number one chair. This was the chair that gave the best view of the affiliate service edit room across the hall and, consequently, of Shelley, the stunning young woman in brown corduroy hot pants and a sheer nylon shirt who worked there. Rick was sure that Shelley would never do anything as uncool as talk to a courier, but that was OK. He wasn't interested in much more than an occasional glimpse. He could enjoy it later.

In this, Rick's photographic memory was a blessing – most times, it was a curse. If he relaxed his guard, stepped out of the world of the immediate for even a second, he was back in the Ia Drang Valley.

In the tall grass.

The searing heat of a tropic sun, the drag of the thick dust on his boots as he struggles to keep up with his unit, almost hidden by the windblast from the choppers scrambling out after the drop-off.

Artillery explodes to his left, and he ducks. He notices that none of the men in front of him do. They've been hammered for three days already and just stand there, smoking cigarettes and watching the treeline with wide-eyed, unblinking stares.

Suddenly, on the left, assault weapons begin their deafening rattle. As he turns, he sees a wave of Viet Cong running towards him.

Shit, those aren't Cong. They have real uniforms and good weapons. Those are North Vietnamese regulars – real fucking soldiers, not half-trained farmers.

Then, it seems as if every weapon in the First Battalion goes off at once. Two Skyraiders scream in, strafing and dropping napalm insanely, incredibly close.

Without even deciding to move, he is down on his knees, scrambling for cover. He can't hear; he can't see through the smoke. A face appears to his right – Asian features. Shit, he's raising his fucking AK – and he pushes his rifle out with one hand and just squeezes the trigger blindly. The face is blown apart, and the body falls back into the smoke.

●●●

"Rick?"

He jerked in his chair. The pretty production assistant was looking down at him. "I'm sorry. Did I disturb you?"

"No problem. Must have drifted off."

"I'm looking for the Hadley film. Did you drop it off?"

Rick glanced up at the clock over the courier desk. "Sure. Over an hour ago."

"Darn." Shelley sounded disappointed as she held up a plastic film can. "I've got the can, but there's nothing in it, and Moretti says it was empty when he picked it up. Hadley still hasn't shown up, so they knocked it out of the Global Report, but we still need to cut it for the affiliates." She headed towards the crew room in her usual headlong rush. "Well, it's got to be somewhere. Thanks!"

"No problem." Rick said to her retreating back. Then he remembered. "Hey, the Hadley crew's not back yet?"

Shelley turned around but kept walking backward. "Not yet."

"I've still got Pete's Bolex."

"Just keep it. If you leave it in the lounge, it'll get lost. Or one of those bigoted jerks will swipe it just to make him look incompetent." She spun on one high-heeled boot and waved as she turned the corner. "Got to go. See ya."

Rick stuck the small camera into one of the desk drawers, then sat back and rubbed his hands over his face. Well, he thought, she was willing to talk to a courier after all. The problem, he suspected, might be ever getting her to stop.

The moment of simple enjoyment faded as he remembered the dream. It had been bad enough to live through his tour in Vietnam once. Reliving it was just unfair. He felt a dull ache spread through his right arm and down his side – the places that had been ripped apart, the places that still had bits of steel, lead, and other people's bones buried deep inside.

He reached up to where his jacket hung on the edge of the partition and pulled a small pink rubber sphere – about the size of a tennis ball – out of a pocket. Holding it in his right hand, he began the familiar ritual of slow squeeze, hold, and slow release. The first time he tried it back in the hospital in Japan, even a single repetition was agony, and the ball kept dropping from his numbed fingers. Now he could do it for hours, a small part of the endless labor required just to keep his body functioning.

OK, that took care of the physical; now he needed something to occupy his mind.

He reached into the desk, pulled out a small, thin box, then got up and wandered through the halls to the back door, where a young black security guard stood, looking official in his short-sleeved uniform shirt and dark pants. Briefly, Rick thought that there were worse jobs for a returning vet than riding a motorcycle.

"Hey, Larry, you ready to get your butt kicked?" He wiggled the box over his head.

"Bring it on, man."

Rick looked around. "It's too busy out here, and I need to hear the phone. Can you come on back to the courier desk?"

"Sure," Larry laughed. "It's not like there aren't three other doors into this building that aren't guarded. I don't know why they even have me stand around looking like a damn fool. I don't check ID, and for minimum wage, I'm not about to get physical with someone who wants to get in. Let's go. I'll give you white and two free moves and still kick your butt."

Rick laughed, and they headed back. Chess would occupy his mind; keep the monsters at bay for a while.

They were just starting a fifth-game tie, when the phone rang.

"Courier desk."

"Anyone else there?" It was Casey Ross up on the Assignment Desk.

"Nope."

"Well, then you'll have to do both runs. Come on up."

Rick hung up the phone. "Sorry, we'll have to resume your inevitable defeat later."

Larry laughed. "Bullshit. It's been weeks and we're still dead even."

"I'm just taking it easy on you. Make you feel like you're all safe and secure and then… *blam*. You'll have more holes in you than the point man in a snuffie jungle stroll."

"Yeah, like the Marines didn't have to save your sorry GI butts about once a week." Larry was the only other Vietnam veteran in the building, and even though they didn't talk about their war, they quickly dropped into the familiar joshing banter.

They walked together to the center hall, and when Larry turned left to his post at the back door, Rick headed right. He opened the rear door, crossed a narrow alley that lead to the courtyard where the courier bikes were kept for the night, and continued into the next building. The ABN bureau took up the bottom floors of two buildings back-to-back and stretched all the way across the block between 18th Street and Connecticut Avenue.

This side was the old news bureau, built when ABN had just begun, running a distant third to the other two networks. Rick walked through a dusty studio with outmoded equipment and an equally antique control room with a picture window that looked out onto Connecticut Avenue.

More to the point, people on Connecticut Avenue could look in. Rick supposed that it might be entertaining to watch the news being produced, but he knew that the sunlight made it difficult to see the monitors, so the directors usually closed the curtains. That and they didn't like anyone looking over their shoulders while they worked.

So much for public relations.

To the left was the main entrance where the hyperkinetic receptionist spun endlessly from checking out everyone who came in to answering calls on an old-fashioned PBX, complete with cloth-covered cables and brass sockets. Rick had learned how to run it so he could give the operators a quick break from time to time, but it was all he could do keep from doing an atrocious Lily Tomlin impression to every caller.

A quick turn to the right and up two flights of worn green linoleum stairs, and he was at the

Assignment Desk. A small room, it was filled with the usual jammed-together collection of scratched beige desks covered with stacks of paper, newspapers, and punch-button phones, several of which were ringing. Typewriters sat on small right-angle extensions at each desk.

Along the far wall, another full set of wire machines hammered steadily. They were inside custom-built cabinets that were supposed to be soundproof but fell far short. A desk assistant was hanging wire copy on one of a row of clipboards marked AP Domestic, AP International, UPI, and Reuters. Most of the reporters would stop by and leaf through the news at least once a day.

Right above the wires was a row of clocks with neat signs underneath – London, New York, Tokyo, and Beirut. Rick assumed that they were meant to show the different time zones, but ever since he'd worked at ABN they had been set to random times, all of them incorrect, and the one for Beirut didn't run at all.

Another young kid just out of college was in the back, laboriously fitting a sheet of paper onto the drum inside a fax machine about the size of a big city telephone book while cradling a phone on his shoulder and cracking jokes – Rick assumed with his counterpart in New York. Suddenly, he shut the lid on the fax, said, "OK, three, two, one," into the phone and then jammed the handset into the rubber cups at the side of the machine. He watched nervously until the cylinder inside started to spin, and then sat back with a grin. It would take about two minutes to feed this page, so he could relax before he had to start again.

Dave Ross was leaning back in his chair on the other side of the room, facing the door where Rick had come in. He glanced up, nodded to Rick, and went back to scrolling through a roll of wire copy, bending what he'd already read in a slight curve so that it rose toward the ceiling at about a forty-five-degree angle. Two other editors had phones to their ears – one was apparently taking dictation, typing furiously as she listened, and shouting "Go" whenever she caught up.

Rick edged between the typewriters, wire machines, and desk assistants and sat on the edge of Ross's desk. "What's up?"

"Just a second." The column of paper folded over and collapsed. "Damn, I almost made it to the ceiling." Ross tore the end of the wire off on the edge of his desk and jammed it into an overflowing trash can at his side. "I need you to do a pickup at the airport. It's a pigeon coming in from Boston on Eastern in… thirty minutes. Can you make it?"

Rick knew that a "pigeon" was a random passenger who had been given fifty bucks to carry a can of film onto the plane, and if he or she wasn't met right as they came out of the gate, it was just as likely that the film would end up in a trash can as be handed off.

"Yeah, I'll have to go a bit fast, but you'll cover my ticket, right?"

Ross smiled. "I'll ask Smithson if he has any of his bonus money left. Better yet, just don't get caught. And, on your way, make a stop at the Palace."

"No sweat, boss." The Seoul Palace was the only Korean takeout place downtown. As far as Rick knew, it was the only Korean restaurant in the city, and a favorite of journalists who wanted to be reminded of their glory days in the overseas bureaus. It wasn't strictly part of the job, but the traditional payment for a Seoul Palace pickup was dinner for the lucky courier.

"Won't it get cold?" Rick asked.

"Yeah, but they're going to close, and cold food is better than no food." Ross stood up and pulled some bills from his pocket. "This should be enough. Hey, you brought in Hadley's film, right?"

Rick took the bills and nodded. "I put it right in George's hands."

"Well, no one can find it, and neither Hadley nor his crew has shown up. New York went apeshit when he missed the show. If he's out doing another of his 'top-secret' stories, his ass is going to be in a serious sling. Did he say anything to you about another shoot?"

"Nope. Didn't say he was and didn't say he wasn't. We're not close."

"Who is?" Ross pushed down on the switch at the base of the large microphone attached to a two-way radio on the left side of the desk and said, "Hadley, Farr. This is the desk. Please respond."

There was no answer, and he picked up the microphone and slammed it back down on the desk. "Damn, I wish these worthless radios worked."

Rick grinned. "Hey, I can't hear anything but static on mine anywhere but up on the Hill, but if he is off on another story, I'm sure they turned all the radios off anyway. You know how reporters hate being bothered by 'those morons on the desk'." He turned toward the door. "I'll bid you morons adieu. I need to get going if I'm going to be there before that guy lands."

As he walked away, the second editor looked up from her phone and, without taking the phone from her ear or pausing in her own typing, said, "After you meet that pigeon, there's a shipment at REA."

Rick waved his hand in the air to indicate he'd heard and kept on walking.

CHAPTER 7

There were no parking spaces on F Street, but parking on sidewalks was one of the unofficial perquisites of being a courier. Rick pulled the BMW up on the sidewalk in front of a row house that had a small illuminated sign with a large Pepsi logo and – in much smaller type – the words "Seoul Palace". He pulled the bike up on the center stand so it was parallel to the street.

Don't block pedestrians, he said to himself, they might be paying customers. It was a rant he'd heard so many times from the people at Seoul Palace, he knew it word for word.

He didn't take off his helmet as he went up the steps two at a time. The door opened just before he reached it and a man in a gray suit came out and roughly brushed past Rick without a word. Rick stood there for a second, watching him walk away, and idly wondered what had ticked him off. When he gave the BMW a sharp look, Rick thought: maybe he doesn't like motorcycles messing up the sidewalk.

After a second, Rick shrugged and went inside.

"I'm here for Mr Ross's order." Rick handed over the

money Ross had given him. "Hey, where is Anastasia?"

The girl who usually worked the counter was cute, and he liked to chat whenever he did a pickup. Tonight, however, it was a severe older woman with a bouffant stiff with hairspray and an old pink scar along her left jaw. She looked at him intently, briefly distracted from making change.

"You mean So Yun? She has to work hard, no time for talking. She's going to law school now."

"Law school at night?"

"Yes, night school. George Washington."

Rick knew that GW Law's night school was tough. Half of the people who actually did the work in DC's political world were graduates. "Well, wish her luck for me."

The woman looked doubtful. "Maybe. What's your name?"

"Just tell her it was the motorcycle guy from ABN. She'll know."

The woman took two steps back into the entrance to the smaller dining room and looked towards the back.

"So Yun, motorcycle boy from…" She paused and turned back to Rick. "Where do you work?"

"ABN"

"… from ABN wishes you good luck in law school."

A voice from inside the dining room said, "Thank you, Mrs Jin. Tell him I appreciate it."

Mrs Jin turned back to Rick. "OK?"

"That's great, thanks."

A thought crossed the woman's face, and she asked, "ABN? The television?"

Rick nodded, but as he picked up the bag of food and turned to go, he thought the woman looked startled.

With the Korean food zipped inside the leather jacket warming his chest, the ride to National Airport was pleasant, despite the steadily dropping temperature. After pulling into the airport, he turned left and then swung down the hidden road beneath the arrivals area, where the buses ran. After parking at the loading dock under the Eastern shuttle, he pushed open the swinging doors and walked up two flights of stairs to the regular Eastern arrival area.

A quick check of one of the monitors told him he was right on time, so he took off his helmet, turned it so the ABN sticker was in front, and held it up on his chest the way limo drivers did when they were meeting a client. An overweight man in a business suit and a tan raincoat came out of the door marked "Arrivals", looked around until he spotted Rick, and walked up with one of the ABN mesh shipping bags in his hand. Inside, Rick could see a couple of small film cans – both with the red tape that meant they were undeveloped.

"Here's your film. Now where's the rest of my money?"

Rick knew he was being scammed. Ross would have told him if he had to make another payment to the pigeon. He looked at the man innocently. "Sorry, but I'm flat broke. You can call the bureau in the morning if you want."

"Ah, forget it." The businessman thrust the bag at him. "Here, I've got to get home."

Rick smiled and headed back to his bike, tucked the film into his bag, and then drove to the left, onto the small road that led to the Railway Express Agency depot at the far end of the main runway.

The depot was a strange place, a leftover from the days when trains were the only way to ship anything. Now REA put urgent shipments in the baggage compartments of virtually every major airline, but it still had the timeworn and faded feel of a rural whistle-stop.

Tonight, the rollers that stretched the length of the main room were filled with white cardboard crates, about the size of pizza boxes, stacked eight high. They were marked "Live Animals - Handle With Care", and when Rick peered through the twine mesh over the air hole in the side of one, he saw it was filled with dozens of white mice. There had to be a couple of thousand mice stacked up on the roller belt. Rick guessed they were destined for short lives in a research lab somewhere.

He turned toward the beat-up wooden counter on the left and heard barking. Behind the counter was a motley stack of metal crates with an assortment of dogs and a couple of cats, all very excited by the two young women in front of the crates who were kneeling down and opening cans of food.

He asked the beefy man in the REA uniform shirt with "Ace" embroidered on the pocket, "What's with all the dogs?"

"Lost in transit." The man turned and looked disinterestedly at the animals. "Lucky for them, those SPCA volunteers come down to feed them because I

sure ain't about to. I can't tell you how sick I am of
their damn barking." He turned back. "What can I do
you for?"

"Pickup for ABN."

"Yeah? I'll go look."

Rick leaned on the counter. Watching the animals,
he wondered where they had come from and how
a family could lose a supposedly beloved pet on an
airplane flight. Ace returned with the inevitable blue-
stenciled ABN mesh bag.

"Here you go. Sign for it right here."

Rick signed and left. He stuck the bag in his canvas
sack, reset the bungee cords, started the engine, and
headed back toward the terminal. He'd only gone a
hundred feet when he heard a rising roar behind him
– a car engine accelerating hard. In his side mirrors,
he saw headlights flaring as the car bounced on the
rough asphalt. He moved to the right to let it go by;
he didn't feel like racing with all the junk he was
carrying. What if I dropped the Korean food,? he
thought.. Now, that would be a real tragedy.

He saw in his mirrors that the oncoming car was
also moving to the right – still heading for him – so
he pulled up and over the high concrete curb, across
the sidewalk and stopped next to the chain link fence
that encircled the runways. The car kept coming, but
when it hit the curb, the angle between car and the
curb was too shallow and the entire front end was
thrown to the left with a shriek of tires.

Rick recognized the black Impala as the same car
that had gone through the light at 18th and L. He
could see the driver wrestling with the steering wheel

but couldn't get a good look at his face.

Rick remembered an incident in college when – as he was just cruising around behind campus enjoying the warm spring weather – this jerk had cut him off on a turn. Rick wasn't angry, but had flipped him the bird just to make the point. The idiot had then tried to run him off the road three times in total fury.

When Rick had finally parked his bike with some dumb movie-born expectation of a fistfight, the driver – a stocky guy with a black shirt and patterned black tie – had gotten out of the big Lincoln with the Jersey plates, stomped over, pulled a nasty little pistol from a belt clip, and stuck it in Rick's stomach.

As it happened, Rick only had to endure fifteen minutes of inebriated but relatively innovative cursing, but it left him convinced that stopping to take on a crazed driver in a fair fight was a lousy idea. After all, a motorcycle could lose just about any car on anything but a long straight – it seemed wrong not to take full advantage.

He kicked the shifter all the way down into first gear, twisted the handlebars sharply left, and gunned it, shooting up a rooster-tail of grass and dirt until he caught traction on the sidewalk and shot off the curb and into the road. The black car stopped and slammed into reverse, but Rick was already past his rear bumper and swerving back onto the road – now in front again. The Impala screeched to a halt and spun its rear wheels for a second before it gained traction and leapt forward.

The Impala had better acceleration in the low end than the dignified – if not downright stodgy – BMW and quickly caught up, passed, and once again cut viciously in front of the courier. Rick slammed on the brakes – feeling as though he were tipping up on his front wheel like a trials rider – and swerved right, passing behind the Impala again.

Rick had left the bike in first gear and both cylinders were screaming. When he popped the clutch, the rear wheel spun and smoked, but now he had the torque he needed as he kicked it up through the gears. He looked back and saw that the black car was still fishtailing on the road behind him with no chance of catching up.

Blue and red flashing lights exploded from a side road hidden between two airplane hangars. Ah, my old friends, the airport police, Rick thought.

Given a choice between a ticket and whatever this maniac behind him had in mind, Rick would take the ticket. He braked hard, pulled well over to the right, and waited for the police cruiser to pull up – shielding him from another assault.

The Impala slid past as slowly as any other law-abiding citizen, and Rick watched the car's taillights dwindle and then turn left onto the highway back to the city. When the car and its still-unknown driver had disappeared, he turned and put an apologetic look on his face for the benefit of the airport cop still struggling out of his cruiser.

Rick thought that there were probably fifty police forces in the capital area, and, clearly, the airport police were scraping the bottom of the applicant pool. This policeman was so fat that his shirt was bulging open between the buttons, and by the time he got out of his car and straightened his gun, his nightstick, his hat, and his flashlight, his face was bright red with the effort.

Things should go pretty well according to the usual script – a demand for his license followed by ten minutes of stern warnings, vague threats, and a hefty fine – so he reached into his inside jacket pocket and pulled out the slim wallet he only used for traffic stops. When the cop had finished chewing him out, Rick drove off with a fifty-dollar ticket that he crumpled and tossed into a Dumpster as soon as he was out of sight. After all, what was another fifty bucks compared to the several thousand dollars he already owed?

Once again, he thanked the incompetent staff at Columbia Women's Hospital. When he was born, his birth certificate had read "James Richard Putnam". His mother, who certainly didn't intend to have her husband's father's name ahead of her own father's name, sent his dad back two days later, and he'd returned with another birth certificate – this time correctly emblazoned with the name "Richard James Putnam".

Even as a teenager, it had been clear to Rick that there were many advantages to having a second identity, so he'd applied for a Social Security card when he started both his first and second jobs and taken his driving test at two locations. "Jack" Putnam had already run up so many points that there were bench warrants out for his arrest, but Vietnam veteran "Rick" Putnam was an upstanding citizen without a single black mark on his record.

Deciding that being a bit late getting back was preferable to running into that jerk in the black Chevy, he took the back exit from the airport and danced his way back to the bureau through dark Pentagon parking lots, past the brightly lit Iwo Jima Monument, and over Key Bridge.

He rode with his usual caution and concentration regarding other drivers, but with most of his mind turning over the same question.

Why would anyone be out to get him?

CHAPTER 8

Still warmed by the peppery combination of *kimchee* and Korean beef, Rick barely felt the chill as he drove up North Carolina Avenue onto Capitol Hill. As usual, he was struck by how nice a place Washington was to live in – almost a guilty secret, considering that many of the amenities, the parks, the museums, the open public spaces came from the lavish use of other people's taxes.

On Capitol Hill, the tidy row houses were divided evenly between brick that had been left in its original colors and brick that had been painted in blues, whites, and some surprising yellows and pinks. Tall trees lined the road and provided shade that was a blessed relief in the hot and humid summer months. It was a quiet neighborhood – much like a small town even though it was only three blocks from the Capitol; Rick could almost imagine the government clerks of post–Civil War Washington in their Homburgs and spats as they walked with their wives, holding parasols, and admired their new homes.

Of course, there were some pretty awful housing projects just a few blocks to the south. He could feel the smoldering resentment every time he crossed the invisible line that separated white from black. Even so, projects were unusual in DC – an error made by well-meaning liberals in the sixties. Most of the poorest areas were still quiet streets of small houses – far different from the cramped industrial ghettos of northern cities like Philadelphia and New York.

He pulled up to a brick house on the corner of North Carolina and 3rd Street SE. It was a surprisingly roomy two-story place, which had been home for at least three sets of housemates that Rick knew of, and there may have been more. What he did know was that whoever had actually signed the lease to the Foreign Service couple who owned it now was long gone. Apparently, so long as the cashier's checks were deposited in the house bank account and no one burned the place down, the owners weren't about to change things.

He jumped off the BMW, leaving it in first gear. Feathering the clutch, he ran alongside as the engine ran the heavy machine over the curb and up the board placed on the side of the three steps up to the backyard. He jockeyed the bike over to the back of the small rear courtyard – just a concrete patio, really – put the front wheel up against a solid metal drainpipe, and secured it with the chunky padlock on a heavy chain looped around the pipe. Yanking on the chain to be certain it was secure, he took off his helmet and went up the wooden steps to the kitchen.

Corey Gravelin – one of his housemates – sat at the kitchen table, eating Special K and reading *The Wall Street Journal*. He was tall and slim with chiseled features, hair just this side of too long, with a neatly trimmed mustache. Corey wore his usual after-work outfit, which in his case simply meant that he had removed the jacket from his blue three-piece suit, carefully folded back his French cuffs, and fractionally loosened his tie. He was one of those men whose good looks made other men wonder if he was gay.

Rick would have been entirely sure Corey was gay if not for the fact that he worked for an extremely conservative Republican congressman and was always accompanied by a stunning woman when he attended events like a Kennedy Center gala or a charity dinner. In either case, Corey's sexual orientation didn't concern Rick. There had been a few guys in the Seventh Cavalry who Rick had been fairly sure swung that way, but they could be counted on in a firefight, and that was all that mattered.

Corey looked up. "How's it going, Rick?"

"Not bad. Anything new in the world?"

"Well, the last guys to walk on the moon are heading home; the President has stopped being Mr Nice Guy to the North Vietnamese. He's got B-52s going all the way to downtown Hanoi this time and…" He paused to look at the paper. "Yeah, the White House is going to take away the *Post*'s TV stations if they don't cut out their bullshit crusade over Watergate." He sat back in his chair. "That whole thing is just overblown, don't you think?"

Rick smiled, and then stuck his head in the refrigerator to see what was there. "Man, you know I don't do politics."

"Yeah, but you were in Vietnam. You must see how the left wing is making it easier for the communists with all this crap?"

Rick grabbed an apple and turned around, leaning back against the counter. He took a bite and chewed for a moment.

"I'll tell you, the main thing Vietnam taught me was ignorance. I went in thinking I knew what I was doing, and that the President and the Pentagon knew what they were doing, and I came out pretty sure that no one had a clue."

Corey turned back to the paper. "Well, I'm glad my boss is on Banking, and I won't have to deal with the circus they're setting up in the Senate. Sam Ervin is a grandstanding fool – 'simple country lawyer', my ass."

"Hey, a nice scandal will mean longer hours and more dough for me, so I guess" – Rick's voice took on a stentorian tone like a politician on the stump – "they should follow the trail wherever it leads."

His voice back to normal, he said, "Let's go from the sublime to the ridiculous. What are the Three Musketeers up to?"

The Three Musketeers were the other housemates, computer programmers who kept the mainframes running at places like General Electric, Westinghouse, and Riggs Bank. At least that's what they claimed. Rick was pretty sure from their conversations that they spent most of their time playing *Spacewar!* on the powerful machines.

"Who knows? I haven't seen them, and I can't figure out what they're doing when I can see them."

Still eating his apple, Rick wandered out into the living room. It was empty, but he could hear excited voices coming from the half-finished basement downstairs.

The three computer techs were sitting around a wobbly folding table, fiddling with what looked like a typewriter in a small suitcase. Steve Lord, a slow-speaking South Carolinian with a full beard, was wearing a T-shirt from a Sly Stone concert, cut-off jeans, and sandals. Rick knew that this was what he usually wore to work and had once asked if that was the way most people at GE dressed.

Steve said that his bosses hated his clothes but knew their computers would go down in a week if he wasn't there.

Neither of the other men had Steve's self-confidence, or much of any self-confidence at all. Zeke Pickell was a short, hyperactive kid from Oregon with bushy red hair and a tendency to wear patterned sweaters. He was known as "Eps", which Rick gathered had something to do with "Epsilon" being computer-guy code for something small.

The last of the trio, Scott Shaw, had been commanded to "Beam me up!" so often that he'd good-naturedly taken the Star Trek engineer's nickname as his own and would occasionally refer to "dilithium crystals" in a thick Scottish burr. With his buzz-cut hair, short-sleeved white shirts, and pocket protector, he looked older and perhaps a bit more deliberate than his friends. Rick knew Scotty was probably the brightest of them all – he'd graduated from MIT in only three years at the age of eighteen.

"What's going on?" Rick said. "And what the hell is that?"

"This is so cool. It just came out, and we got one of the first off the assembly line. This" – Eps swept his hand towards it like a model on a game show showing off a Cadillac convertible – "is a Digi-Log Remote Interactive CRT. With this, we can use a phone to go right into the computers at work."

"Why in God's name would you want to?"

Steve replied, "Mostly so we don't have to drive all the way to Bethesda every time the PDPs go down and everyone starts running around with their hair on fire." He turned back to the table. "See, it's got a full keyboard, a monitor. Everything you need."

Rick pointed at the odd rubber cups at the back. "What are those for?"

Scotty, who was peering deeply into the tiny green letters on the tiny green monitor, silently shook his head at this display of ignorance.

Eps piped up. "Those are for the phone. You call up the computer and stick the phone right in there."

"Computers have phone numbers?"

"Sure." Steve grinned. "And we've got their phone book. That's really what we're doing – seeing what other computers we can get into."

"Again. Why?"

"It's fun. Hell, it's a game. We programmed most of the systems in town and friends of ours set up the rest. Consequently, we know most of the backdoors and system hacks."

Rick held up a hand. "Stop. 'Backdoor' almost makes sense, but what is a 'system hack'?"

Scotty didn't even look up. "One system hack is putting in a backdoor."

Rick stared at him for a moment in mock anger. "OK, don't explain it to me." He turned back to Steve. "So, what are these games?"

"They try to protect their systems, and we try to break in."

"What do you get when you break in? Military secrets? Unlimited checking?"

Scotty finally sat back from his intense scrutiny of the monitor. "No, we just go in and look around. See if the other guys have any cool new tricks. Maybe leave them a note."

"It doesn't sound like fun to me, but what do I know? I think a good time is riding motorcycles way too fast." Rick headed back upstairs. "Good night, guys."

In his bedroom, Rick stripped, put on a pair of running shorts and a T-shirt, and began the long ritual of going to sleep. Sleep, especially dreamless sleep, was a hard target. Memories were the enemy and exercises were the weapons of battle.

Except for his bed, which he still made with military precision, the only furniture in the room was a weight bench with carefully laid-out bars, collars, and plates. He began with some stretching, concentrating on his right arm and side, where scar tissue tended to tighten up during the day.

Then he began the hour-long workout he had developed and specifically structured for strength, speed, and power rather than muscle bulk. The VA doctors had been pleasantly surprised when he regained the use of his right arm and hand. After one of his regular exams, a doctor had told him that his body was held together by a web of muscles that had grown stronger to take up the work of all the cartilage and tendon lost in battle and the long series of surgeries that had followed. The doctor predicted that Rick would end up a cripple anyway – explaining that, over time, most people lost interest, stopped working the muscles, and lost the use of the limbs they'd regained with such difficulty.

Rick thought that since military doctors became officers the moment they signed up, the chances were good that he could prove this guy wrong – just like any other officer. Vietnam hadn't left him with a high opinion of military leadership and judgment.

He'd been working out steadily since he got out of rehab, weights at night and his little pink rubber ball all day. Not only had he retained the use of his arm, but he was also pleased to find that he was now surprisingly strong. The other day, one of the secretaries had asked him to move a typewriter from one side of her desk to the other. He'd stood on one side, reached over, grabbed the typewriter and the typing table together, lifted both straight up and over the desk, and then gently lowered them to the floor in front of her. He hadn't missed the looks that almost everyone in the newsroom had given him for that stunt.

Time passed, and he fell into the calm mental state that came with steady exercise. He went back over the incidents on 18th Street and at the airport. If they were connected, who was the driver, and why would anyone want to hit him? It was serious enough in regular city traffic, where the drivers acted as if he didn't exist, but he couldn't shake the feeling that this time he was a target.

Eventually, the exercise took over his mind completely, and he stopped thinking about anything. When he finished, he took a bath – one of the few failings of this house was a single bathroom and no shower – got into bed, and fell asleep immediately.

It's full night, and he's lying on his back on damp ground. Around him, the soft sounds of others trying to hide under the fragile cover of darkness. Suddenly, someone yells in Vietnamese and then there are screams.

The fucking Cong have found another wounded grunt. The screaming is going on and on, and then a burst of gunfire and silence. They've taken to firing directly into the poor bastards' wounds after jabbing a bayonet or the barrel of an AK-47 deep inside.

Another American starts begging, "No. No. Please don't." The voice ascends into wordless screams, and then gunfire.

Trying not to make a sound, he reaches around him, searching with his fingers, but his rifle is gone. Lost.

Where the fuck did he lose his rifle?

Slowly, he moves over to his left. Sergeant Cook had used his .45 to blow the back of his head out a couple of hours ago. It should still be here.

The searching fingers hit metal.

The .45 feels sticky but solid. He hopes the blood and brain matter haven't jammed the mechanism.

There is a rustling in the grass. A boot touches his leg.

They have AKs. The .45 is useless.

He tries to hold his breath, stop his heart, and freeze the blood pounding through his veins.

Then the boot hits him in the right arm and drives the shrapnel deep…

Rick woke with his throat locked, straining to hold back the scream. His heart was pounding and the bed was soaked in sweat. The yellow sodium light from the streetlights outside filled the room. He'd taken down the curtains when he first moved in – their moving shadows were too lifelike. He needed his environment to be fixed, solid, and without nuance.

He looked at the clock on the windowsill.

Three hours.

Not bad. Three hours would get him through the next day.

That's all he could expect. Most days, it was the best he could do.

Gradually, his heartbeat slowed, the screams in his throat retreating to wherever they went in the sane times.

He swung his legs off the bed and sat, rubbing his face with his hands. Then he got up and paced, taking slow, deep breaths and shaking the tension out of his arms and back.

Eventually, he stripped and remade the bed with the clean sheets he'd left neatly folded on the closet shelf. Then he dressed – making sure that he put on all the insulating layers he owned.

It was time to dance.

First, the sharp twists and blind turns up Beach Drive in Rock Creek Park and then a slash run back through the early morning traffic on Reno Road. That should work.

It was still a couple of hours until dawn. He could still be on the steps of the Lincoln Memorial in time – right when the sun came up.

Rick moved quietly, so as not to disturb his housemates, and headed downstairs and out the back door.

His housemates heard the back door lock click and relaxed in their beds knowing that now they could finally sleep without sharing the tortured agony of Rick's war.

CHAPTER 9

Wednesday, December 20, 1972

After the battle in the Ia Drang Valley, after the long, painful journey through aid stations to MASH units to hospitals in Japan and, finally, VA centers in the United States – after he took off the uniform and folded it away in a box at his father's house – Rick had gone to college.

He didn't wear his old GI jacket, didn't write letters to newspapers, didn't march in protests or counterprotests, didn't throw his medals away – in fact, he didn't look at them at all. His classmates knew he was older, quieter; he asked a lot of questions in class, but they were real questions, not opinions disguised as questions. He didn't make many choices, like a career or even a major. He just took whatever classes seemed appealing.

The image of a career – or marriage or a future of any kind – had been erased in the battle that had wiped out so many of his friends. He almost didn't graduate, but a professor whose son was never coming back from the war approved him for a general studies degree, saying with a note of sadness that Rick would have lots of time to figure out what he really wanted to do with his life.

He spent a year living in a dorm before he rented his own apartment. The young guys who lived on his hall learned not to make loud noises – his response to the idiot who had set off an M-80 firecracker right outside his window had been particularly impressive.

He had to explain to Andy, his roommate, why he should simply *tell* him that the dining hall was about to close. Shaking him awake triggered automatic battle reflexes. He had to buy the poor guy a nice tie to cover the finger-shaped bruises around his neck. Andy said everything was fine, but for the rest of the semester, Rick noticed that his roommate would only speak to him from the safety of the doorway. After that, he made sure to live in places where he could at least sleep alone.

He was adrift, looking for a new life where the sun shone and there were fewer terrors in the shadows. Living within the memories of Vietnam was too painful, so he tried desperately to be normal – much like his dad in 1946 – just someone trying to get on with an interrupted life. The people around him caught the request implicit in his silence and did not ask to share his thoughts or try to ease his burden.

Except Dina Scholten.

He was sitting alone at lunch one day, and she sat down with her tray, looked straight at him, and said, "Tell me about your war."

Rick had looked at her for a long moment. He saw a chubby girl with a severe haircut and brown eyes that were sharp but, as far as he could see, still open.

Her mind wasn't already made up. It was just possible that she had meant what she said, that she wanted to know about his war – not to harangue him about the one she saw through a political lens.

So, he told her. Not all of it, and not the worst of it, but for the first time, he talked about some of what had happened in the green shadows under the thick jungle canopy.

She listened and asked thoughtful questions about the things she didn't understand. She was interested but didn't show any sympathy or pity or outrage or any of the other cheap emotions he had feared.

She was back at lunch the next day, and the day after that. She began to talk about her childhood as a "red diaper" baby raised by aging revolutionaries in Brooklyn, her work at a legal clinic in a housing project, and her dreams of a career in politics. They eventually discussed the Meaning of the War – from morality to political reality, to patriotism, to what it meant to those fighting it, and those marching against it.

After Dina was accepted at Georgetown Law School, they continued to have lunch once a week, sharing a Greek appetizer platter at the Taverna Cretekou, just east of the Capitol. Dina said that the smashed caviar was better there than anywhere else – even in the Greek neighborhoods of Queens.

Rick blinked as he came in from the bright sunshine. He scanned the dining room crowded with aides and interns making the most of their fifty minutes away from the halls of power. Dina waved from the back of the room, but he'd spotted her customary outrageous hat and was already heading to the table. As he walked up, he caught a brief glimpse of the other woman seated across from Dina. She was much shorter, slim, with an interesting body. A round face, with solemn dark eyes, was framed by long, straight black hair.

Dina introduced her as Eve Buffalo Calf, a Northern Cheyenne law school graduate working as a legal adviser with the American Indian Movement while studying for the bar exam. Rick didn't know much about AIM except that their "warriors" had taken over the abandoned Alcatraz Prison in San Francisco for a while and then occupied the Bureau of Indian Affairs down at the Interior Department a month ago and trashed the place on the way out. On the other hand, he had known and liked a number of soldiers who came off the reservations and certainly was open to the idea that the government had thoroughly screwed the tribes.

The waiter came for drink orders and both the women ordered Irish coffee. Rick asked for just plain coffee as strong as they could make it.

The dark-haired girl said, "You don't drink?"

"I'd love to, but it's never worked out for me."

Eve gave him a quizzical look. "What's that mean?"

Rick liked her directness. "Well, it's how I ended up in Vietnam, for one thing."

"You got drunk and enlisted? That's a fairly popular way to spend a Saturday night back home."

Rick laughed. "No, I wasn't the one drinking. My mom was an alcoholic, and… well, a lot of children of alcoholics simply run away – usually emotionally. I ran away for real and ended up in the Army. It seemed like a good idea at the time."

"And now?"

"Well, I guess it still seems like it was a good idea, or at least better than living in a household with a drunk. I watched my mother try to escape into a bottle to get away from her problems, and all the problems just got worse, and eventually her liver blew, and she died. By that time, she'd driven away everyone who'd ever cared about her. They got in the way of her dedication to drinking. I didn't wait to be driven away – I ran. When she was dying a couple of years ago, I visited, but there wasn't any emotional scene. Didn't like her when she was alive and don't miss her now she is dead."

Dina said, "Isn't that a bit cold?"

Rick looked her straight in the eyes. "It's the only advantage to being the child of an alcoholic. From what I've seen, healthy people feel terrible when a parent dies."

Dina just shook her head, but Eve nodded. "Alcohol is a huge problem back home. Most Native Americans tend to have trouble with alcohol – apparently, it's genetic. Plus, the stress of poverty and… hopelessness eats our people up inside, and drinking is a cure or at least it dulls the pain for a little while. A lot of the guys coming back from the war seem to be drinking to forget."

"Yeah, well, there are some things that happened in Vietnam that I would drink Drano to forget, but short of that, alcohol just doesn't work. I end up hung over and still remember everything. The worst of both worlds."

She looked at him seriously. "So, what do you do to forget?"

"When I manage to forget a single second of my time over there, I'll be sure to let you know."

"But you can't go on like that," she said. "At home they'd say you were sick, poisoned. The elders know how to fight an illness like that, but you have to be willing to fight along with them."

"Smoke and feathers?"

"My dad's the only licensed psychiatrist on the Montana reservation." There was a flash of anger in her eyes. "Sometimes he uses smoke and feathers, and sometimes he uses psychotherapy. Occasionally, he just knocks the patient upside the head once or twice."

Rick grinned. "Sounds like my kind of guy."

They might have continued to talk about each other, but Dina was fighting for a position on the Senate Special Committee that was about to start hearings on the Watergate scandal and she was bursting with the latest chapter of the story that had been delighting – or infuriating – political Washington since the "third-rate burglary" had happened six months ago.

More cash had been discovered. Dina said that the wife of one of the arrested burglars had been in a plane crash and turned out to be carrying thousands of dollars in cash.

Rick said, "Everything about this Watergate thing seems to have something to do with cash."

"This is the tip of the iceberg," Dina responded. "Everyone knew that Nixon was calling in all his chips for this election. The money was just flooding in. Corporations, industry associations, old friends. You name it."

Eve looked curious. "But don't they know the names of everyone who gives money to a campaign? I thought they just passed a law on that."

"They did, but it didn't go into effect until last April and under the old law – and I love this name, The Corrupt Practices Act – you didn't have to identify any contributions to a candidate before he was nominated."

Rick had watched the convention coverage like a soap opera, since there wasn't much else going on when all the politicians were out of town. "And Nixon didn't officially get nominated until August."

Dina smiled. "Bingo. My Republican friends say his money people started beating the bushes the day after the election in 1968. There must be millions of dollars sloshing around. Hell, he certainly didn't have to spend much to beat McGovern."

Eve smiled. "I could have beaten George McGovern."

The women went on with their conversation. Rick said enough to not to be called on the carpet for inattention by Dina, but he was actually just enjoying watching the dark-haired woman talk. He felt that sitting next to her was like sitting under a warm sun and dropping off to sleep. When he was a kid, his favorite time at the beach had been late afternoon, when most of the people had left and the surf and sun merged into a golden haze, and he would doze off and wake up to find that he was alone in the twilight.

"Rick, Rick, Earth to Rick. Come in."

He brought his attention back to Dina. "Hmm?"

"We were talking about the war, the peace talks breaking down, and now the carpet-bombing of Hanoi."

"And you almost let me miss that?" Rick snorted. "Thanks a lot. They've been having peace talks since they started this war, and I don't know which particular idiots are planning those air raids, but a lot of those B-52s are going down. More downed planes means more POWs – just what we need."

Eve looked at him. "But I thought this war was over. Kissinger said 'peace is at hand' months ago."

"Yeah, but South Vietnamese 'President for Life' Nguyen Van Thieu and his boys seem to have had other ideas, and they blew up the talks." Rick shook his head. "I'm just glad that most of the ground troops are out. That means fewer American grunts on the front lines, and as far as I'm concerned, that's a good thing. I'm not saying that the war was right or wrong, but I do think we've had enough good men die over there. Let the Vietnamese work it out."

Eve turned back to her salad. "Dina said I'd be surprised how different you were from my idea of a Vietnam vet."

"Most of the vets I know are different from all the other vets I know. Except in one thing – given a choice, we'd rather talk about something else." He smiled. "So, what are you doing for the 'noble red man'?"

She looked at him sharply and then realized he was being ironic – not insulting. "Well, as a 'noble red woman' and soon to be a 'noble red lawyer', I'm working on getting charges dropped, people released, and things settled so that I can get back to winning back some of what was stolen from us."

"Like Alcatraz?"

"Hey, it's not like anyone else was using it. And there's some good fishing off there."

Rick laughed.

Dina gave him a funny look, looked as if she was about to say something, but didn't.

The conversation wandered from topic to topic and, when lunch was done, Eve went looking for the ladies' room, and Dina immediately turned to Rick with all the subtlety of a Manhattan prosecutor.

"Wait one damn second. In all the time we've known each other, I can count the number of times I've seen you laugh. Today, you've laughed, talked, and generally acted like a normal human. What's up?"

"Nothing's up." He held his hands up, palms out. "See, I've got nothing to hide."

"No, you like that young girl, and she likes you." She shook her head in mock disbelief. "I thought I'd never see it. All these years that I've watched women throw themselves at you without even scratching that smooth surface, and she just walks in and… wham!"

"There is no wham. There has been no wham, and there will be no wham."

"Only if you're a lot dumber than I think you are." Dina gathered up her things. "Well, like any good lawyer, I can see when it's time to lose gracefully, so I'm going to get out of here. Why don't you walk her home? She's staying right around the corner from your place."

He did try, but Rick couldn't think of a good reason not to follow Dina's advice.

As they walked through the quiet of a Capitol Hill

afternoon, Eve asked why he was a courier.

"Why not?"

"Isn't it dangerous?"

"Nah, the statistics for accidents on a motorcycle are about the same as a car after the first six months, and... well, I just like it."

"What is it you like? It's cold. It's wet. Why not sit in a nice warm car?"

"Well," Rick paused. "It's all about turns. Everyone thinks that motorcycling is just going real fast in a straight line, but it's not. The bike is just a big gyroscope, so it bends against a turn. The harder you turn, the more it leans over."

"Like a sailboat?"

"Who knows? I've never sailed. Are there a lot of sailboats in Montana?"

Eve made a face. "Let me think... On an average day, I'd say there were approximately... none."

They both laughed. "Well, a bike going through turns is like... It sounds dumb, but it's like dancing. You swoop, drop your weight down so far you think you're going to scrape the road, and then come up and drop over to the other side and do it again. If you go slowly, it's a terrific way to see the country."

"And if you go fast?"

"Well, if you go fast, it's a very different thing."

She turned her head. "How so?"

"Hard to describe. It's something you need to feel."

"Well, that's not going to happen."

They had arrived at the enormous subway dig that had replaced D Street. It was only a block from Rick's group house.

"I'm staying just over there in that pink house," Eve said. "You don't have to come all the way to the door. There isn't room for two people to walk on these damn rickety catwalks."

Rick looked over the wooden beams that served as a fence around the enormous pit. "I can never believe how deep this goes. It's got to be ten to fifteen stories down."

The entire street was simply gone – ripped out and trucked away. Trees, sidewalks, and even front gardens had been lost – and what remained was a deep, dark space filled with girders, stairs, and work lights. Big mobile cranes were working at both ends of the dig and at the bottom, acetylene torches flared.

"From what I read, this is where they dropped the mole in to dig the tunnels."

"Mole?" Eve asked.

"Yeah, they're using a monster drill that cuts out the whole subway tunnel at once with room for both train tracks. That's the mole. Every day they just goose it forward a bit more and lay concrete in behind it. At least most of it's underground up here. Downtown it's all cut-and-cover, and the streets are just boards."

She smiled. "Tough on a motorcycle, I'll bet."

"Damn right. If it's raining, it's like trying to drive on an ice rink. Last week, a taxi missed the turn at Connecticut Avenue and just slid right over the edge. He was lucky that he caught on the exhaust pipes after the front wheels went over. They had to pull him out with a crane." He looked over the edge again. "And it's not nearly as deep as this."

"The girl I'm staying with says that they're afraid all the houses are just going to fall in someday." She pointed at one of the pastel-colored brick-fronts that sat only a few feet from the edge of the pit. "See, they've had to hammer in I-beams like that to brace up a number of the houses. The walls were beginning to crack."

"Well, if your place starts to topple, I'm just over there." Rick pointed. "You're welcome to drop by anytime. Just don't let my roommates frighten you off."

"Are they bikers, too?"

"Worse, computer hackers and a Senate staffer."

She gave a fake shudder. "Yeah, that's worse. If anything happens, I think I'll just go ahead and fall in."

Then she smiled, gave him a quick wave, and walked quickly down the flimsy walkway over the incredible drop.

CHAPTER 10

Rick didn't have to start his shift until 1 o'clock. Mornings were slow, and the couriers didn't have to go into all-out crazy speed mode until after noon, when the push to the 6 o'clock deadline began to pick up speed. He drove slowly up 14th Street – bemused by how the blinking lights and inviting signs of the gaudy nightclubs and the leering come-ons of the sex shops were only blocks from the White House.

A man in a wrinkled raincoat, whose hat just happened to be covering his face, came out of the Olympic Baths and scurried away. Across the street, two tired hookers, one in ripped fishnet stockings and the other in a tiny denim skirt, were sitting on the stoop of a house between two strip clubs: This is It and The Butterfly. One of them waved at him without any real hope. He just waved back.

Ahead, he spotted the rundown town house and garage on H Street where Motor Mouse Couriers was located. At least there was a sign outside that claimed that Motor Mouse was a courier company, but to his knowledge, no one had ever hired them.

Certainly, no one who had ever actually visited their office.

The chopped Harleys outside the garage doors proclaimed its real occupants, the Dawn Riders Motorcycle Club, a group far less violent than the gunrunning Pagans in Prince George's County or the black bikers of the Galloping Gooses, but still dangerous people to run into late on a Saturday night.

He parked the BMW at the end of the row of bikes and took off his helmet. Two men with filthy denim vests and peaked leather caps were slouched in a couple of plastic chairs on the sidewalk. Rick thought the caps were dumb-looking, but at least they weren't wearing leather fringes. He did wonder if there was a dress code among outlaw bikers that required all of them to wear T-shirts advertising Harley dealers.

The biker on the right – a goateed and pimpled man with a beer gut straining the inevitable black Harley dealership T-shirt under his vest – got up and walked slowly over. He walked around the BMW, examining it with a sour expression.

"What the hell is that on your front wheel?"

Rick looked at his front wheel, sat back, and pretended to think about it for a moment. "Earles front suspension."

"Weird fucking thing."

"Yeah, I suppose it is, but it means that BMW can put the same shocks on both the front and rear wheels. As a matter of fact, the front and rear wheels are the same, too." Rick smiled. "They designed these bikes to ride across Africa. This way you only have to carry one set of spares."

"Who the hell wants to ride across Africa? It's already like Africa in this city, anyway. Why don't you get a real bike?"

The biker was clearly looking for a fight, but Rick didn't feel like obliging, "Maybe someday. Is Hector here?"

"That whackjob? Watch out for him. His brains got scrambled bad over in Nam."

"Yeah, I've seen that happen to a lot of people. Is he here?"

The biker just jerked his thumb toward the garage door as he headed back to his chair in the sun.

Coming from the bright sun into the gloom of the garage, Rick was unable to see for a moment until his eyes adjusted. Motorcycles and scavenged skeletons of motorcycles littered most of the filthy floor, and a bright red, immaculately clean mechanic's toolbox stood out all the more in contrast. Beside it was a candy-coat green chopper with elaborate swirling chrome exhaust pipes – also immaculate.

Hector was bending over the engine from another bike, hitting an impact wrench with a ball peen hammer.

"Hey, *Gordito*."

Without standing up or looking around, Hector said, "I hate that name," and slammed the hammer down on the wrench again. "What the fuck do you want, Zippo?"

"That green chopper is a really sweet bike."

Hector glanced over at the bike. "You know what that is? That's what I thought about every night over in Nam. Designed every inch of it in my head." He walked over and rubbed at an invisible speck on the tank. "When I got home, it took three years of nights and weekends to build it. I'd never been a biker, but that taught me how to keep other guys' hogs running and led me to the position of leadership I hold today." As Hector stood up and started to wipe his hands on a red shop rag, he used his chin to indicate the garage. "*El jefe* of the Dawn Riders – the world's most sorry-ass motorcycle club."

He spat on the floor and then turned back to face Rick. "Now, let me say it again: what the fuck do you want?"

"I need some help."

Hector looked at Rick for a long moment. Then he spoke. "I don't like you. Why the fuck should I help you?"

"Because you and I were both there."

"Being fucked up in the same firefight doesn't make us buddies."

"I don't want to be your buddy. I wasn't your buddy when we were over there. But we counted on each other when we were in the shit, and I don't know about you, but I can't say that about too many people out here in the world."

Rick looked the mechanic in the eyes. "I think someone is trying to kill me, and I need your help."

Hector pulled out a cigarette pack, took one, and, after a pause, offered the pack to Rick. Rick took a cigarette, then pulled out the Zippo and lit it off his leg.

Hector scoffed. "You still doing that dumbass trick? You still think it's going to keep you alive?"

"Worked so far."

"Guess I can't argue with that." Hector took a light from the Zippo, then sat down on a half-dismantled Harley and slowly blew out a cloud of smoke. "OK, what do you need?"

When the door to the restaurant opened, Mrs Jin looked up and saw the man in the gray suit come in. For an instant, she could feel how much she loved this man showing in her eyes. She started, remembering that she could never let him know that. If he knew, he would leave. Never come back.

So, she stripped all emotion from her face, returning it to its usual blank mask, and motioned for him to follow her into her office.

"So Yun, take the front," she snapped. "Those drunks from the GSA will be in soon. Don't let them just sit at a table and waste our time with drinking. Make them buy food so they can walk out of here without being carried."

Opening a door next to the swinging double doors that led to the kitchen, she stood aside and let the quiet man in the gray suit into her office. It was a tiny space with barely room for a desk and two chairs, almost entirely devoid of character. The walls were bare, the two shelves behind the desk held no books or mementos, and the surface of the cheap desk was empty except for a single blue ledger placed precisely in the center.

The man, with an oddly courtly manner, waited until she was seated behind the desk before sitting down in the other chair. They looked at each other in silence for a moment, and then he said, "It's good to see you again."

She frowned. "Yes, it is good, but dangerous. You shouldn't come again during the day."

The man nodded once in agreement. "It's necessary, or I wouldn't have put you at risk. I'm having problems tracking down all the parts of this puzzle. I think the twins would be helpful."

There was another period of silence.

The woman appeared to be considering his request, but in reality, she would always do what he asked. Her mind drifted back to the hot day more than twenty years ago, when the smell of the filthy river had combined with the stench of cordite and death, and this man had saved her life.

Carefully keeping any evidence of these memories from her face, she returned to the present. "Of course, I will have them contact you. Remember that they need very close supervision. They can be impulsive."

A small smile crossed the man's face. "I'll try to keep them from killing any more people than strictly necessary."

There was another silence; it might even have been called "companionable".. Then Mrs Jin shook herself back to the present. "How bad is the trouble? I've already told the club owner to go to ground."

"Going to ground won't help. It's not about what

he's doing now, but what was done years ago." The man shrugged. "I've dealt with worse after the Bay of Pigs and Dallas. This will end the same way."

She nodded slowly. "With silence, yes."

"With silence," he agreed.

CHAPTER 11

Rick always thought of Georgetown as a sad part of the city. Sure, there were many neighborhoods that were more run-down – most of them, to be honest – but Georgetown had been the home of the Kennedys and the center of Camelot not all that long ago.

Now, it had a defeated air: there were too many young kids with backpacks or blanket rolls, sitting in doorways and asking for spare change with dead eyes. The stores were all covered with so many layers of new paint laid over old paint that they looked thick and pulled out of shape. The few high-end restaurants that had arrived with the Kennedys were struggling to survive next to stores selling marijuana papers, elaborate bongs, and multicolored glass pipes.

Rick made the turn at Wisconsin and M streets, marked by the Riggs Bank with its trademark copper turret on one side and Nathan's – a legendary DC watering hole – on the other. Halfway down the block, he turned into a narrow cobblestone alley and then made a hard right turn into the courier company's garage.

He had the bent brake pedal replaced and waited impatiently while the Ecuadorian mechanic changed the oil. The company mandated that couriers stop by and have the oil changed every week. Rick guessed that that was the reason so many of the BMWs had been driven over a hundred thousand miles, and a couple upward of two hundred thousand.

It could be that they just didn't want anything in the engine to ever go wrong – they were as stingy on repairs as they were on his paychecks. Almost every other Friday the dispatcher used every excuse in the book to stall until the couriers couldn't get to the bank before 3.00pm to cash their checks and the company would have the weekend to come up with the payroll. They were terrible bosses, but then again, they had all used to be couriers, so it shouldn't come as a surprise.

He chatted idly with one of the commercial couriers while he waited. The commercial riders were paid on a commission basis – the more they delivered, the more they earned – and consequently tore through town like complete maniacs. Rick had started out as a commercial courier but had decided on the second day that he wasn't going to die to deliver some lawyer's brief in record time. Luckily, on the same day, the dispatcher had decided that Rick was never going to ride fast enough to make money for the company, so they sent him over to ABN, where they were paid $7.50 an hour no matter how long it took him to deliver a roll of film.

Well, Rick thought, it was that and the fact that the previous ABN courier had been caught with an unlicensed .45 while he was working the night shift at a convenience store. Gun and drug arrests were all they checked for at the White House, but it was definitely one strike and you're out. Rick might have been new to Washington's confusing network of streets, but at least his record was clean.

On the other hand, he felt a bit guilty about bumping the guy – having a gun under the counter in an all-night market seemed reasonable when you realized that everyone except the most desperate and disoriented junkies knew that all the money was kept in a drop-safe. A buddy in the army who had pulled the graveyard shift at several all-night stores told him that anyone so fucked-up that they would even consider such a low-profit crime was so far gone that shooting a clerk over a twenty-dollar bill would simply strike him as the sensible thing to do.

After his oil change, he cut down to the waterfront under the Whitehurst Freeway – usually the quickest way back to the bureau. Today, however, the three coal cars that made up the only train that ever used the Georgetown Branch rail line – a beautiful right of way through the trees along the Potomac – had just arrived. It was a ridiculously wasteful way to deliver coal, but the small power plant under the freeway was where the White House got its electricity.

It was a bad place for motorcycles. It was the one area in the city where the company had ruled that any crash damage had to be paid by the rider – and the only place that Rick had seen a diamond-shaped danger sign with a picture of a motorcyclist. Even with all these warnings, every month or so,

Rick would hear of a rider getting his front tire jammed in a sunken railroad track and flying over the handlebars.

Consequently, he picked his way slowly through the maze of coal cars and cobblestones, feeling like he was following the flags that marked the safe path through a jungle minefield. Rick was almost a half hour late when he finally got to the bureau. Being late meant that there was no room to park with the other bikes just outside the 18th Street entrance, and he had to scout out a space behind a bar in the alley that ran through the center of the next block.

The minute he walked into the bureau, he knew something was terribly wrong.

All around the newsroom, there were small groups of men talking earnestly in low voices, and the secretaries were sitting at their desks with red eyes and streaked makeup. Rick asked Moretti what had happened.

"Hadley and his crew are all dead. They went off the George Washington Parkway last night. You know, where it's way up high over the river." Don shook his head and continued. "The crew wagon was so smashed up that the cops didn't even identify the bodies until late last night. What a fucking mess." The editor turned and went back into his small edit room – sitting on a high stool with his head in his hands.

As a courier, Rick wasn't really considered a part of the newsroom, and he was guilty but grateful that this allowed him to skirt the emotional chaos and make it back to the courier desk. Between his mother's destructive methods of child-raising and an unhealthy dose of battle trauma, he'd realized long ago that he just didn't react to this kind of emotional situation the way most people did.

Just another way that I don't act like a normal person, he thought.

The courier phone rang as soon as he sat down, and he was sent to the White House. Yes, everyone was upset, but there was still a show at 6 o'clock.

To avoid having to talk to anyone, Rick took the garage exit next to the courier desk. As he walked across the street to his bike, he saw the slim silhouette of a Datsun 240Z parked a bit farther down the alley. He considered the 240Z to be about the best-designed car on the road, so he was looking at the car, not paying much attention to the two men seated inside. But as he started his bike and pulled out, he realized that the men in the Datsun, two young Asians – almost certainly Vietnamese – had stopped talking, and both were staring straight at him.

After he turned the corner and started up the alley toward 19th Street, he heard the Datsun's engine start up. It sounded like it was fitted with glass-pack mufflers, and the ripping snarl of the engine echoed off the surrounding buildings. He decided that even if he wasn't sure they were following him, they'd shown an unhealthy interest, and putting a couple of dozen cars between the red sports car and his bike couldn't hurt. By the time the Datsun reached 19th Street, he had already made the left onto L and was out of sight.

Arriving at the southwest gate of the White

House, he waved at the guards, and they opened the black iron gates to West Executive Avenue and let him through. As always, he was amused at the idea that a helmet and a radio could get you into just about any place in this town. He parked next to three other courier bikes at the bottom of the stairs leading to the West Wing and jogged up to the guard booth.

The bored Uniformed Service officer inside said, "ID please."

Rick thought for just a second, and then reached into his jeans pocket, pulled out a wallet, and handed over the license with his real name on it.

"Birth date?"

The answer surprised Rick. "Today!" He'd totally forgotten.

Promptly, the guard in the booth and another officer standing just outside proceeded to sing a chorus of "Happy Birthday". Rick smiled. He'd be able to tell his kids someday that he'd celebrated his birthday in the White House, or more accurately, on the White House grounds. He took back his license and walked over to the pressroom.

Inside, it was hot and steamy. The camera crews had strewn their winter gear in heaps across half of the seats in the back of the briefing room and were either napping or smoking in the others. Rick turned left and headed through a maze of cubicles and down a set of stairs to the ABN booth. He opened the door and said "Hi" to the two reporters, a producer, and a radio engineer who all shared a space so small that their shoulders touched.

Jamie Mayweather, the lead White House correspondent, was on the phone and thrust his forefinger up in an urgent signal for Rick to shut up and wait.

"Answer me this," Mayweather roared into the phone. "If you don't know what's going on, who the hell does?" After listening for a second, he broke in. "Don't just tell me 1701! For Christ's sake, are you guys running the White House or are they? OK, *whom* at 1701 should I talk to? Oh, never mind, just forget it. I'll find out on my own." Mayweather then slammed down the phone and spun around to face the courier.

"What the hell do you want?"

"I don't want anything. You wanted a courier pickup."

The reporter glared at him for a second and then became distracted by something in the *New York Times* spread out on the counter to his right. "Well, just wait a damn second," he yelled over his shoulder as he began to read an article.

"What is '1701'?" Rick asked.

Mayweather acted as if no one had spoken, but the other reporter – a genial and slightly rumpled man named Ken Garrison, who seemed to have accepted the fact that he would always stand outside the spotlight that Mayweather seemed to carry around with him – said, "1701 Pennsylvania Avenue. The headquarters of CREEP. You know, the Committee for the Re-Election of the President that's already re-elected the President but doesn't seem to know when to go away."

"Ah," Rick said. "Less interesting than I thought. What else is going on?"

"Well, let's see. We've lost two more B-52s over Hanoi and there's a new boss over at the FBI, but the real lead story is that even the President can't get the NFL to lift the blackout on the Redskins playoff game."

Rick smiled. "Now we know where the center of power in this country really is."

"Did you ever doubt it?"

Mayweather shot up out of his chair, roaring, "Can't you people be quiet for two seconds?" He shoved a red-taped can of exposed film in Rick's general direction. "Here, take this back to the bureau. I won't use it tonight, but it will get you the hell out of here."

The phone rang, and Mayweather grabbed it and yelled, "What the hell do you people want? I can't get anything done if you keep calling me with your stupid questions!"

Rick looked quizzically at Garrison, who grinned and mouthed, "New York."

Rick headed back to his bike with the sound of Mayweather's shouting fading away behind him.

Rick searched but couldn't find anything to read at the courier desk except an old copy of *Sports Illustrated* he'd already flipped through twice. Technically, there was another magazine there, but it was one of the other couriers' copy of *Easyriders*, which, in Rick's opinion, was the only publication actually written by functional illiterates. He could only guess that the editors dictated it to some poor secretary or perhaps to one of the many girlfriends who were photographed wearing skimpy underwear and caressing their boyfriends' bikes. They always looked a bit uncomfortable, and Rick suspected that the heavy-handed symbolism was a bit much even for them.

"I found it, I found it!"

Shelley bounced out of the affiliate newsroom with a smile on her face, then suddenly stopped and burst into tears. Rick stood up, and she buried her face in his chest. He thought that he probably should give her a hug, but she was wearing the same sort of sheer nylon shirt as yesterday and, clearly, nothing underneath.

He was reduced to awkwardly patting her shoulder.

"Oh God, can you believe it? Joe, Ed, and Pete? They're dead. They're all dead. How can that happen?"

Rick was far too familiar with how death happened and didn't want to dwell on it, so he tried to change the subject. "You said you found something. What was it?"

She held up a red plastic film can. "Oh, I found Joe's film. Not that it matters anymore, I guess. But Ed, the operations producer, told me to find it no matter what it took, so I stayed here all night and looked and looked and couldn't find it, and then I started rolling every piece of film in the bureau through the Moviescope just to be sure."

Rick thought only a young kid trying to prove herself would work that hard. Of course, it was hard for any woman to prove herself in this business. There was only one female producer in the entire bureau, and the sole female correspondent was only ever sent to cover news events like the First Lady's teas.

"Where was it?" he asked.

"That's the weird thing. It was in a can marked as a Senate committee hearing from last week, and the head and tail of the film were labeled the same. I mean, the lab techs never make that kind of mistake, but I guess they did this time. I went through it all, and I could see Joe in the suit he had on yesterday and Pete moving around in the background of one setup shot, so I know it's right."

"Did you listen to it?" Rick asked. "Joe said it was a good story."

"I couldn't." She looked a bit guilty. "I'm not really supposed to use the Moviescope much less the Steenbeck, and you can't hear anything on the edit table. There were just some reverse shots of Joe, and "B-roll" roll' of the guy and the outside of his house, and then this long interview."

She spun around and headed off down the hall at a trot. "I'm going to tell Smithson. Maybe we can still do Joe's last story."

Rick called after her. "Wait a minute. There was 'B-Roll' on Farr's film?"

"Yup. They shot it before the interview."

Rick stood there and watched her go. Then he sat down, opened the drawer of the desk, pulled out the Bolex camera, and stared at it. If the crew had already shot cutaways and reverse shots with the primary camera, what was in the film Moten had given him?

After some thought, he stood up and yanked the heavy desk away from the wall. Reaching over, he carefully slid the small camera down so it stopped against the baseboard, making sure it couldn't be seen from the floor, and then gently pushed the desk back into place. He shoved a random pile of newspapers and net bags over the gap, and then lit a cigarette, sat back down, and stared into space.

CHAPTER 12

"So, the dispatcher can't figure out why the Dulles cops are laughing when they're telling him that one of his guys crashed." Sam Watkins was holding forth. "So, he gets the van and goes out to pick him up. And he goes into the police station and he finds his guy sitting there with a blanket around him."

A heavyset black man with patches of lighter-colored skin spotting his face, Sam held up a finger for emphasis. "Only a blanket."

He coughed, lit a cigarette, and continued. "What happened, you see, is that he'd gone under this bridge by the Pan Am freight terminal where the wind is always blasting straight in from the side. When he came out from under the overpass, it caught that damn metal fairing bolted to the front forks, and that bike was gone. He was scooting right along, and when he went down, he popped off the bike to keep his leg from being chewed off, but then he went skidding and rolling along for damn near a hundred yards."

Sam pursed his lips and popped his eyes for comic effect. "He was one hundred percent naked. He'd scraped every scrap of clothes he had on right off. Boots, jeans, jacket, everything. He wasn't really hurt, just scraped up, but the cops just fell out when they found him."

Rick laughed. Sam had been an ABN courier since 1963. According to him, he'd been hired the day before Kennedy was assassinated and ended up sleeping on top of desks in the bureau for two weeks before he got home again. Sometimes, Rick thought he'd learned more from listening to Sam's rambling stories than in four years of college.

He pulled out a Winston, offered one to Sam, did his up-down trick with the Zippo, and lit both cigarettes.

"Hey, move over and make some room," said a voice over his shoulder. It was Kyle Matthews, the third courier currently assigned to ABN. Kyle was a skinny kid with a tattoo of a shamrock on his left arm and a sort of "twitchy" look – as if he were always playing an angle. He was just out of junior college or, Rick suspected, just flunked out of junior college. Kyle was OK to hang out with, but not someone you wanted to depend on.

"And exactly where do you expect us to make this room?" asked Sam in an arch tone. "I suppose you could sit in the ashtray. Or in one of the desk drawers."

"Well, you could start by taking all this crap," Kyle said, grabbing the pile of raingear and heavy coats that were sitting on the remaining chair, "and putting it carefully in the proper location." He dumped the wet mass into the middle of the hall, threw his own gear on the top of the pile, and sat down. "Now there's plenty of room."

He opened a bag of Cheez Doodles and began to eat.

"How is it out there?" Rick asked.

"Completely shitty with a fifty percent chance of incredibly shitty," Kyle responded. "It's stopped raining at the moment, but it's right at the freezing point and the roads are slick as hell. I almost lost it just making the turn into the side entrance off Connecticut Avenue."

Sam intoned, "Another beautiful day in Paradise."

The courier phone rang.

"You, sir, are up." Sam gleefully pointed at Rick. "And with any luck, I won't get another run before I can get out of here. For once, I might actually get home with my toes unfrozen."

Rick picked up the phone. "All-Night Couriers, We Go In Snow."

"I damn well hope so," said Casey Ross, "because you get to slalom your way out to Suitland for the weather film."

"Casey, don't we have a car I can drive? I figure I've got about a fifty-fifty chance of making it back alive in this temperature."

"I already checked. We don't. Just take it easy. It's not like it's worth your life." Ross laughed. "Of course, you have to make the local feed, so I guess you do need to take a reasonable amount of prudent chances. On the other hand, if you lose your life, we'll miss the feed, so–"

"This must be the way you used to talk to guys you were sending out to hot zones in Vietnam. Glad you care so deeply."

"Empathy, my friend, is what has made me the award-winning journalist I am today. Bring the film right up when you get back." The phone line clicked off.

Rick hung up and began the long process of suiting up. In reality, the run wasn't going to be that bad – a little cold, but there wasn't any snow or ice… yet. If he had really thought he might die on the way, the weather film could sit in Suitland forever.

He mused, "Does anyone know if they feed that stuff down to the Weather Service, or do they drop the film from the satellite?"

Sam cocked his head and pretended to think for a moment. "I haven't the slightest clue, old man. I just know that the entire nation is depending on you to bring them those pictures of fluffy clouds in time for the 5 o'clock news."

Kyle slid into the seat Rick had just vacated and picked up the paper. "Hey, look at this. This place in Virginia just blew apart. Cool."

Rick glanced at the paper. He recognized the trees behind the pile of rubble that his perfect memory told him had once been a brick Colonial. "Was the owner inside?"

"Ummm. Yeah." Kyle read a bit more. "Or at least they think so. Everything was pretty much vaporized, according to this. They say it was a gas leak."

Rick turned and headed for his bike, but his mind was on the events of the day before. Hadley and the crew had an accident, and now the guy they'd interviewed was a mist in the wind. *And* the film had gone missing. Had the can been incorrectly labeled on purpose? He felt a chill and imagined he heard the rustle of someone moving closer in the tall grass.

As he began to light his cigarette, Paul Smithson realized that he had two already burning – one in the ashtray on his desk and one in the ashtray on the credenza behind him. He looked at the one in his hand a moment and then went ahead and lit it, shaking out the match with a snap of irritation, and sat back in his deep leather chair, rubbing his forehead and sighing deeply.

He sure as hell hadn't signed up for this.

He regarded the red plastic film can on his desk with a mixture of fear and hatred. Why couldn't that goddamn film just stay lost? he thought.

After all, film that people actually wanted to find disappeared every day into the river of pictures that passed through the ABN bureau, so why did the one goddamn reel he never wanted to see again keep popping up?

It reminded him of his ex-wife.

That little hippie bitch was the real problem. Why couldn't she have just given up like a rational person?

Everything had been simple, deniable, and easily explained even if it became known. The film was hidden in plain sight. He'd just gone down and taken it from where it sat in the crew room before the editor came to pick it up. Not that it mattered – the bureau chief could go anywhere – but no one had even seen him.

It had only taken a moment to step into the office across the hall and replace the markings on the head and tail ends, slap on the new label he'd prepared, and then go back into the crew room to put it in with the other old film cans that no one had ever picked up. God knows no one would ever have willingly screened through that boring damn hearing.

Now there it was, sitting on his desk like a fucking rattlesnake. And even worse, that dumb blonde had screened it, so he couldn't just make it disappear again.

Damn her, I'd be doing her a favor by firing her. She should be out having babies or getting laid or something. Not working overtime. Women just aren't right for this kind of work.

He swung around to look out the window at the dreary winter street. It had all seemed so easy: a cushy job as a respectable member of the press after all those years of political warfare. His stomach no longer required a daily dosing of Pepto, and he'd kick the cigarettes anytime now, and, God, the money was so sweet. At this rate, it would only take a couple more years to pay off that little place near Key Biscayne – a proper reward after all those years of public service.

Damn it, he'd left politics behind him. They had no right to just call him up and expect him to jump like a fucking monkey just because they said "national security" like those were magic words. Hadn't he ripped Hadley a new one after they called bitching about that story on the money getting laundered through that bank in the Bahamas? Hell, he'd made the prissy bastard do a public apology for that one.

The good old days were gone, and those bastards had to wise up. Sure, he'd gone along when a story just had to be spiked or his old boss wanted him to go after some liberal faggot on the Hill, but things had changed.

He spun around and jammed his cigarette into the ashtray. Damn it. He simply wasn't going to do it. This was the news business and, goddamn it, this was real news. Hadley was dead, but he could hand it off to Mayweather. That grouchy son of a bitch would run with it.

Running his fingers through his hair, he stood up and grabbed the film can. The phone rang, and he picked it up. "Smithson."

At the sound of the voice on the line, he closed his eyes and felt helpless resignation wash over him. He sat down heavily. When he finally spoke, his voice was flat and lifeless.

"Yes, sir. I do remember who gave me my first job. Don't worry; it will all be taken care of."

CHAPTER 13

The Suitland Federal Center had been built like many things around Washington – during World War Two to house whatever needed to be housed. From what Rick could tell, they didn't plan things back then. It was more that a branch of the military saw a piece of vacant land, grabbed it, and built something just in case they might need it. They seldom seemed to give any of it back.

He remembered that it was only a year or so ago that they had finally knocked down the "wartime emergency offices" that had covered both sides of the Reflecting Pool between the Lincoln Memorial and the Washington Monument with row after row of poorly built wooden shacks.

Suitland seemed to be where government departments were dumped when no one could think of a better place to put them: a Federal Records Center, Naval Intelligence, and the Census Bureau. One of the cameramen had told Rick that the Library of Congress even kept thousands of feet of old newsreel in hardened munitions bunkers out there. The reasoning being that since old film was essentially

TNT on a reel, it was probably a bad idea to store it next to the Capitol with the books, documents, and other equally flammable cultural artifacts.

The Weather Service had also ended up in one of the drab concrete buildings that seemed to have been all anyone had built in the 1940s. On the bright side, wartime urgency meant that the government had built a road dedicated to military use from Washington to Suitland, or, more correctly, out to Andrews Air Base, which was right next door, and which had originally been meant for fighter pilots to get to their planes quickly in case of a German attack making its way across the Atlantic.

In the absence of any likelihood of *Luftwaffe* bombers suddenly appearing, Suitland Parkway was open to civilian traffic, but it remained one of the hidden roads used exclusively by people who lived and worked in Washington. Like Beach Drive in Rock Creek Park, or the Whitehurst Freeway around Georgetown, they were the secret ways you could slide right through crowded neighborhoods and past the stoplights where tourists waited in increasing frustration.

It was an easy cruise through downtown, past the gay dance clubs, warehouses, and battered housing projects of Southeast and over the Frederick Douglass Bridge. From runs to Frederick Douglass's home, Saint Elizabeth's Hospital, and other places in Anacostia, Rick knew it had once been well-to-do suburban living for government workers, but that had been long ago. Now Anacostia was a nightly war zone between rival drug gangs – a place where innocent children were caught in the cross fire on a regular basis. He had read that the shooters called the children "mushrooms" because they just popped up everywhere and got in the way.

Rick was perfectly content to use the parkway to bypass Anacostia.

Once on the quiet, tree-lined four-lane road, the commuter traffic thinned out, and Rick opened up the BMW. He wasn't really dancing – it was too slick for that – but he didn't see any point in taking his time.

Suddenly, there was the thunder of a powerful engine only inches from his rear bumper. In the side mirrors, close-set headlights blazed. He felt a jolt, and the bike went crazy. The front pushed out of line and swerved wildly. Rick fought the handlebars and grabbed more throttle – speed would help straighten him out.

He risked a fast glance behind him. It was that Datsun he'd seen earlier, the glass-pack exhausts roaring and the two guys inside grinning. Grinning, damn it!

He heard a crunch from the rear fender, but no shock. They must have dropped back before they hit the tire. For a moment, the rear fender made dangerous noises. It was obviously cutting into the rubber. Then there was a backward jerk from the rear, and the noise stopped. Rick realized with a sense of relief that the end of the fender had folded under. At least it was off the tire.

Rick abandoned any ideas that this was just random road rage. The fact that he'd spotted them before meant these morons were clearly out to get him. He kicked down two gears and the engine screamed in protest. BMWs weren't really made for speed, but now Rick was thankful that they were very well-designed for stability and durability. For a moment, he drew away from the sports car as the speedometer needle crept upward. He crouched down over the tank, continued to nail the throttle to the stop, and kicked back up to top gear.

He was coming up fast on two cars driving side by side – blocking both lanes. Rick split between them like they were standing still and smashed the side mirror of the car on the right with the end of his handlebar. Let's see the Datsun do that, he thought.

The Datsun swerved right, passing the cars on the gravel verge, then smoked the tires as it fought its way back onto the parkway and straddled the centerline, catching up once again.

Rick shot a quick glance to his right. Too damn steep; he'd never make it. Without conscious thought, he locked his legs around the gas tank and whipped the bike down in as hard a left turn as he'd ever taken.

Time seemed to slow. Rick could feel the front tire bucking and slipping as he slammed across the grass median. Thankfully, the ground was still iron hard from last week's hard freeze, or the front end would have rammed into mud and he would have flipped over for sure.

Behind him, the Datsun's tires screeched as the driver slammed on the brakes and the sports car spun on the slick concrete.

Rick could see a car coming fast from the opposite direction, but it looked like he would get across the road in front of it, so he concentrated on trying to make out what was on the other side of the road. At first, it was just a solid wall of trees and bushes.

There. A hole in the wall. Some kind of path.

He went airborne for a few feet when he hit the curb of the southbound lanes, but he held the bike in alignment by shifting his weight with his butt, and as soon as he hit concrete again, he began struggling to turn toward that tiny empty space in the trees. The BMW's inertia was immense, and he had to use all the strength in his shoulders and arms to muscle it out of what was a clear intention to shoot straight into an enormous tree trunk. He backed off the throttle, but was afraid he'd lose control if he hit the brakes, so he slammed down through the gears instead.

Time accelerated as he ripped across onto the gravel and then the grass. The oncoming driver flashed by his rear bumper, and he saw a streak of red zip just behind him on his right, and heard a car horn voice fear and anger. He'd forgotten all about the oncoming car, but, luckily, he had been right about who would get there first.

For a long, terrifying second, he thought the bike would miss the path. Then his front wheel shot upward as the bike hit the clear slope. He threw his weight forward over the gas tank to keep the front down, and trees began whipping past. Still belly-down to the tank and peering just over the handlebars, he realized it must really be a footpath because he hadn't hit a tree yet – a lot of branches, but not a tree.

Not yet.

Now he could use the rear brake, feathering it just

on the edge of breaking into a skid. He fought to bring the heavy bike under control, which was a relative term. The BMW was never designed to be a dirt bike, and he stood up on the foot pegs as it bucked and banged beneath him.

He kicked through neutral to first gear and gave it some gas. The rear wheel threw up a fountain of dirt and leaves as he began to surge up the slope. A log across his path almost took him down, but he managed to bounce the front wheel up and power the rear wheel over it.

A final screen of bushes tore at his arms, and he was clear – alone in an open field.

He skidded to a stop and carefully put down the kickstand. Slowly, he swung off and turned around. The woods were dark and silent behind him, no headlights following him up through the trees. Around him were the quiet, carefully tended expanses of grass and the rows of small, dignified white headstones of a military cemetery. He walked over and read one of the stones.

Andrew H. Sturris, LCpl. US Marine Corps, World War II, Sept. 24 1921 July 16, 1943. Silently, he apologized to Lance Corporal Sturris and anyone else he might have disturbed, and then he dropped to the ground and just lay there – catching his breath.

After a while, he stood up and walked around the BMW to look at the damage. The rear fender was screwed, but the useless radio was still firmly attached. He pulled some branches out of the front end and marveled at how much damage that weird triangular front linkage could take.

Both mirrors were shoved back, but only the left one was cracked. Otherwise, the bike was in miraculously good shape.

He bent the mirrors back into place and used the small tire irons from the tool kit tucked under the seat to beat the rear fender to a reasonable semblance of its original shape. Swinging his leg over, it took three tries to start the engine. The familiar rumble was like the voice of an old friend.

Staying close to the backs of the headstones to avoid running over anyone – alive or dead – Rick drove slowly across the wintry grass until he found a gravel road and followed its solemn curves to an open entrance leading to a main road. Looking both ways, he spotted the enormous satellite dishes of the Suitland Federal Center to his right.

As he drove to the pickup he was wired as tight as a point man in country – focused on everything around him. The Datsun didn't reappear. Maybe they had just picked him up on the street in DC and didn't know his destination. He hoped that was the case since any other explanation would require someone at ABN ratting him out.

At Suitland, he moved slowly through parking lots and wove in and out of the old buildings – even stopping and cutting the engine at one point – but he didn't hear that distinctive sound of custom exhaust pipes – so he headed for the Weather Service.

He picked up the small can of film that held thirty seconds of clouds racing across the North American continent from the bored old woman at the counter and returned to his bike. As he put the can in his bag, he felt another round shape. Pulling it out, he read the Magic Marker on the red tape around the edge.

"Hadley B-Roll."

Thinking back, he realized that this was the can of film that Pete Moten had handed him at the bookkeeper's house on the day they died. It had slipped to the bottom of his bag, and he'd forgotten about it because he was concentrating on the Bolex camera and that damn twelve-hundred-foot magazine. It hadn't ever made it inside the bureau and couldn't have been developed.

Or lost.

Lost twice.

He slipped the can into the inside pocket of his leather jacket and took a different way back – north to Pennsylvania Avenue, across the John Philip Sousa Bridge, and through back streets and alleys to the bureau.

On the way, he made a quick stop at his house and hid the can marked "Hadley B-Roll" under the back steps.

CHAPTER 14

The Omega Restaurant had been a part of Washington's secret history for decades. A Hungarian, smart enough to get out before Soviet tanks crushed his fellow revolutionaries, first opened it in the 1950s. In those days, the tables were filled with conversations in German, Czech, and Polish, and the air laced with code words and watchful silences.

Now it served Cuban food, and if the name's resemblance to the Miami paramilitary group Omega 7 didn't make it clear enough, the sign out front spelled out "O-m-E-g-A". In 1962, when a Cuban refugee bought out the Hungarian owner, the Organization of American States – OEA in Spanish – expelled Cuba and declared Fidel Castro's government illegitimate. Some say this gave legal cover for the disastrous invasion at the Bay of Pigs.

A small room next to a little grocery store on Columbia Road at the edge of the Adams Morgan nightclub district, it was worth a visit even if you weren't there for a secret meeting or some revolutionary fellowship: the menu was one of the finest in Washington.

The quiet man in the gray suit was at his usual table in the back, where he could sit with his back to the wall and an escape route through the kitchen was only a few steps away. He looked around at the small oilcloth-covered tables and thought the place had recovered well from the firebomb that had smashed through the main window a year or so ago. He knew that the owner wasn't frightened by something as trivial as a firebomb, and it appeared that the cooks were cut from the same cloth.

He was eating pork with a bitter orange sauce, and though he resisted nostalgia as much as he did any other emotion, it was impossible not to be reminded of days in Miami when brave men had stood by his side and planned how to free their island nation.

He would go to his grave convinced that they had been betrayed.

It was in the aftermath of the failed invasion that he took on a different line of work. Silent violence in the shadows with no one by his side. Cut adrift from all contact with the Agency; those on the inside could go on fighting the forces of tyranny abroad while he cleaned up messes here at home.

There was always a mess. Today was no exception.

The door to the street opened and two young Vietnamese men came in. They stood there for a moment, clearly looking for someone until the man in the back raised a hand. They came to his table, bowed slightly, and sat upright in their chairs with their hands carefully folded on the table.

For a time, there was silence. The young men stared at the tablecloth as if it held some great secret, or perhaps just a reasonable excuse for failure. Despite their working name, they were not twins. Nguyen Vien was slightly taller and heavier than his partner, and had his long hair pulled back into a loose ponytail. Today he was wearing a white T-shirt and jeans. Quan Tung looked older and more businesslike in a shirt and tie, and, indeed, he usually took the orders and made the deals.

Today, they both had scrapes and bruises on their hands and faces. These would heal and fade away, but when you looked in their eyes, it was easy to see that both men had many older, deeper scars.

The quiet man sipped his coffee – sweet and almost violently strong in the proper Cuban fashion – and ran his eyes over everyone in the room.

Then, without looking at the two men seated across from him, he spoke. "The courier got away?"

"We hit him twice!" Tung burst out. "He should have crashed, but he put that goddamn bike right into the goddamn trees. We tried to follow, but we would have smashed the car. Then we ran through the bushes on foot. Look at us."

He made a dramatic gesture to the damage on his face.

The deep blue eyes blazed. Tung fell silent and his hand fell back to the table.

"The courier got away."

Sullenly, Tung said, "Yes."

"So."

The man in gray raised a finger and ordered another coffee. He didn't offer to get anything for the other two. There was another silence until the coffee arrived. The man took a sip, carefully put the tiny cup back in its saucer, settled back in his seat, and folded his hands in his lap.

He spoke. "There will be no more mistakes. None. Do you understand me?"

Both men nodded, keeping their eyes on the empty table in front of them.

"We need to clean this up. All of it. The courier, the film – everything has to be taken care of." He sighed. "It's gone too far to be kept utterly silent. We'll just have to hope that it gets lost in all the other bullshit going on in this town." He shook his head. "Jesus, the Watergate operation was a complete screw-up. I still can't believe they couldn't handle a basic black-bag job. They certainly weren't that stupid when I worked with them. At least everyone is looking at them and not at us. We just need to make absolutely damn sure that there are no loose ends – none."

The two Vietnamese nodded again.

"Look at me," he said. There was another silence as he stared at first one, then the other. "I do not want to have to consider both of you expendable. Do you understand?"

This time they didn't nod; they just stared into his eyes and saw the bottomless cold of a Korean winter.

"Good. Now leave."

The two men got up and left without a word.

The man in the gray suit took another sip of his coffee. Damn, it had gone cold. He raised his hand for another cup.

Rick carefully drove the BMW across the sidewalk and up the narrow passage next to the bureau. In the center of the block, he turned and bumped over the wooden walkway, then parked in the courtyard between the buildings. No one would accidentally spot the BMW here, he thought.

If those two were waiting for him when he came out, he'd know that someone in the bureau was to blame.

He swung stiffly off the bike and walked around the tiny courtyard for a couple of minutes, limping as he stretched out the places on his legs where they'd been pummeled by branches or battered by the jolting motorcycle. Then he stood still, straightened up his spine, took a deep breath, and headed for the back door.

When he entered the bureau, he was walking without a limp and had his usual half smile on his face. He passed the main studio, glancing inside to see one engineer up on a stepladder setting lights, another engineer puffing on a cigar and idly holding the bottom of the ladder, and yet another engineer sitting in a chair and observing. For a moment, he thought how nice it must be to have a union job.

He continued to the main newsroom, where the pre-show chaos was in full swing. The anchor wasn't in his chair and Tom Evans, the senior producer, was sitting back with his feet on the desk, just looking at the ceiling and smoking.

He looked down at Rick and raised one eyebrow.

"Nothing interesting, just the weather film. What's going on?"

Evans picked up a sheet of paper from his desk. "Well, here's the first lineup, which we know will change, but let's see. We'll begin with the war. The B-52s hammered Hanoi again, but the bastards are parading the aircrews who were shot down yesterday in front of the cameras, so that is at best a draw. Then Hopson over at State will talk about the diplomatic situation, which is, to put it simply, entirely screwed up. Even he can't stretch that out, so that should only take a minute."

He drew on his cigarette.

"OK, then we've got Apollo 17 pulling off the final moon landing, and Marcus will tell us how much money we wasted on that little project."

He paused and ran his eyes down the page.

"Well, after that, we pretty much run out of news except for that poor bastard at the *LA Times* who's getting locked up for refusing to give up his Watergate interviews, and… that's it. We plunge headfirst into the land of cuddly kids and even cuddlier animals."

He looked up and smiled, squinting a bit from the smoke. "All in all, a tip-top newscast."

Rick laughed. "Well, you could always run the weather loop."

"We're not that desperate. At least not yet." His smile vanished. "Oh, and we're going to do a story about Hadley and the guys at the end of the broadcast. Almost forgot about that – wishful thinking."

Don Moretti's voice came from his edit room. "Hey, Rick, did anyone ever find Hadley's film?"

Rick turned. "I thought that Shelley from the affiliate group found it."

"Nah, that turned out to be some other interview from months ago. Smithson's not happy about it, either."

"That sucks. She's a good kid."

Evans nodded. "She is. However, you'd better drop by and say your good-byes. Smithson fired her."

"What about Hadley's story? Anyone else going to take it?"

The producer looked at Rick for a moment, then said slowly, "One of the things you learn in this business is that some stories–"

One of the secretaries called from her desk, "Tom, New York's on line four."

Instantly losing any interest in speaking to Rick, Evans picked up the phone and said, "What do you want now?" Listening intently, he lit another Lucky and started making notes on a yellow pad.

Rick knew he should deliver the weather film directly to the affiliate service instead of the processing lab, since it had been developed before he picked it up. The moment he walked in, a weeping Shelley hit him like a linebacker.

"I screwed up," she sobbed. "They're going to fire me and…"

Any intelligible words were lost against his chest in a storm of tears. Rick realized that, again, she was wearing one of those damn sheer nylon shirts, so, thinking that it was probably a good thing that he still had his leather jacket zipped, he once again began patting her on the shoulder.

When she paused for breath, he broke in. "I have the weather film."

A big smile instantly replaced the tears. "Oh, great. That needs to go out right now." She brushed past him on a dead run, and Rick, with the vague feeling he'd just narrowly escaped a disaster, went across the hall to the courier desk. Sam was sitting in the number one chair with a big smile on his face.

On second thought, Rick thought it looked more like a leer.

"Damn, man, you look like you're going to get lucky." Sam said.

Definitely a leer.

Rick gave him a raised eyebrow and went to hang his riding gear on the end of the cubicle partition.

Sam chuckled, and then his face became serious. "Hey, did you hear about Kyle? He got busted."

"For what? Driving while stupid?"

"No, that's not a crime in this city. Grand larceny."

"You're kidding. What did he do? Rob a bank?" Rick immediately answered his own question. "No way. Kyle's not smart enough to even plan something that big."

"Yes, as you point out, our friend Kyle isn't too bright." There was a certain relish in Sam's voice – this promised to be a good story. "But he is persistent. Three weeks ago, he went to a car dealer and stole two tires for his new used Volkswagen. Jacked their car up and took 'em in the middle of the night – got away clean, no problems." Sam paused for dramatic effect. "Well, the new tires looked so good on the front, he starts thinking how much better it would be if he had matching tires on the back."

Rick collapsed into the other chair. "Please don't tell me he went back."

"Yes, indeed. It's only been three weeks, but that doesn't stop the brainless fool from going right back to the same dealer – he goes to the same damn car! And surprise, surprise, the lights go on, and there are police everywhere."

"Is he in jail?"

"No, it happened a couple of days ago, and he managed to talk his way into getting bail – first offense and like that. Or, at least, it's the first offense he got caught at." Sam pointed at Rick's chair. "He was sitting right where you are now, moaning about being broke and needing a lawyer and how unfair it all was."

The courier phone rang. Sam picked it up.

"I'm sorry. No one is available to take your call. Please call back tomorrow."

Clearly, whoever was on the other end of the line wasn't buying it. After a couple of minutes of listening, Sam put down the receiver and stood up with an exaggerated groan.

"Well, it's off to the OSOB for me. Payment for my sins. See you later."

"Later."

Rick smiled as he remembered his first day at ABN. He'd been told to get up to "the OSOB" on the double, and he'd responded, "Yes, sir!" and almost ran out of the building. He waited until he was a block away and out of sight before he stopped the bike, pulled out a map, and struggled to find his destination. After an hour and several conversations with passers-by and bemused Capitol Hill cops, he finally identified the Russell Senate Office Building as older than the Dirksen Senate Office building and therefore called the "Old Senate Office Building" or "OSOB".

Just another example of how this town was designed to confuse anyone who wasn't born here.

Since he was usually assigned to the late shift, one of Rick's regular runs was to Union Station. Sort of like a diplomatic pouch, ABN sent bags every day on the last train up to New York and the last train down to DC. They usually held archived films that someone had ordered from the library, but the contents could be almost anything, from stacks of memos or expense reports to parts for some broken machine.

Rick had always liked Union Station. It felt like only yesterday thousands of young men in green woolen uniforms had passed through on their way to the battlefields of Europe or beach landings on remote Pacific islands. Walking in through the wooden swinging doors, he looked up at the vaulted ceiling. Once painted white, smoke and dust had turned it a splotched yellowish gray. On a balcony that ran around the sides were statues of Roman warriors in robes and togas holding shields in front of them. Rick smiled, remembering that Sam had told him that at least one or two were "anatomically correct" behind their shields.

The main hall had an echoing marble floor and dark wooden benches that appeared to have been designed for maximum passenger discomfort when steam engines still smoked and whistled out in the rail yard. Rick waved at the two cops who stood on the side, amiably observing the passing crowds. The fatter one smiled back and touched the brim of his cap in mock salute.

The baggage checkroom was in the back, behind the ticket counters, where the floor changed from marble to worn linoleum tile. Rick leaned on the wooden counter while the elderly black attendant made his usual laborious search for the brightly colored mesh sacks that Rick had immediately spotted right in the front section of the second set of shelves. He wondered briefly if he should say anything, but then realized that he wasn't in any real hurry and decided to just relax.

Instantly, he froze. The very act of relaxation had triggered all his battle reflexes – letting down for even a second could mean a quick death in combat. He didn't move, but he was suddenly acutely aware of every movement, every sound around him.

It saved his life.

There was a quickening in one set of footsteps approaching from behind him, and he whirled and jerked to one side as a knife slammed through the space where his back had been. He grabbed his attacker by the neck as the man lost his balance – betrayed by the lack of resistance to his knife thrust. Pulling hard, Rick used the man's momentum to slam his head against the wooden counter and then into a stumbling sprawl on the slick tiled floor. A long, thin knife went spinning across the waiting room and disappeared under a heating unit.

His assailant spun to his feet and faced him. For an instant, Rick thought he was back in the Ia Drang Valley, caught in another flashback. In front of him was a Vietnamese face twisted in rage – like in every one of his nightmares. Then the man reached into the small of his back, pulled out a pistol, and cocked it as his arm came up to aim.

Without conscious thought, Rick dodged to the side, jerked the heavy Motorola radio off his belt, and threw it hard at the man's head. Without even looking to see if he hit his target, he turned and ran.

When it came down to it, he didn't care if this was real or a flashback. If he got away, he could always figure that out later.

And if it wasn't a dream, who the hell was this guy?

He raced toward the back of the station, where hundreds of passengers were lined up, patiently waiting for the attendant to unhook the velvet rope and allow them to board their train. Concentrating on keeping his footing – motorcycle boots weren't made for running – Rick heard the sound of his assailant's soft shoes coming up fast behind him and realized he wasn't going to win in a footrace. Not after all those damn Winstons.

He rammed past the passengers, knocking two businessmen at the front of the line flying, their briefcases exploding in a shower of paper. Then he cut sharply to the left, stopped by slamming into the wall beside the open door. He grabbed the brass pole that held the velvet rope and – without looking – swung it behind him as hard as he could.

The Vietnamese caught it right in the stomach, grunted, and went down. Rick dropped the pole's heavy metal base on the man's head and took off again. He thought, I don't want to kill, but I don't mind slowing him down.

He shot through the open door to the train platforms.

He looked left and saw forklifts and freight and, behind them, a solid stone wall. No escape there, so he headed down the concrete deck to his right, looking for a street and a way back to the motorcycle parked out front. After he passed the front of two trains, he heard the slam as his attacker came through the door behind him and then a bang and the simultaneous *zip-whistle* sound of a bullet going by his head.

Damn, that son of a bitch is serious!

Instantly, he went left, between the trains, weaving around the green iron columns that ran down the center.

A bullet chipped thick paint off a column he'd just passed.

The last car of the train was on his right, so he dodged left, and then went right; throwing himself off the platform and down onto the rails and loose stones of the rail bed. He almost lost his footing but managed to stay upright through sheer momentum. On the other side of the railbed, he scrambled up onto the next platform and started running again.

There was no train on his right this time, only a short iron fence and a drop-off to more tracks. Suddenly, he realized where those tracks went. He turned to the fence and paused, looking down at about a ten-foot drop to more damn loose rocks.

Behind him, he could hear the gunman's running footsteps, so he swung his legs over the fence, climbed down to the concrete ledge, hung by his hands as far as he could, and dropped, bracing for the shock.

He was amazed when he didn't sprain an ankle, but he wasn't going to question his luck. He couldn't keep running out into the open rail yard – he would be an easy target – so he reversed course and headed back toward the station. He hopped over the rails and jumped up on another platform. This one had a roof that gave him cover – a good thing, since there was another shot and a round smacked into the wood above his head. After pounding down to the end of the platform where the stairs led back to the station, he jumped back on the tracks and followed them into a tunnel.

He knew that this tunnel went right under the Capitol and was the only way through DC for southbound trains. The tunnel was old and dark, with only occasional metal-caged bulbs casting orange pools of light. It curved to the right, so there was no light at the end, and he knew he wouldn't be backlit for an easy shot once he got out of the light spill from the entrance.

He slowed to a fast walk, worried that he'd twist an ankle on the rough and unstable footing.

He looked back and saw his pursuer. The bastard was still coming. Well, let him come. He was tired of running.

He realized that he wanted a cigarette and was amused that not being able to satisfy his nicotine habit made him angrier than being shot at.

As he expected they would, the two tracks soon merged into a single line. He'd seen from the Southeast Freeway that only one track led out on the other side, heading for the railroad bridge over the Potomac. He kept up a fast pace, looking for something to use as a weapon.

Almost simultaneously, he heard the sound of a northbound train in front of him and saw a two-foot length of metal pipe in the trash alongside the track. He used the pipe to destroy the next two overhead lights and pressed himself up behind a support beam right where the gloom gave way to the next pool of light.

He thought: This guy will be cautious in the dark, but he'll start feeling better with the light, and his attention will be focused up ahead.

He snuggled in close to the wall, hidden by the beam, and waited, forcing his breathing to slow. His body ached from the abuse he'd just put it through, but the core strength from his nightly workouts had protected him from any serious damage.

Then he could hear cautious steps on the other side of the beam. The Vietnamese man took only one step too far, but it was enough – the pipe slammed down on his wrist, and the pistol went skittering off into the darkness.

The man immediately attacked with the knife in his other hand.

Rick held the pipe across his chest and blocked the first thrust. Then the light from the coming train filled the tunnel with actinic fury. The Vietnamese man shot a glance at the train and moved in – away from the tracks. Rick caught his opponent's knife hand in his right fist and rammed the pipe into his chest with the left.

Years of patient squeezing of that rubber ball had served him well. The knife stayed locked in place even when his attacker tried to put his hip behind it and push with his legs. The train's whistle began a frantic series of warning blasts – painful in the small tunnel.

For a second, the two men remained locked together, immobile as they strained against each other. Then, slowly, Rick began to push the other man back – back into the path of the oncoming locomotive. His attacker jerked his head toward the train, becoming frantic as the slow-moving train came steadily closer. Finally, he tried to jerk backward, making a desperate plunge to the safety of the other side of the tunnel.

His knife hand remained locked in Rick's grip, and the courier was slowly pushing the metal bar forward, pushing the Vietnamese man directly in front of the oncoming locomotive.

Rick stared into the other man's eyes.

He shoves his rifle into the angry face only inches away and pulls the trigger. The lever is set to full rock and roll, and a stream of bullets shred the face into a mist that merges into the smoke of battle.

Rick shook his head to clear it. He was damned if he was going to see this bastard's eyes every time he went to sleep.

He reversed his effort and pulled his attacker close to his chest just as the train shot past with shrieking brakes and that damn whistle screaming. An engineer up in the cab was frozen in an instant of shocked surprise.

Using the momentum of the pull, he twisted and slammed the back of the man's head into the tunnel wall. Then, he spun the pipe and rammed it viciously into the other man's crotch. As the Vietnamese crumpled forward, Rick released his knife hand and, grabbing his opponent by his pony tail, spun him around again and slammed his face into the steel support beam – once, twice, three times – until the man's body went limp. The knife rattled on the rocks underfoot.

The train was still pounding and swaying only inches away. Rick jammed the pipe between the I-beam and an electrical conduit that ran down the tunnel wall, pinning his assailant solidly. He exerted an extra burst of strength to shove it down another inch, ensuring the pipe wouldn't move.

He stood rigid until the picture of what he had almost done was packed carefully away in a corner of his mind along with the mud and blood of war. He knew it wasn't gone, and he was sure to see it replayed many nights, but it was safe for the moment, and the moment was the small place where he could still remain alive – and relatively sane.

At least this time he hadn't killed anyone.

When his attention returned to the tunnel, the train had almost stopped, but he guessed it wouldn't take long for one of the crew to work their way back to investigate. More likely, they were radioing DC Metro to close off both ends of the tunnel – train crews weren't paid to investigate things like this.

The cars were beginning to slow, so he began to make his way along the tunnel wall – heading south because there sure as hell would be cops coming in from the station after all that noise they'd made. He came out of the tunnel on the other side of the Mall, jumped the fence into the parking lot of the Market Inn, and walked back across the Mall to the station, looking like a rather smudged tourist.

He even felt like a tourist as he gazed with a new appreciation at the white glory of the glowing Capitol dome and the long expanse of grass that ran down to the Washington Monument.

When he got back to the train station, he took off his leather jacket and stashed it behind a bush near his bike. At the front of the station, the only redcap was patiently waiting for an elderly woman to work out how much to tip him for putting her in a cab. He didn't see Rick take a small suitcase from the pile behind him.

Rick carried it through the doors and past the transit police. No one grabbed him, so he dropped the suitcase next to the locked door marked "Lost Luggage" and headed for the baggage counter.

This time, he didn't wait on the attendant. He pointed out the ABN sacks, signed for them, quickly picked up his radio from the dark corner of the floor where it had gone unnoticed, and left. He smiled as he thought that this might have been the first time that the damn radio had been useful.

CHAPTER 15

As the adrenaline washed out of his system, Rick felt as if everything around him was closed off behind a wall of thick plastic, and he had to pay close attention to be sure that he did everything correctly as he finished up at the office.

"Correctly" in this instance meant acting like a person who hadn't just come very close to being killed. When he reached the group house, he saw that all the lights were out, so he came in quietly and began to look for something to eat.

He'd cut off a chunk of Jarlsberg cheese and was leaning against the sink, eating it, when he suddenly stopped in mid-bite. After a pause, he went back outside, unlocked his motorcycle from its usual parking place in the backyard and rolled it down and into the alley behind the house. He pushed it along until he found a gap between two garages and backed it in. He rechained the front wheel around the handle of a metal trashcan, figuring that it would serve as a burglar alarm if not as much of a real theft deterrent.

He walked to the front of the alley and stood in the shadows thrown by the big tree in the backyard. He looked and listened. Situational awareness was vital – it had kept him alive in combat, and now it appeared that he would need it here at home. There were no pedestrians and few cars at this hour, and all of the cars drove by without changing speed. He scanned all the parked cars from which someone could watch the house. After a time, he took a slow walk around the block.

When he no longer felt the itch of anxiety, he returned to the house, where he finished the cheese and then went through his nightly routine – the weights, the bath, and bed – and fell asleep.

His friends' blood flows across his face. He is hiding under their bodies – silent and still as the Cong move around him. They throw more dead GIs on the pile and then a machine gun – using the bodies as sandbags.

He feels the bodies above him shudder as return fire slams in.

My God. His own unit is going to kill him!

He's going to get up and fight. To throw himself on the machine gunner. Tensing to push off the body that covers him, his hand sinks deep into a gut wound. It feels like raw hamburger, and the smell of shit is suddenly everywhere.

He settles back.

He plays dead. He doesn't even move when the grenade shrapnel pierces his side.

He clenches his jaw and holds his breath to keep the screams in.

He plays dead.

He is dead.

CHAPTER 16

Thursday, December 21, 1972

Rick woke to the sweats, the shakes, and all the rest. He looked at the clock. Three hours again. Well, if he couldn't change it, he would just have to continue living through it.

He got up, dressed, and headed out into the predawn darkness. He decided against taking out the bike. Walking just felt better for some reason. It also just felt better to go up a block and down D Street, his boots loud on the wooden walkways over the subway construction.

He could see what Eve had been talking about. One of the town houses had three I-beams driven into the ground to hold up the front. She hadn't given him the whole picture, though. There were cracks in the brick large enough to put your fist in and massive cables and turnbuckles were woven between the beams.

"You're up early."

He spun around with his fist raised and only barely stopped himself from going on the attack. Eve was standing right behind him. He could see her whole body brace against the blow, but she stood her ground, raising her chin as she looked into his eyes.

He lowered his fist, took a deep breath, and relaxed. "You never know; I could be up late."

She looked at him closely. "Nope. I can still see the dreams in your eyes. Bad?"

"No worse than usual."

She brushed past him on the narrow walkway and said over her shoulder, "I'm heading down to the Washington Monument."

He could see that they both were going to pretend that nothing had happened – that he hadn't almost assaulted her. He turned and walked behind her.

And observed.

She stopped at the end of the block. "I hope everything back there met with your approval."

He grinned and then pointed with a thumb to the construction. "I was checking everything closely, and Metro seems to have everything well in hand."

She just looked at him without expression for a moment, then gave a snort of laughter and resumed her walk. Once they'd gotten off the wooden catwalk, Rick pulled up alongside and they walked in silence up First Street toward the Capitol, passing the dark windows of the Rayburn Building.

At the base of the Capitol steps, she stopped to look down the Mall. "It reminds me a little of home," she said. "Well, very little, to be honest, but at least there is a bit of ground without trees. I really miss open sky." She looked back up at the Capitol and asked, "What's all that?"

Looking up at the construction that was beginning to cover the West Front, Rick said, "They're starting to build the platform for Nixon's inauguration." He pointed over to the right. "See that semitrailer? That's the TV pool truck. They've been working to get that ready for about three weeks."

"So, the bastard gets to stand up there and pretend that nothing's wrong?" She turned her back on the scene. "What a waste of time and money."

Rick didn't see that her statement required any response. She glanced at his face and then set off across the Mall. Rick caught up, and they walked in silence the rest of the way to the monument, moving fast enough to put a burn into his leg muscles.

Standing beneath the snapping flags at the base of the monument, he offered her a cigarette and lit it with the usual up-down snap of the Zippo on his leg. She caught his wrist with her free hand and stared at the lighter.

"Garryowen?" she read.

"It's the nickname of my old regiment – after a song they used to play going into battle."

She began to whistle the old bagpipe tune, and then stopped. "That's the song that Yellowhair's soldiers played on their way to the Battle of the Greasy Grass. That's General Custer and the Little Bighorn to you."

"We both went to college. Let's just take as a given that we remembered most of American History 101."

"Sorry, I've been told that I get defensive a bit too quickly." She smiled and changed the subject. "I'm named after one of the women at the battle. Women were warriors then."

They started back toward the Capitol.

"Are you a warrior?" Rick asked.

"I don't know." She was silent for a moment. "I think I have to be. They're killing us."

"Who?"

"The CIA, the FBI, the Tribal Police, the sellouts on the tribal councils. We're making trouble for them, and so they're going to kill us – or put us in prison. Last year, my half brother was killed organizing for the Movement in South Dakota. I'm pretty sure that it was the government, but I can't prove it."

She shook her head as if trying to shake off a thought, and then continued. "That's why I'm studying law. We need to adopt the weapons used against us. Just like the rifle replaced the bow."

"Makes sense."

"OK, new subject. That one isn't right for a morning walk." She pointed to his pocket. "So, what is Ia Drang? It's on your lighter."

"Yeah, that's definitely a better topic." He looked at her and then decided to keep going. "I suppose it was another Little Bighorn. We weren't wiped out, but it came damn close. We came in on waves of slicks. They were calling it 'air cavalry' for the first time, and when the first units landed next to the Ia Drang River, they were hit hard by North Vietnamese regulars. It was also the first time that real North Vietnamese soldiers had entered the war in battalion strength. I got there a day or so into the battle, when the Seventh Cavalry was sent in as reinforcements."

He walked in silence for a moment. "I guess we won. I don't know that I did."

"Is that what the dreams are about?"

He took a deep breath and let it out. "Yeah, I lived

through it. I had to watch almost everyone else die, and I don't know why I didn't die, but I didn't, and so… now I get to live through it again every night. I didn't enjoy it then, and I'd be quite happy to forget it now, but… it's just buried in too deep."

He looked over and smiled. "Motorcycles help."

"They do?"

"Yeah. You go fast enough, and it fills your mind. Makes it so you can't think of anything else. Can't remember, can't hear the sounds…"

"Can't grieve for your friends." There was the slightest glint in her eyes, but there were no tears of sympathy. He was grateful for that.

"It all gets blown away in the wind and the speed and seeing how close you can come to the edge without going over."

"OK, if you're going to put it so poetically, I'd like to try it sometime."

"You're on."

As they walked past the reflecting pond at the base of Capitol Hill, the morning sun hit the ornate greenhouse that was the National Botanic Garden and exploded in gold shards off the glass panes.

Rick felt warmer, as if the light were the flame of a campfire.

"So, I've got this film. Any of you guys know where I can get it developed?"

Rick was drinking coffee with Corey, Scotty, and Steve and spinning the silver can on the dining room table. He had retrieved it from under the back porch on the way in from his morning walk.

Steve smiled. "What do you think guys like us did before we got our hands on computers? I built a darkroom when I was eight."

Scotty topped him. "I was seven."

Steve looked at his friend. "Well, I spent time working on ham radio first, OK?" He turned back to Rick. "Anyway, we can build a darkroom and a developing tank in the basement. It'll be easy to find the chemicals we need and read up on the timing. Apparently, most porno films have to be developed... um... privately, so the instructions have to be out there somewhere."

"You sure you're good with doing this?" Rick paused. "People seem to be taking an intense interest in this stuff, and I don't think it's because I got my hands on a particularly good sex flick."

"And you think these mysteriously 'intense' people are going to worry about a bunch of four-eyed wimps like us?" Scotty snorted. "I seriously doubt it."

Corey got up and rinsed out his coffee cup. "Well, you've convinced me. I'll be away for the evening. As far away as possible." He put on his suit jacket, adjusted his cuffs, and picked up his briefcase. "Don't wait up."

He headed briskly for the front door.

Steve scratched under his beard. "Well, I think it's an interesting problem." He looked at Scotty, who nodded agreement.

"OK, let's go for it. Let's get the research done and the chemicals ready by seven tonight, and we'll get started. I think we can do at least as well as your average hairy-palmed porn freak." Steve stood up with a dramatic sigh. "And now I have to go and be abused by GE's finest managers for my bad attitude. It's time for my annual review, and I suspect they don't like my work clothes." He looked down at his T-shirt, ragged shorts, and sandals, then looked up with a big grin. "I got to tell you, I'm tempted to go in naked just to see what would happen."

That afternoon, Rick had one of those days that happened from time to time when it seemed as if the Assignment Desk had simply forgotten him. He was sent to the White House to pick up some press handouts, but when he got there, it turned out that one of the reporters had already taken them back to the bureau. He called in and was told just to stay put and wait – there would be a stand-up to take back later.

He was sitting on a leather couch in the back of the briefing room, reduced to reading a year-old copy of *The Atlantic*, when Jamie Mayweather slumped into the seat next to him and growled, "What the hell are you doing?"

"Reading about the war."

"Screw reading about it. I was there. Ask me about it."

Rick didn't bother to mention that he'd been there as well. "Why'd the peace talks fold up?"

"You mean after they'd finally settled on a shape for the table? They probably went to hell for the same reason as they did in 1968. Thieu pulled the plug." Mayweather leaned back and stretched his shoulders. "About a week before the elections, it looked like maybe Johnson would get a deal and Hubert Humphrey – the Happy Warrior – would coast into the Oval Office. But the South Vietnamese suddenly got a bug up their butts." He snapped his fingers. "Presto chango. No more peace talks and Tricky Dick's moving truck is pulling up outside the front doors of the White House."

"You think Nixon had anything to do with that?"

"I think lots of things. I only talk about things I can prove." After a second, Mayweather continued. "But it was damn convenient. On the other hand, you'd think that President Thieu would have a good reason to like Democrats. After all, it was Democrats who pulled the rug out from under his predecessor and gave him the keys to the palace."

Rick nodded. "Yeah, I'd heard that, but it was never proved."

"None of this shit is ever proved. Watergate isn't proved. The fact that there are stacks of hundred-dollar bills sitting around in peoples' safes isn't proved. Hell, Oswald being a team player isn't proved." Mayweather jumped to his feet and headed back to the booth. "Time for me to prove that I can pull a rabbit out of my ass for the 6 o'clock."

Like most of Rick's conversations with Mayweather, it ended without a goodbye.

The sounds of hammering and boisterous conversation were echoing up from the basement when Rick got home. At the foot of the stairs, a set of thick black curtains tacked to the exposed ceiling joists blocked his way. He found the place where two curtains overlapped and pushed his way into the basement. The three computer techs were standing around a large folding table placed securely against the back wall and covered with bottles of chemicals, beakers, measuring spoons, books, and dozens of pieces of plywood in different shapes and sizes. More black curtains hung over the three small windows high on the walls.

"How's it going?" Rick asked Eps.

Eps looked up. "Great! We've almost got the tank processor built, and most of the chemicals are mixed. We're just checking to see how much sodium sulfite we need in the second developing bath."

"Sul-*fide*. Sodium sulfide," Scotty said firmly.

"Right, whatever. Anyway, we should be ready to go in just a few minutes."

Rick wandered over but understood neither the chemicals they were discussing nor what they were going to do with them. For a while, he examined what looked like an intricate puzzle box made out of a metal can, rubber tubing, and a lot of carefully cut plywood squares boasting an assortment of notches, slots, and smooth curves.

Apparently, Steve had built all of this. He was now consulting a ring binder filled with diagrams. As Rick watched, Steve put on a pair of thick plastic lab goggles and began to carve notches in a new piece of plywood with a small electric jigsaw. The sound was deafening in the enclosed space.

One of the things he learned in the army was to let experts do what they knew how to do, and his housemates were pretty damn good. He went over to one of the battered reclining chairs that made up the bulk of the basement furniture, and settled in to watch. The chairs didn't actually recline, but you could only expect so much from furniture you found sitting outside on trash day.

In a much shorter time than he might have predicted, the three had mixed the chemicals and constructed what turned out to be the processing tank. It was a metal can with the top cut off, replaced by an intricate wooden lightproof cover with a hole in the center. At the bottom, a rubber hose ran out of another, smaller hole sealed with caulk, up the side, and was firmly clipped to the top.

Eps showed how the black curtains would block all light from the windows and the stairs, and held up a second set of curtains that would go up as a backup before the process began. There was even a layer of black cloth tacked across the ceiling to prevent any light leaks coming through the floorboards.

Scotty then proceeded to explain in detail how the film would be wound emulsion-side up around the wooden spool. When the one layer of the film covered the spool, two plywood spacers would go in to keep the second layer of film from touching the first layer, and the winding would resume. When all the film had been wound on the square spool, it would go into the metal tank and the top would be sealed and lightproofed.

"And so up until that point, you're doing all of this in complete darkness?" Rick asked. "How are you going to do that without being able to see?"

"Braille," said Steve. "No, we all learned how to do

this kind of stuff a long time ago. Didn't you?"

Rick just shook his head.

The others laughed. "Anyway, once the film is safely in the tank, we can turn on the lights." Steve pointed to the recliner. "Your place is right where you are so you don't get in the way."

Rick obediently did as he was told and spent a pleasant hour or so sitting in the dark listening to smart guys work as a team – a lot like the atmosphere he liked so much in the newsroom. Eventually, the winding was finished and, after turning on a dim red light, they poured in developer, checked temperatures and stopwatches, emptied the tank by unclipping the hose and letting it run into the laundry sink, and started all over with fixative and then a water rinse.

It took several hours, but eventually the film was fully developed, or at least they hoped it was developed, since they hadn't opened the tank yet. Finally, it was left to dry overnight.

Rick began to apologize for putting them to so much trouble.

"Trouble?" Eps laughed. "This is easy. From what I read, the pervs who make *feelthy peechures* used to do all this inside a garden hose, sliding the film in and then pouring the chemicals through. Now that sounds tricky."

"Only if the hose had 'kinks' in it," deadpanned Scotty.

The three techs laughed and headed off upstairs, while Rick did a final circuit of the neighborhood. Nothing sparked his sense of danger, but he was still tense and wary. He decided to ease his fears with an extra half hour of weights.

It must have worked because he actually slept solidly for four and half hours. He paid for it when he awoke – the echoes of his screams were still bouncing off the bedroom walls.

CHAPTER 17

Friday, December 22, 1972

It had been a beautiful dawn. He had sat on the Capitol steps and watched the city slowly emerge as the morning mist withdrew to the Potomac. Then a golden wave hit the top of the Washington Monument and slid down to light up the white marble buildings that lined the Mall.

He headed back home, but by the time he had crossed Independence Avenue, the sun was gone and the sky was once again the unbroken gray of a Washington winter. Nothing appeared to be out of place at the house, but he did a recon around the block anyway.

When he came in the back door, Corey was sitting at the kitchen table, drinking coffee. "Tom Swift and his Bionic Buddies are downstairs," he said dryly. Rick poured himself a cup and headed for the basement.

They'd obviously been hard at work. They had extracted all the film from the makeshift tank and tacked it carefully to the joists with thumbtacks through the sprocket holes. It hung in long loops back and forth across the basement. Steve and Scotty were using a Tensor lamp to backlight a section, while Eps was putting away the chemicals and equipment.

"What does it look like?" Rick asked.

"Well, first off, it doesn't look like movie film." Steve shook his head. "I don't get it. You didn't bring us some sort of half size photo film, did you?"

"Don't think so. Let me look."

Where Rick expected to see the repetitive pictures of someone's head or the outside of a building that were typical in developed film, the images looked more like the microfilm you'd see in a library. Most of the reel appeared to be shots of an open book – a ledger, possibly. The images only changed toward the end, where there were tight shots of what looked like currency.

"Wait a second," Steve said and snapped his fingers. "Does the Bolex shoot 'single frame'?"

"Sure," Scotty answered, "that's how we did clay-figure animations back in high school."

"That's what it is; they shot single frames of something. Who's got a magnifying glass?"

Rick was completely unsurprised when both Eps and Scotty indicated they had one upstairs. When they returned, Corey followed, curiosity winning out over his usual cool and uninterested demeanor.

After a few minutes of intense scrutiny, they confirmed that the majority of the images were indeed shots of a ledger with what Corey said looked like serial numbers in the left column and totals and subtotals on the right.

"Well, now we just need to print these out," Steve said. "I can do that over at a buddy's darkroom this afternoon."

"Don't you have to work?" Rick asked.

"Nah, I've got their computers working so well that half the time, I have to insert errors just to keep the bosses from thinking they don't need me around. I can't have that. Maintaining an image of infallibility is half the battle in this business."

Rick spent most of the Friday in safe places – the White House, the Senate, places like that. He called in favors and traded runs to avoid any assignments that would leave him exposed. He stuck to big streets like K Street and Wisconsin Avenue and was on constant alert.

Since he was prepared, nothing happened.

He checked the papers and even glanced at the local newswires, but there was no mention of a death on the tracks or a disturbance at Union Station. A tall young man with curly hair had replaced Shelley over at the affiliate service.

Finally, he called the Assignment Desk to say he was checking out for the day. Casey Ross said that was fine in a bored voice, and then, "Hey, someone tried to reach you yesterday."

"Who?"

"Do I look like your secretary? I don't know. Probably your ex-wife."

"Or a bill collector. Did you tell them anything?"

"I don't know anything. Nobody knows anything about you."

"That's great. Thanks."

"Don't mention it. Good night."

Rick hung up the phone, thinking how glad he was that he hadn't given the desk his home address. He put on his cold-weather gear and headed out. He stood in the shadows of the curtains in the picture window watching Connecticut Avenue for a long time. The only person of interest was DC's only bicycle courier, a gray-haired black man with one leg shorter than the other who slowly but steadily pedaled a battered bike loaded with rolls of blueprints around town.

Eventually, he went back and got the BMW. He came down the narrow sidewalk to the street and drove slowly over the tarred boards of the Metro construction – watching for anyone pulling in behind him – and then sped up and went into a series of high-speed turns and alley cut-throughs. Finally satisfied he wasn't being followed, he headed home.

Rick did a slow cruise around the neighborhood before he pulled up behind the group house, where the lights were shining brightly in the dining room. Once again, he slid the bike into the crack between the garages and then stood, watching the street. His silent inspection revealed no lurking menaces, no knife-wielding assassins. He was anything but disappointed.

Inside, all his housemates were sitting around the dining room table, staring at stacks of eight-by-ten photograph prints. Pizza boxes on the counter showed that dinner was already over. Rick found a couple of pieces that hadn't already had the cheese and pepperoni pulled off and sat down to eat.

"We cleaned up downstairs and rewound the film," Steve said as he handed him the can. "Then we figured it was time to bring in an expert."

Eps interjected, "And since we couldn't find an expert, we asked Mr Gravelin to take a look."

Corey only snorted at the joke, his attention fixed on two of the photos. "As far as I can tell, it's a record of deposits," he said. "But I don't understand why it's set up this way."

"What way?" Rick mumbled around his pizza.

"Careful, don't smear sauce all over the table," Steve ordered. "I didn't spend all day balancing sixteen-millimeter negatives in a thirty-five-millimeter holder just to end up with the photos stained with red sauce."

Corey was slowly moving a finger down one of the photos. "Well, it looks like a record of cash donations. These are probably serial numbers of the bills over here, but no names of fund-raisers or state committees or corporations. You can't tell where the money came from or where it went. There's a column here that must be some sort of code. It has 'BBR' or 'MEX' on some rows, but mostly it just says '1701'."

"'1701'?" Rick finished his slice and wiped his hands. "Mayweather told me that the Committee for the Re-Election of the President is known as '1701'.1701'. 1701 Pennsylvania Avenue."

Corey looked up sharply and seemed about to say something, but Eps spoke up first. He'd been examining the photos from the end of the roll. "These are hundred-dollar bills, but the serial numbers aren't in sequence, so they can't be traced."

"Sure they can," Corey responded. "That's how they got the Watergate burglars. The Federal Reserve and the banks now track large transfers of hundred-dollar bills by the individual serial numbers."

"See, that's exactly the kind of dumb things bureaucracies begin to do as soon as you give them a computer." Steve shook his head in mock sadness. "No one would record all the serial numbers of all the hundred-dollar bills washing around in the system if you had to do it by hand, but it's tailor-made for a mainframe."

Scotty nodded. "Stupid, simple, repetitive actions done real, real fast."

Rick shook his head. "Great, but that doesn't help us. We're not the FBI, and I don't see a warrant around here."

Corey clearly made a decision. "That's it; I'm out of here. If you want my opinion, this is almost certainly a record of cash contributions to the Committee, and if it is, it's radioactive." He almost threw the photos he was holding down on the table, then brushed his hands as if he could remove the information he'd seen. "The FBI and CIA are stonewalling the committees so hard that they've got to have dirty hands, and the White House is playing full-court hardball."

"Mixing a few metaphors?" Eps interjected.

"This is really not the time for dumb jokes." Corey got up and grabbed his coat. "Take these photos, burn them and the film, and pretend you were never here and never saw anything at all. And do me a favor," he said, as he headed out the back door. "Forget you ever knew me."

He slammed the door behind him.

Rick looked thoughtful. "Listen, I need to warn you guys. You might want to follow Corey out that door. He's right. There are guys trying to kill me, and now" – he gestured at the photos spread across the table – "I'm pretty sure it's because I ended up with this film.

At first I thought I was just paranoid, but I think they tried to take me out with a car three times, and two nights ago, I got chased through Union Station by a guy with a knife and a gun."

There was silence. Then Scotty asked quietly, "And you didn't think to mention that piece of data?"

"Well, I'm pretty sure he's still alive, but as long as there was a chance that he ended up under that train, I didn't want to get you guys involved."

Steve fanned his face with one of the photos. "Interesting way you have of defining 'involved'."

"Yeah, but helping with the film is one thing, and being accessories to murder is another." Rick held up a hand. "*If* that guy is dead. I don't think he is, and I don't think he's the type to go filing a complaint with the DC police. No, I'm worried that whoever is after me is going to go after you guys."

"Does anyone know we're involved?" Scotty asked.

"I can't see how," Rick answered. "I think they picked me up once when I was first given the film and again when I came out of the bureau. I think they might be getting information from someone at the bureau, but I've never given the Assignment Desk a phone number, and they don't have this address on file."

"And you've been playing Daniel Boone all over the neighborhood the last couple of nights," Steve mused. "Spot anything?"

"Not a whisper," Rick answered. "For once, my continuing state of jumpy paranoia might be coming in handy. I'd swear this place is clean."

Scotty spoke up. "It's probably a good thing that none of us are actually on the lease."

Eps added, "I never thought that having to get all my mail at work was anything but a pain, but now, almost nobody knows we live here."

"And, looking at it logically, it's impossible to 'unknow' a thing, so we're already involved." Steve looked at the other two men. They nodded in agreement.

"So, that's decided. Now, let's turn to possible solutions. When I play Dungeons and Dragons, I've always preferred to take the offensive." Steve smiled. "Maybe we can turn the tables and start putting pressure on these bastards."

"How exactly are you going to accomplish that?" Rick asked.

"We are talking computers here, and we" – he waved a hand to indicate the three techs – "are the Athos, Porthos, and Aramis of the digital realm. I can go to the office in the morning–"

Scotty interrupted. "We don't have to wait until morning. Fire up the Digi-Log, and let's do it tonight."

"But you guys don't work for the government," Rick said. "Steve, your computers are over at GE, and you two work at Riggs."

Scotty smiled smugly. "Yes, but we know all the secret codes–"

"Because we've written most of them," finished Eps.

"ARPANET?" asked Steve.

"Fuckin A," said Eps. "You know they've hooked in the Federal Reserve by now."

"Of course. Moving this kind of financial data around after a nuclear war is what it was invented for."

Rick knocked on the table. "Hello? Earth to computer dudes. Speak English, please."

Scotty got up and headed downstairs as Eps explained. "A-R-P-A. Advanced Research Projects Agency. The Defense Department's own version of Thomas Edison's labs at Menlo Park, except instead of the phonograph and the electric light, they're thinking about stuff like making sure you can still pay taxes after a nuclear attack and how to pack a transmitter in a cocktail olive."

"That one's from James Bond," Steve said. "And he's fictional."

"So they say," Eps continued. "Anyway, they formed ARPA right after Sputnik, when it looked like the US was about to get buried just like Khrushchev said we would, and they've been throwing money at people like us ever since."

Rick was dubious. "And just how does this help us?"

"Well, ARPA invented the ARPANET. That's a way of connecting computers in a self-repairing network so communications can survive a major disaster – like a nuclear attack. It's all very secret, but again, we're the guys who run it, so they can't very well keep us out."

Steve looked smug. "Yeah, we had a nice computer conference call going during Kent State, with antiwar messages and information on the shootings flying from coast to coast."

Scotty walked in lugging the heavy briefcase. "Just because the Defense Department puts up the money to invent it doesn't mean they get to play with it all by themselves. Pull the phone over, Eps."

The three got busy with keyboards, monitors, and phone couplers and, in an amazingly short amount of time, were ready to go.

Eps picked up the phone and listened for a dial tone. He got a funny look on his face as he listened. "Wow, there is some strange noise on the line tonight."

Rick asked, "Will it screw up the connection?"

"Nah, the system is using checksums. That's when–"

"Please, leave me in blissful ignorance," Rick said. "Just get this show on the road. How long will it take?"

Steve sat down to the keyboard and cracked his knuckles. "Probably most of the night. We have to hack our way out of one system and into another. We'll get there. They don't have much security because… well, because there isn't anyone to secure it against. But it's going to be slow."

Scotty grabbed a cola from the refrigerator. "Yeah, why don't you get your usual three hours, and by the time you finish the nightmares, we'll probably have an answer."

"You know about the dreams?" Rick asked.

"We've lived through most of the battle a couple of times. I looked it up in the archives and diagrammed it out a few months ago, and now we can follow along." Scotty smiled. "It's not a problem. We might have to hear it, but you had to live it."

"And relive it and relive it again," Eps added. "We agreed a while ago to help you out if we could and stuff pillows in our ears if we couldn't. I mean, other than the screaming, you're a pretty good housemate."

Rick found his throat had tightened, and he couldn't

say anything, so after a second, he headed upstairs, leaving his friends alternately typing on the keyboard and staring at the tiny green-glowing screen.

CHAPTER 18

Saturday, December 23, 1972

Bodies surround him. Soldiers with their legs blown off, with huge pieces of their skulls gone, with little holes in the front of their torsos and enormous craters in their backs.

Some were clutching their stomachs as if, by keeping their intestines in, it would magically hold in their life.

It hadn't.

There are ants on the blood-covered ground. Ground so soaked with blood that it's changed from brown dust to terrible red clay.

Ants are crawling in the deep wounds in his legs.

No one could live in this place. No one could. But he's alive. He has to go on living. Has to continue fighting the hidden enemies.

Fighting the pain that isn't hidden at all.

Wait, there's a helicopter!

It's turning away… They haven't seen him.

Rick woke and checked the clock.

Three hours.

He got up, stripped the sheets, and remade the bed.

It was all very simple. His friends had died. He had

lived. That was what had happened. There wasn't any reason for it. He couldn't deny it, and he couldn't accept it.

After he dressed, he picked up the pink rubber ball and walked down the stairs. Slow squeeze, hold, and slow release. Slow squeeze, hold, and slow release.

Downstairs, it looked like his housemates had indeed been up all night. Scotty was still pecking on the tiny keyboard, eyes fixed on the blurry green screen. Eps was asleep on the floor with his head on a pile of black curtains left over from the developing.

Steve was sitting at the table with the stack of photographs in front of him, making tiny, precise notes with an engineer's black calligraphic pen. He looked up as Rick entered. "Well, good morning, sunshine. I'd ask if you slept well, but I'm afraid we already know how that went."

Rick found the coffee, poured a cup, and sat down across the table. "I never was much of a morning person. What did you guys find?"

"Well, when you add up all the information, it's a pretty disturbing picture." Steve tugged at his beard as he put a period at the end of a sequence of notes, and then sat back. "I guess if I were even slightly political, I'd say I was shocked."

"Shocked?"

Scotty spoke without looking up from the tiny monitor. "'Saddened' might be a better word. 'Sobered', possibly, but certainly 'shocked' would be appropriate."

Eps spoke without opening his eyes. "Appalled. Thunderstruck. Concerned. Gobsmacked."

Steve threw a pencil in Eps's direction. "OK. He gets the picture. We've looked at all the possibilities and tried to apply all the possible explanatory scenarios, but..." His voice trailed off. Rick could see something besides exhaustion in his eyes.

Steve stacked up the photos, put his pages of notes on top, clipped them neatly with a binder clip, and slid it all across the table to Rick. "Dates, amounts, places... we've noted it all. We don't have a printer here, but we've written down all the systems we... uh... 'accessed', and the appropriate databases, so any halfway competent technician can find everything again. We even made it straightforward enough for a government auditor. It's essentially a road map for a real investigation complete with people's names and addresses to simplify the process of sending out subpoenas."

Rick ignored the photos, looking at Steve's eyes. "So, what's the story?"

"The short version is that our President took campaign money from the South Vietnamese government." Steve rubbed his eyes. "The records show that it goes back a long way – at least back to the 1968 election. But the largest amounts came in" – he sighed heavily – "right after Kissinger announced that peace was at hand this October."

"And then the talks went to hell and the B-52s started pounding Hanoi," Rick said in a flat voice.

"Yes."

"Let's back up. OK, Thieu gave the White House a fucking bribe–"

"'Campaign contributions', technically," Steve said. "Although I think you could still say 'fucking campaign contributions'. No matter what we call it, I think it's undeniable that a good deal of the money sent to South Vietnam as US aid simply made a round trip back to the campaign."

At Rick's questioning look, he continued. "Yeah, we're certain. Scotty tracked a sufficiently large sample of the cash all the way there and back to prove our theories."

Rick felt like he was still asleep, except that his usual dreams were a lot more believable. He rubbed his eyes. "What did they get in return?"

"I don't know. At least not with a similar degree of certainty. It's not like there are specific actions listed next to the contributions." Steve thought a moment. "But no one pays that much money without an expectation of return. What has the South Vietnamese government wanted?"

"They've wanted the war to continue, and American troops to stay in the fight." Rick's voice tightened. "If the North Vietnamese win, each of those guys is dead if he stays, and just another refugee if he bugs out."

"To give it the most positive spin possible," Scotty sat up from the screen. "They're patriots, and they were trying to guarantee the most American support at the highest level for the longest amount of time."

"But in the end, no matter how you look at it, the money bought a longer war." Steve's voice dropped. "And the inevitable conclusion is that a longer war meant that more Americans were killed or wounded than would have happened otherwise."

Rick stood up, took the reloaded can of film and put it in the inside pocket of his leather jacket. Then he stuck the photos inside his belt in the front so that they lay against his chest, put the jacket on, and zipped it up. "So, guys just like me, grunts who might have fought beside me or were flying air cover overhead or…" He stalled and then continued. "These guys have ended up dead or had their ass blown off or whatever – not because we had to win the war or stop Communism or whatever bullshit we were told. Not because of that, but because someone…" Rick stopped again and then began to bite off each word. "Because. Someone. Took. A. Fucking. Bribe."

Rick took his helmet and walked out, leaving only silence behind him.

CHAPTER 19

The BMW howled through the empty city streets.

Rick was flying through the turns, ignoring stop signs and traffic lights, not even registering the horns of the few cars he passed. Only pedestrians were still on his radar, and he slowed and stopped on M Street to let an old woman hobble across with her shopping cart. Then he took off again.

On upper 16th Street, a police car lit up behind him, but he slashed across a park lawn and into Carter Barron, popped over a couple of curbs, and down into Rock Creek Park. Soon, he could no longer hear the siren.

Finally, he slowed down – not because the dance had worked its usual magic but because it wasn't working at all. His chest was tight and tears were building up behind the windburn in his eyes. Mechanically, he pulled into a roadside picnic area far up Beach Drive and parked. He got a yellow rain jacket and pants out from the canvas bag on the side and pulled them on.

It was only a slight disguise but there was no point in being arrested when he wasn't dancing.

Driving smoothly, reasonably, he made his way back down Rock Creek Parkway, under the Kennedy Center, and up onto the Southeast Freeway. Pulling off on to 4th Street, he cruised back to the house.

As he stopped at the stop sign on the corner of 3rd and E, a half block down from the house, Eve stepped right in front of him and slapped him on the helmet. He realized that she'd been calling his name, but it just hadn't registered.

"Stop." She grabbed his right hand and stopped him from turning the throttle. "Someone is in your house. Something is wrong. I know it."

He looked at her as he struggled to understand. Then, methodically, he backed the bike into the curb, set the kickstand, and put his helmet on the handlebars.

She stood quietly until he was finished. "I came over to see if you wanted to walk. Oh hell, I just came to see you." She was wearing gray sweats, and her hair was loose rather than in the thick braid she'd worn before. "As soon as I came around the corner, I saw two guys on your porch, and then one of them broke the glass in your front door and they went in. I think they had guns."

She took a deep breath and continued. "A minute or so after they went in, there were sounds inside. I've done a lot of hunting, and I think they were gunshots."

Rick felt a cold wave run down his spine. "Did they see you?"

"Maybe. I kept on going on the other side of the street and then came around the block. If they saw me at all, I made it look like I hadn't noticed anything wrong."

Rick looked down 3rd Street to his house and spotted the 240Z parked illegally out front. He crossed the street and headed for the back, letting the other houses block any view from the windows.

"Wait!" Eve was right behind him. "After that. There was a much bigger bang, like an explosive."

"Damn it. The guys – I shouldn't have left them." Rick spun around. "You stay right here where it's safe."

She looked at him calmly, and when he turned and started up the alley, she was right behind him. He looked back, and she just shook her head. Short of breaking her leg, he didn't see any way to stop her.

They cut between the garages, and as soon as he could see the back door, he stopped. He stood watching for a long moment and then started walking slowly and carefully toward the house. He wasn't trying to crouch or hide, just move at a slow, steady pace that he hoped would not stand out from the background.

The house was originally built with the first floor about three feet above ground level to give more light to the basement. That put the bottom of the dining room windows about six feet off the ground. They came up next to the first one and stood with their backs to the brick wall of the house for a second. Rick slowly pivoted to look in with his eyes just over the bottom sill.

The first thing he noticed was the blood.

It was smeared along the white-painted wall of the hallway and glistened in a large pool on the floor in the dining room.

Simultaneously, the window shattered in front of him and he heard the *zip-whine* of a bullet. He felt his hair move from the wind of its passage.

He was dropping even before he realized it, ducking below the sill, grabbing Eve's hand, and sprinting around the house – staying close to the brick walls.

Eve gasped, "But your bike – it's back there."

"No time. I think the guys are dead. There's blood everywhere. We have to get out of sight or we're going to be dead as well."

He heard the front door slam open, and another shot went high as they dropped down the three steps to the sidewalk. Rick didn't look back, just raced up 3rd Street and into the shelter of the next row of houses.

At the corner, he pulled Eve to the left and onto the walkway over the subway dig. "We can't go to my place," she panted. "Joyce is there with her kids."

"Not going to your place," he said without stopping. "We're going down. Too many straight lines up here. We need to make turns. Lots of turns."

He heard racing footsteps behind him as their pursuer came off the concrete sidewalk and onto the hollow, booming plywood of the walkway.

On his right, there was an opening in the railing – a platform cantilevered off the side with a chain-link gate about three feet in that was locked now that all the workers were gone for the weekend. He pulled Eve sideways onto the platform just as the footsteps behind him stopped and he heard another shot go wide.

He let go of her hand, took two steps, and launched both boots right at the gate's latch. He ended up on the wooden floor but the lock gave, the entire left side bending back and the gate crashing open.

They were at the top of a square staircase built into the scaffolding. Three fast turns brought them back under the wooden platform and blocked another shot. Two and three stairs at a time, he pounded down, half pulling, half carrying the smaller woman.

When he heard their pursuer come through the gate and start down the stairs, he picked Eve up in his arms and began leaping down from one platform to the next, skipping the stairs entirely.

Jump. Crash to a landing and spin. Jump again. He was holding Eve in front of him, but his back slammed into the massive wooden sidewall on every third jump. He had to be careful not to break right through the makeshift railings on the other three sides – all that blocked the drop to the construction work far beneath.

The dig was at least fifteen stories deep, and after a few flights, the morning sun was blocked, and most of the light came from yellow work lights on every other landing. He grabbed a quick glance at the bottom without slowing and saw the tunnel entrance over to the right.

"The tunnel is to the right," he panted. "When we get to the bottom, head for the tunnel."

"What about you?" she said in a jolting stutter as he continued his spinning descent. "I'm not leaving you."

"I'll be right behind you."

He could tell by the sounds behind him that they were descending faster than the gunman. The guy must not be completely crazy, he thought.

Then they were on the concrete floor of what would someday be a subway station, and he shoved Eve toward the tunnel through a litter of boards, beams, and concrete mixers.

Rick turned back. He had to slow down the shooter – it was too much of a straight line to the tunnel. They'd never make it. He looked at the wooden stair and saw that it was solid, but clearly temporary, meant to be knocked out and removed when the work here was over. At the bottom, only a couple of long nails in each riser fastened it to a wooden crossbeam laid directly on the concrete.

He reached down, bent his knees, and lifted the lowest step. Years of concentrated effort had made his upper body strong – strong enough to overcome the damage the Cong had done.

To that strength, he added rage. Rage against the asshole behind him who had killed his friends, rage against the chickenshits who had sent him to that goddamn jungle, rage against the President who had sent his friends to die.

And who had taken fucking money for it!

The nails at the bottom pulled out with a scream, and he twisted the whole stair to the side, wrenching the flimsy supports, and pulled two flights down into a pile of boards.

"Jump that, motherfucker!" he screamed and took off toward the tunnel, jerking from side to side, and changing speed as he ran. He fully expected to be shot, but he heard a last bullet *sprang* off a pile of rebar, and he was in the tunnel, in darkness, running on the smooth concrete floor where the rails would eventually go.

Eve, who was waiting inside the tunnel entrance, caught up, and ran by his side. "Who the hell was that?"

"I don't know." Rick caught her arm and pushed her onward, catching her look of disbelief. "I'm telling the truth. I really don't know. I'm in the middle of something. Something big and ugly. I'll try and explain, but right now, we need to get out of here."

Running at any speed in the raw and unfinished tunnel was almost impossible, since the floor was crowded with piles of raw materials and construction debris. The best they could do was a fast walk. Every ten yards or so, the workers had strung bulbs in protective cages. Rick picked up a piece of steel rebar about four feet long and began to smash the lights.

"Adding vandalism to your crimes?" Eve said over her shoulder as she concentrated on where she was placing her feet. Twisting an ankle would be a real problem.

"Yeah, that will definitely be what gets me in trouble, but I have to admit it's getting to be a habit lately." Rick crossed to the other side of the tunnel. "Keep switching sides at random. If this guy makes it down, I don't want him to have an easy shot." He smashed out another light. "And if I can knock out enough of these lights, we'll be in darkness, and he'll be outlined against the light from outside."

For a few minutes, they were silent, concentrating on their footing. As in the open section behind them, there didn't seem to be any construction workers.

They saw no lights moving up ahead, heard no sounds of air compressors or heavy machinery. Apparently, the workers had Saturday off.

Eventually, Rick looked back and said, "I guess our buddy couldn't find a way down. I didn't think he was properly dressed for running around construction sites, anyway."

"Who is these days?"

Rick looked at her face. She was intense and serious, but didn't seem to be terribly concerned. "What's going on?"

"What do you mean?"

"Don't get me wrong, I appreciate the effort, but you just saved my life, got chased by some random shooter, and damn near got killed. Why?"

She looked at him, studying his face in the dim light, and then turned back to the way ahead. "I told you. My half brother was killed by the tribal police. They said he was trying to escape, except that his leg was broken long before he was killed. I got lost in my head for a long time after that, and I only came back to life through work. I defend activists who are being beaten up and killed on a regular basis by the FBI and the BIA. So, I guess calling the cops just wasn't my first reaction."

She was silent for another few steps. "And as for warning you, I guess you could call that a calculated risk."

"A 'calculated risk'?"

She glanced back, and he could just see the smile in her eyes. "Yeah, you seem like a good person." She sighed. "Or at least a person who is trying to do the right thing. In any case, the kind of person who deserves to be warned."

"I don't know what the right thing is anymore. Right now, everything I ever believed in has just been thoroughly trashed."

"I know a lot of guys like you. Warriors who came back from the jungle with terrible wounds – except that the wounds don't show on their bodies. The worst scars are in their souls. They have nothing to believe in. Nothing greater than themselves." She glanced back again. "Most of them start drinking and don't stop."

"I told you, if booze worked for me, I'd be right in there with the best of them. But it doesn't."

"Good. You might as well just put a bullet in your brain." She laughed. "Maybe that's not the best metaphor to use right now. Sorry, put it down to excess adrenaline."

She continued. "I don't think you've given up. You're still fighting – trying to find out what will give you a reason for living, trying to figure out what's the right thing to do."

He reached out and put his hand on her shoulder, turning her toward him, and kissed her. It lasted a long time. Then she put her arms around him and laid her head on his chest.

"OK, that was the right thing to do." He could feel her smile. "You're making progress."

He spoke with his head buried in her hair. "I just found out that all the reasons I thought I went to war were bullshit. I don't want to believe that. I want to believe that there were good reasons for going. I want to believe that there was some glory in what we did."

He pushed her away a little so he could look in her eyes. "I'm giving you fair warning. I'm about as screwed-up as they come. Three good people have just been killed for helping me. I'm in the tall grass watching the Cong kill my buddies about as often as I'm here on the streets of Washington. I can't promise you anything."

She looked at him gravely. "You forgot to mention that real people are really trying to kill you."

"I keep trying to ignore that part."

She reached up and poked him between the eyes. "OK, that's just all wrong. When the war inside your head is worse than the war you're fighting outside your head." She shook her head, her long hair bouncing. "I don't know, Trooper; maybe I'm just a sucker for last stands."

Rick laughed. "That's right. You guys did the Seventh Cavalry in the last time."

"So maybe it's time to reconsider which side is really worth fighting on." She gave him a quick kiss, turned, and began walking up the tunnel again. "Come on. I'm assuming you have a plan for getting out of here."

He followed. "Not as much a plan as a logical guess. I'm guessing that they've already built the next vertical shaft – there is a construction site up on Seventh Street."

"Oh, so we're looking for a light at the end of the tunnel?"

"You mean like that?" Rick pointed at the blue color of daylight ahead.

"Beats a train coming at you."

"I doubt that. Even I don't have two trains coming at me in a single week."

She shot him a questioning look.

"I'll explain later."

The construction debris got worse as they approached the access shaft, and sandwich wrappers and milkshake cups were piled on all sides. Clearly, this was where the Metro workers ate lunch.

One of the piles moved. Three rats shot from it, scurrying off in different directions.

Rick jumped. "Damn it!"

"Scared of a few rats?"

"I'd like to think it's more about sudden movements," Rick said. "I knew there were rats down here. One afternoon, I stood at the corner of Connecticut and K and counted over twenty just down in that section of the Metro alone."

"Counting rats. Now there's my idea of a fun afternoon."

He looked at her, shook his head, and took the lead as they approached the light coming down the shaft. He slowed and moved to the side before he reached it, trying not to appear in the obvious spot if someone were looking down with a rifle.

After a cautious observation, he couldn't see anyone waiting at the top. There was a construction elevator bolted to one side, a red-painted steel cage that slid up and down on a vertical rail. There were only two buttons – up and down. Once they headed to the top, there would be no way to stop and reverse if there was trouble.

Rick put an arm in front of Eve, blocking her

from getting in. "Maybe I should go up first in case someone's waiting."

"And leave me with the rats? Not on your life." She pushed his arm away and slid the steel mesh door open. "*Vamanos*, cowboy."

CHAPTER 20

There was no one at the top of the shaft. The elevator emerged into a jumble of construction machinery, office trailers, and supplies surrounded by a solid green-painted wooden wall. The gate was padlocked, but that gave way to Rick's piece of rebar, and they quickly walked outside and pushed the plywood door closed.

Rick tossed the rebar over the wall with a bit of regret, but it would attract attention – no matter how much safer it made him feel to hold even this most basic of weapons.

"What's your plan, now, Yellowhair?"

He grinned. "Custer jokes are going to get old, you know."

"Haven't yet." She took his arm and shoved him into a walk. "Let's go. We should at least look like a normal couple while you detail your brilliant plan. Once again, I'm assuming you have one."

They began to stroll through the evening quiet of a weekend on Capitol Hill. Rick looked around. "We need somewhere to sit down and think. Doesn't Dina live up here somewhere?"

Eve had Dina's number and called her from a pay phone next to a bar called "Mr Henry's". Rick looked at the upcoming events and saw that Roberta Flack would be playing tonight. Then he remembered Sam telling him that Flack had been playing there every night for years and seemed to have no intention of leaving.

Eve hung up. "I told her we were in trouble and needed to get off the street. Dina said to meet her outside this bar around the corner on 8th Street."

Rick frowned. "Why outside?"

"I have no idea, but she was very specific. Let's assume she has a good reason."

Rick shook his head but didn't argue as they walked down Pennsylvania Avenue and turned right on 8th Street. On both sides of the broad street were storefronts, mostly garish bars and nightclubs mixed in with a Chinese laundry and a couple of corner stores with heavy chain-link on their windows. The neon lights and colored bulbs along the street were all lit and flashing even in the bright daylight.

Rick noticed that one place they passed was advertising a "Mr Miss America Contest."

Eve pulled him to a stop. Rick looked at the storefront in front of them. It was painted green with no windows, no sign, and no indication of what it was or if it was even open. "Are we at the right place?"

"It doesn't look like it, but this is the street number Dina gave me." Eve looked up the street. "OK, there she is."

Dina, in a bright red coat and one of her signature hats, swept them through the green door in a whirl of deliberately meaningless chatter. It was, in fact, a bar, dimly lit with a long polished oak-and-copper counter on the left, tables on the right, and two pool tables at the back. Rick realized that, except for the bartender, everyone in the bar was a woman and, from the glances being shot his way, not particularly friendly.

"Is this a gay bar?" he asked.

"A lesbian bar, to be precise." Dina shoved them toward a table in the rear. "I couldn't think of anyplace someone would be less likely to look for you, and I'm known here. No one will talk. Hell, no one ever talks. We've all got too much to lose."

She waved, hugged, and kissed her way through the small crowd, and by the time they sat down, the pool games had restarted and the noise level had risen back to normal bar chatter.

"Most of the people in this place would lose their jobs if anyone knew they were gay." Dina shrugged off her coat and sat down. "Including me. These women don't particularly want you here, but that doesn't mean they'll go to the cops. It just means they don't want you to hit on them, so keep your hands to yourself."

"Damn. Grabbing at random women usually works so well for me." Rick sat down and, for the first time in hours, relaxed slightly.

As soon as he did, the images of his housemates snapped into focus. In his head, he just kept repeating, goddamn it, all three of them – dead. Their friendship, the way they'd accepted his personal war, the sheer loss of potential in those brilliant minds. All gone.

He straightened up, took the pink rubber ball out of his jacket pocket, and concentrated on the steady rhythm of slow squeeze, hold, and slow release. Slow squeeze, hold, and slow release.

Eve put her head in her arms on the table and began to shake. When Rick and Dina both moved to comfort her, she put up a hand, palm out. Without raising her head, she said in a quavering voice, "Just give me a minute to fall apart. Then I'll be just fine, really."

Dina patted her on the shoulder and stood up. "I'm buying a drink for you anyway. The usual coffee, Rick?"

He nodded.

They sat without talking until Dina returned balancing the drinks. "Here, sweetheart, think of this as medicinal," she said as she put a glass of scotch in front of Eve. Then she put a steaming coffee mug in front of Rick, and a shot and a beer back for herself.

She sat down, knocked back the shot, took a sip from the bottle, sighed, and said, "OK, you've had your moment. Could someone please tell me what the hell is going on?"

Eve scrubbed her eyes on her sleeve, raised her head, and reached for the drink. "You know, I was about to ask that question myself." She looked at Rick and raised a quizzical eyebrow.

Rick kept pumping the rubber ball for a few more seconds, trying to make sense of all that had just happened. He began with a warning.

"I think you both can still walk away at this point." Rick looked hard at Eve and then at Dina. "After you hear the explanation, I'm pretty sure that people are going to try and kill both of you."

"Kill me?" Dina's eyes widened. "Then this isn't about the DC cops finally nailing you for all those speeding tickets?"

"Well, I've got those too, but the cops haven't worked out who I am yet, and a couple of thousand dollars in fines isn't a capital crime. At least not yet." His attempt at humor went flat, and his face tightened. "Three of my housemates are dead because they tried to help."

"Corey?" She looked at his face closely. "No, it's the computer guys, isn't it?"

He nodded.

After a pause, she asked, "Are you the good guys or the bad guys?"

"Shit, Dina, what kind of question is that after all these years?"

"Sorry, I shouldn't have even asked." She took a long drink from the bottle. "OK, if you're the good guys, who are the evil bastards?"

"I don't know. Let's start with the President and work our way down. I know that I haven't done anything wrong, but I've ended up with something that it appears a lot of people think I shouldn't have, and they're willing to kill people to get it back."

"So, give it back."

"I can't. Steve said last night that it's impossible to 'unknow' something. I think that's why he and the others were killed." Rick paused and sipped his now-cold coffee. "And that's my immediate problem. If I tell you two what's going on, you're in just as much trouble as I am. I think I should just say thanks for the coffee." He looked at Eve. "And for saving my life."

"No big thing," she responded.

Rick continued, "And then I should just get out of your lives. They know who I am; it's a bit too late for me to pretend innocence. Anyway, I think they got a whole bunch of my buddies in Nam killed, and I'm not letting that go without some major payback."

Dina's voice lost its usual brash tone. "OK, now it's my turn. After all the time you've known me, do you really think I walk away from friends? Abandon people when they're getting pushed around by the government? Don't ever insult me like that again."

She sat back. "Listen, my dad learned how to practice law from the guys who fought to keep Joe Hill off death row for a murder he didn't do. Dad's first case was the miners in Harlan County after they were beaten by company goons. When those three kids were killed in 1964, he went down south and stood up for the Freedom Riders. He slept with a gun under his pillow every night. As far as I know, he still does. He used to say that you didn't take on a client – you took on their enemies." She shook her head. "As of now, those people are officially fucking with me, and they are going to regret it."

Rick looked at Eve. "What about you? I don't think anyone knows who you are." His eyes softened. "I would like to think you were safe somewhere."

"I'm not going to say this was all part of my future plans, but I'm afraid you're stuck with me, Trooper." She took another drink. "And I'm fairly certain that the people who are after you are the same assholes who are arresting and killing my guys in the Movement – or at least they're close cousins. The government isn't exactly welcome on a lot of the reservations these days."

She started braiding her hair like a warrior preparing for battle, pulling each strand tight.

He looked from one woman to the other. "OK. Let me start at the beginning – or at least what I think was the beginning. It took me a while to realize that anything was going on but random accidents. I did a film pickup out in Virginia for Joe Hadley–"

Dina interrupted. "The reporter who ended up in the Potomac?"

"Along with his crew." Rick nodded and started counting on his fingers. "That would be coincidence number one, since the crash happened right after I picked up the film. At just about the same time, I almost put the bike into a car that jumped a red light. I thought it was just another lousy DC driver, but now I'm pretty sure it was the first time they tried to kill me, and that's coincidence number two." He sipped his coffee. "Number three, the source that Hadley was interviewing had a gas leak explode in his house that night. There was nothing left but splinters. The cops ruled it an accident."

"Are you sure it wasn't?" Dina said sharply.

"Nope, and I'm not sure that Hadley's car didn't just blow a tire on the George Washington Parkway. It could just be coincidence or a run of crappy luck. It's not, but it's at least as plausible as Oswald being the only shooter in Dallas."

He continued. "Let's add some more 'coincidences'. A black Impala that sure looked like the same car that I almost T-boned downtown tried to run me off the road at National Airport later that night. That's four, and it's quite a stretch, but you could still say it's all coincidence."

Rick held up five fingers. "Two Vietnamese cowboys in a 240Z – the same car that the shooter parked outside my house this morning – tried to run me down on Suitland Parkway. At some point, even a sweet idiot like me has to admit people are trying to kill me. Just because I'm paranoid–"

"Doesn't mean people aren't after you," Dina finished. "The question is, why? You're just a schmuck. Why would they be after you?"

"Ellsberg was just a schmuck until he got the Pentagon Papers out to the *New York Times*," Rick said. "It's all about the pickup I made out at that guy's place in Virginia. Hadley was determined to nail the Committee for the Re-Election of the President after he had to apologize for a story about loose cash in someone's safe last week. This was his big score – a bookkeeper from CREEP willing to spill his guts."

Rick thought for a second. "You know, I hadn't put this together, but the primary film of the interview got lost, and Shelley – the production assistant across the hall – told me she had found it. Then it turned out to be the wrong film, and she got canned." He shook his head. "I'll bet she found the right film and someone in the bureau covered it up. Anyway, the 'A-roll' – the main interview – is gone, Hadley is gone, and the source is gone."

"Again, why would they be trying to kill *you*?"

"Because I still have the 'B-roll'." He took the silver can out of his inside pocket and spun it on its edge on the tabletop.

Both women looked blankly at the spinning can, so he explained. "'B-roll' is the secondary film you shoot to make the story look better. Pete Moten, the soundman, gave me a silent camera and this can of film. Said it was important. I dropped off the 'A-roll', but totally forgot about this and only found it in my bag after that Datsun made me take a detour through the woods on the way to Suitland."

Rick felt his face freeze. "That's where I screwed up. I asked my housemates to help me with the film. That's what got them killed."

"No way." Eve shook her head. "You didn't kill anyone. Don't take the guilt away from the people who did the crime, and don't make your friends look like dumb pawns in your game. They chose to do what they did, and they deserve respect for that choice."

"I wish I could believe that. Anyway, they developed the film in the basement, and it turned out to be pictures of pages of some sort of ledger. They printed them out." He pulled the papers from inside his jacket. "Here they are."

Dina grabbed the photos and began to study them.

"Corey identified it as a deposit ledger for CREEP and took off, scared out of his mind. Steve recognized that these numbers" – Rick pointed at a column – "were serial numbers for hundred-dollar bills."

"Yeah, but they're not consecutive. You can't prove where they came from," Dina said without looking up.

"Remember that those three are – shit, were – the best computer techs in the city. Apparently, the banks are just beginning to record all the serial numbers of big bills, where they go and when. So, they got into the banking computers and followed the money trail."

Eve looked doubtful. "How did they get inside a bank?"

"They didn't," Rick said. "They had this briefcase with a keyboard, and they hooked up over the phone. I didn't even know it was possible, but these were the guys who were inventing this stuff." He paused again and then rubbed his eyes. "Crap."

"OK, I see." Dina pointed at some of Steve's microfine annotations. "According to them, these are bills that went from the Federal Reserve directly to the accounts of the government of South Vietnam in 1968, '69... and '70." She flipped through the pages. "There must be five hundred thousand, seven hundred... Shit, there are millions of dollars here."

She tossed the papers on the table. "And you're saying that this is a deposit ledger for the committee? So, the South Vietnamese were taking the money we were giving them."

"And putting it back into the campaign." Rick finished her sentence.

She shook her head. "And no one would know because it was cash and because you didn't have to report who gave cash contributions to a campaign until the Election Law went into effect in April. This makes Watergate look like the 'third-rate burglary' that Mitchell said it was. They were taking money from a foreign government. No wonder President Thieu thought he could blow up the peace talks every time it looked like Kissinger was close to a deal."

"And more American soldiers died." Rick's voice

was low and cold. "They stretched out the war. Hell, they're bombing the crap out of Hanoi right now and losing more planes every day. People are dying just so the bastards in Saigon can go on stealing."

"On the committee, no one thinks they can nail Nixon for Watergate." Dina mused, "I mean, they'll gavel up the hearings and make accusations and hold people's feet to the fire. Maybe they'll even get to impeachment, but no one really thinks they'll get a conviction."

Eve asked, "I thought impeachment was a conviction?"

"No, it's like an indictment. The Senate has to vote to convict, and the votes just aren't there." Dina looked up. "But even Republicans won't stand behind the bastard over this. I mean, everything else can be explained away as just tough politics, but this is treason."

"Admittedly, I just finished law school, but I'm not sure that this" – Eve waved at the stack of papers – "is good enough to hold up as evidence."

"No, it's not. But this is." Dina's finger stabbed at one column of figures. "It's the bank's record numbers of the transactions. Along with these notes – I guess that handwriting is Steve's?"

Rick nodded.

"With Steve's notes, a good forensic accountant can nail these bastards."

"That's what he said he was trying to do – give some prosecutor a road map."

She sighed. "Unfortunately, there isn't a good forensic accountant on the whole damn staff of the Watergate Committee. Just a bunch of political lawyers. And they're so hamstrung by trying to be bipartisan, they won't investigate anything that isn't either printed in the newspaper or handed to them on a silver platter."

"I guess that's a dead end, then." Rick sat back. "All I can do is try to stay alive. It's just like Ia Drang. Everyone is dead, and I'm left trying to stay alive."

Eve smacked his forearm. "Whoa. Stop the self-pity express before you run off the rails completely. You're not in this alone, you know. You've got us and you've got Corey and–"

"Corey! That's it!" Dina snapped her fingers. "He's on the Banking Committee, right? The White House is sending everyone but the First Lady up to talk to the Joint Committee, but they're stonewalling Senator Patman and Banking. The White House even strong-armed the Republicans into denying him subpoena power, and that stopped him cold. Why? Because the staff guys at Banking and Commerce are probably the best money people on the Hill."

Eve nodded her head. "And with these files to work from, they can go digging for the transactions even if they can't admit the film exists."

"Exactly." Dina snapped her fingers. "They aren't going to need evidence that will stand up in court. The White House can't let stuff this flammable even be introduced in an open hearing. He'll have to resign first."

She sat back with a smile. Then her broad face turned serious, and she leaned forward. "The first order of business is to keep you two alive and keep these files from getting 'accidentally' burned or blown up or something. With the disappearance of the other film, there's been too much of that sort of thing already."

Around them, the women at the bar went on talking and laughing, and the taunts and bragging around the pool games sounded like the happy chatter of teenagers. For a second, Rick had the feeling that he was somewhere safe – a place where he was among friends and the rest of the world could just be ignored.

Then, a chill ran down his spine and curled around his scrotum – in his experience, good feelings like this never lasted very long.

CHAPTER 21

Dina went off and talked at some length to the bartender, who kept giving Rick suspicious looks. Eventually, she returned to the table and dropped in her chair.

"OK, Sam has a room upstairs that no one uses." She sighed. "He's not thrilled about having a guy around – much less a straight couple – but I told him you guys were trying to avoid a jealous girlfriend, and he gave in."

She smiled at Eve. "That would be your cycle-dyke girlfriend, of course."

She laughed at Eve's slightly shocked surprise. "It was easier to spin that story since you clearly have a thing for bikers."

Eve opened her mouth to say something, paused, and settled back in her chair.

Dina laughed again. "Rick, you better be nice to this kid. I feel responsible."

"I'll be nice, but I'm not sure I can convince the other players in this game." Rick shook his head. "Whoever they are."

Dina's face sobered. "Yeah, you've got a point there." She shook her head and stood up. "Well, whatever's going to happen, the best thing is to get you guys off the streets and out of sight. You should stay here for the rest of the afternoon and just chill. This place is a tighter secret than the CIA's little hideout under Mount Weather."

Eve asked, "Mount Weather?"

"See? Even fewer people know about this place." Dina dropped a set of keys in Eve's hand. "When it gets late, just go through the door behind the restrooms and up one flight of stairs. It's an empty apartment, and Sam said there were a couple of cots up there, but not much else. Apparently, some of the staff bunk up there on nights when they have a bit too much fun after the bar closes." She smiled. "That might be fine for them, but you kids make sure and get some sleep. I'm going to go home and act extremely normal."

Rick said, "You're pretty good at acting normal. Who'd have ever known you were gay?"

"Rick, you are sweet, but you're also the only friend I have who didn't figure out I was a lesbian within the first conversation." Dina shook her head. "You don't let people get close to you. I almost had to stuff you in a sack just to get you to talk to me back in school. You had a wall up all the way around you."

"Hey, that's not true," Rick protested. "I talk to people."

"If you count 'hello' and 'see ya later' as talking, yes. Actually getting inside your head requires dynamite." Dina stood up and started getting ready to leave. "Lucky for you, I'm training to be a Senator, and that requires digging my claws into people and never letting them go. Especially when they're worth the effort. Call me at home tomorrow."

Eve held up a hand. "I don't mean to be paranoid, but what about the phones?"

Rick nodded in agreement. "There were some strange noises on the house phone last night. And that guy knew just where to go, and I know I didn't let him follow me home."

He paused for a second, realizing he'd forgotten about his dead roommates for a few moments. "Goddamn it."

Dina gave him an awkward hug and patted his stiff shoulder. "Nothing you could have done, sweetie."

Eve stood up, and the two women wrapped each other in a long hug.

Dina pulled back and sniffed, tears bright in her eyes. "OK, I can't think about that right now. Here's how we do phone calls. Call me from one phone and ask for someone else and then just tell me you were looking for another number. Make it the number for another phone. Add a one to the first number and subtract a one from the last. I'll go to a pay phone and call you."

"Hold it, hold it." Rick said. "You're going to have to run through that again, Agent 99. And where did you learn all this spy stuff, anyway?"

"Hey, I told you Dad was on the red list. Our phones were tapped my entire childhood. I used to sing songs to the FBI agents when I got tired of calling them names. This was the only way I could talk to my girlfriends." Dina leaned over and went through the routine step by step, "So, you call me, ask for Joe

Schmoe, then say, 'Isn't this four-four-three-five-one-oh-four?' I'll go and call five-four-three-five-one-oh-three. Add one to the first number and subtract one from the last."

"Now, if we've got that straight" – she smiled and turned to the door – "good night, kids."

The apartment turned out to be a relic of the 1940s with peeling wallpaper, a battered combination stove and sink unit, and a single tin cabinet over the stove layered with decades of brown cooking grease. The bathroom had a claw-footed tub and a showerhead bolted onto an upright pipe that rose from the faucets. There was a yellowed vinyl curtain hanging off a circle of metal attached to the shower pipe. Dust and grime coated everything. All the shades were pulled down in the front room, but the single bare overhead bulb revealed three army surplus wood and canvas cots folded away in a corner.

"Wow, what a cozy little hideaway," Eve deadpanned.

"It's not about where you are," Rick said with mock pretension. "It's about who you're with."

"I'm with a biker who attracts people with guns. What's that say about me?"

"You're clearly the innocent victim of bad companions. Now let me think a second."

Rick turned in a circle. He needed somewhere to put the film and the photo prints. Eventually, he walked into the bathroom, knelt down at the end of the tub, and – carefully avoiding touching the wall so as not to leave streaks in the dust – shoved everything high up under the rim. The prints were bent between the tub and the wall and were sprung tightly enough to keep everything from dropping to the floor.

He stood up and looked at his work. He couldn't see it from the floor and the rim covered it from the top. That would probably work unless someone took the place apart, which he supposed could happen.

He went back to the living room, where Eve was sitting on the floor next to the door with her knees bent and her back against the wall, watching him patiently. Rick turned the overhead light out, went over to the front window, and slowly pulled back a side of the shade.

He watched the street for a long time, just absorbing the people passing by. As the afternoon turned into evening, more began to appear in pairs or groups, and most of the groups were made up of one sex or the other. The men seemed to be separated into two types: those who were wearing outrageous leather outfits, formal evening wear, or extremely tight jeans, and those who were aggressively normal – if that were possible.

He was trying to form a picture of the scene so anything that changed would stand out. He really had no idea if this would reveal another assassin waiting for them tomorrow, but he figured it couldn't hurt.

Then he checked out the other direction for just as long.

Finally, he let the shade fall closed and turned on the light. Eve hadn't moved and was still watching him without expression. The question of who was going to sleep where was on both their minds. Feeling a bit flustered, he began to set up, leaving a careful space between the cots.

She stood up and helped.

When they were finished, Eve sat down on one of the narrow cots, hit it with her fist to verify its rock-like stiffness, and gave Rick a crooked grin. "Well, I guess that eliminates one possible way to spend the night."

"Guess so." He sat down across from her. For a moment, he was silent, still filled with the sense of foreboding he'd first felt downstairs. "Look. I know Dina makes fun of me for being closed up, but I've had too many people who got close end up dead." He sighed. "Jeez, that sounds melodramatic. Everyone who fought over there could say the same damn thing."

"And they'd be right."

"I guess. Anyway, I don't have any right to drag you into this. Hell, I don't even know why I was dragged into it. Nevertheless, I've got skin in this game. Even if they weren't guys I knew – soldiers who were in my unit or whatever – good men died because this bastard stretched out the war when he could have ended it."

He turned over his right arm and looked at the scars that ran down it. "I invested a lot in this war and I'll be damned if I let a bunch of asshole politicians turn it into a campaign gimmick. So, for all those reasons, I've got to keep going. Not to mention a selfish desire to figure out some way to stay alive. But you don't have to."

Her face was still and impassive. After a moment, she said, "No, I don't have to."

Rick could hear the unspoken decision in her voice, and he felt both warmed by her support and chilled at the possibility of terrible loss. They looked at each other without speaking for a couple of minutes.

"OK, let's leave it at that, then." Rick got up, turned out the light, and found his way back to his cot by the yellow glow leaking through the shades.

"Good night."

"Night."

The radio operator next to him falls. He reaches for an arm and tries to pull him to his feet; then he sees that one of the operator's eyes is gone.

Guns suddenly open up from everywhere – snipers in the trees, machine guns on the left flank, assault guns in front. He turns and watches as men around him simply drop. One, three, ten, too many to count.

Even the smashing sound of the gunfire doesn't cover the cries – screams for help, screams of anger, screams that hold no meaning and just go on and on…

Eve was awakened by his thrashing and listened to the noises coming from between his clenched teeth. She sat up and looked at him for a moment.

Then she stood, went around to the other side, and pushed her cot over next to his. Lying down, she reached over, unbuttoned a button of his shirt, and slid her hand inside, skin to skin on his chest.

Slowly, his movements calmed and his breathing deepened.

The wooden edges between the cots were cutting into her back, so she moved over to his, sliding her hand deeper into his shirt so that she could hold him just a bit tighter.

He turned on his side, unconsciously giving her more room. She snuggled up to his back, and they slept spooned together.

CHAPTER 22

Sunday, December 24, 1972
Rick woke slowly.

That was unusual, and the warmth curled around his back and the soft breath on his neck were extremely unusual. For a time, he just lay there.

"I've got to say, Trooper, sleeping with you sure isn't dull." Her voice came over his shoulder; he hadn't even known she was awake.

"It was bad?" he asked.

"Well, you were quiet, which is good because I'd have hated to give all the people downstairs the wrong idea. But there were some times when it did feel a lot like sleeping with a Mixmaster."

Rick could feel her smile against his shoulder muscles. "Sorry to disturb you."

"I didn't say it was disturbing. Just a bit energetic." She slid her arm back. "I think my arm will wake up sometime around noon."

"Again, I'm sorry."

She hit him on the shoulder with surprising strength. "Goddamn it, stop apologizing. It makes me feel like a Sister of Mercy or something. I don't feel sorry for you. It's just that no one should have to go through shit like that alone."

She sat up with her back to him and started to undo and re-braid her hair. "You know, most men in my experience have been quite happy to wake up with me."

He grinned. "Most men?"

She smacked him backhand without turning. "Now you can apologize." She got up and headed for the bathroom. "Then find me something to eat."

Rick stood up and stretched. He hadn't slept this long in years – at least not without some serious drugs. He checked his watch and saw it was almost 2.00 am. He stepped over to the window and cautiously looked out.

Despite the late hour, the street was, if anything, more active than it had been earlier. A few more people were holding hands and he even spotted a couple kissing in the safe anonymity of the darkness between the streetlights. He couldn't see anyone that seemed out of place. Maybe they – whoever "they" were – didn't have any agents who were comfortable blending into this crowd.

Then he spotted Corey.

"I'm going out," he called as he threw his jacket on and pulled on his boots. "Meet you outside."

Rick hurried downstairs and through the near-empty bar. The bartender looked up from where he was scrubbing the sinks. He looked like he wanted to say something, but Rick waved a hand at him and said, "I've got to talk to someone. I'll be right back."

Corey had just come out of the bar across the street with another man. They were walking close together but not quite touching. Rick supposed Corey's companion was dressed like a motorcycle rider, but not like any rider he'd ever seen. He was in full leather, from the tiny Harley hat on his head to the polished boots on his feet and all the fringe and zippers in between. Rick shook his head. The only bikers he'd seen wearing chaps were DC motorcycle cops during the winter.

"Corey!" he shouted.

His roommate turned, recognized him, and a quick look of panic crossed his face. For a moment, it looked as if he might actually turn and run, but that passed, and he said something to his companion, putting his hand on the man's shoulder. The biker gave Rick an annoyed look and turned around, heading back into the bar.

Corey watched him go and sighed. Then he turned to Rick. "What the hell are you doing here? And what in God's name were you doing in there?"

Rick smiled. "You wouldn't think of looking for me in a lesbian bar, would you? We figured no one else would, either." Then he sobered up. "You haven't been back to the house, right?"

"No, I was out all day."

"And all last night, too."

"That, sir, is none of your business."

Rick nodded. "No problem. I'm not trying to pry into your life; I'm just trying to keep you alive. Whatever you do, don't go back to the house."

"I have to," Corey said. "All my things are there."

"Listen, we really need to talk, and I'd like to do that somewhere a bit more private."

Eve came out of the green door of the bar and, spotting Rick, came across the street to join them. Rick introduced her to Corey and then asked again if there was a good place to sit and talk.

Corey looked around nervously. "I'm not sure that you going into any of these places is a good idea–"

Rick interrupted. "Corey, I've already figured out that you're gay. I'm not completely stupid."

"You're not?" Corey gave him a quizzical look, and Rick laughed.

"OK, I'm stupid enough not to have figured it out months ago. Now, where in all these gay hangouts is there a place where we can find a quiet table?"

Corey thought for a second, then sighed and said, "I guess the Townhouse would be best."

They ordered coffee and sat in a corner of the upstairs lounge area. Apparently, the Townhouse didn't shut its doors when the other bars closed, and the downstairs was packed. Rick inhaled the coffee and felt some of the kinks that the army cot had left in his back and shoulders begin to loosen up.

"OK, what the hell is going on?" Corey broke the silence.

"Well, the short version is that Steve, Scotty, and Eps are dead." Rick nodded at Corey's frozen surprise. "Yeah, I think people just walked in and shot them. They probably would have shot me too, but she" – he nodded at Eve – "came along and warned me. Still wondering why she did that."

"You and me both," Eve said, and then turned her attention to her coffee.

Corey let out a breath. "What the hell? Was it a

robbery? Did you call the police?"

"I don't think the police will be any help. It wasn't a robbery; I think the shooters came in planning to kill everyone they found in there. The Musketeers never had a chance."

"You mean they were murdered? Why would anyone want to kill those guys?"

Rick shook his head. "I think they were just collateral damage. I'm fairly certain that they actually wanted to kill me."

"What?"

Eve put her finger to her lips and said, "Inside voices, guys."

"What the hell are you talking about?" Corey whispered fiercely. "What kind of trouble are you in?"

"Enough that we had to run through the Metro tunnels to get away from a shooter who was willing to fire a gun in full daylight on a city street." Rick looked down. "You were right this morning. It's the film. I think these bastards were sent to get the film back and make sure anyone who knows about it was… taken care of."

"Shit, that goddamn film!" Corey put his head in his hands. "That stupid fucking film. It's the fucking committee. I told you it was radioactive."

"Little late to worry about that, but yeah, the answer that makes the most sense is that the government is out to clean up a mess and we're it."

Corey shuddered and then shook himself. "I still can't believe it."

He looked closely at Rick. "You're sure they're dead?"

"There was a *lot* of blood. I can't imagine those guys put up much of a fight."

"I guess you would know if anyone would." Corey turned to Eve. "How did you get involved in this?"

"I was stopping by to see if Rick wanted to go for a walk." She smiled. "I'm an innocent bystander, honest. Not that it's going to do me any good. Now that I know what's going on, I guess I'm just another target."

"You've got to give that stuff back," Corey said to Rick. "Give it back, and we'll swear we didn't see anything."

"You really think that would work?" Rick looked doubtful. "I'm not completely certain, but I think this is the third time someone has tried to kill me since I picked up that film. No one seems willing to stop and talk about it."

"The third time?" Corey's voice got louder, and Eve put her finger to her lips again. He fell back into an angry whisper. "Why didn't you say that before?"

"I didn't want to get you in trouble. Doesn't appear to be working out that way."

Eve put her cup down decisively. "OK, there's a lot of time to assign blame. Let's talk about what we should do right now."

"We need to call the police," Corey said.

"Didn't you hear me? This guy was shooting at us right on Third Street in broad daylight." Rick shook his head. "Do you really think he's worried about the police?"

"But three people are dead!"

"If it's been going down the way I think it has..."

Rick started flicking up his fingers in a count. "They've already killed the whistle-blower who provided this information, the cameraman, the soundman, and the reporter who got the story, and maybe a kid in my office who saw the film. That's five. Add in Steve, Scotty, and Eps and we're looking at eight dead. There is no way that many people get killed and no one notices, unless someone in law enforcement is looking the other way."

Corey shook his head. "That's crazy. You'd have to believe the entire government was in on this."

"I've got no trouble believing in a government conspiracy," Eve said bluntly. "The government has been killing Native Americans – well, they've been killing us for centuries, but lately, there have been at least five deaths of AIM members with no real investigations."

Corey put his head in his hands. "My God, how did I get so completely screwed? What the hell is on this film? You'd think it was an Oval Office orgy with underage girls." He paused. "No, he'd probably get away with that. Boys of any age would destroy him, though."

"He took money from the South Vietnamese," Rick said bluntly.

Corey dropped his hands and stared at Rick. "That bastard. It wasn't bad enough that he's turned the entire government into a political – no, a criminal – enterprise. He sold the war out for campaign contributions?"

Rick spread his hands. "That's what Steve told me. He said they'd followed the whole trail on the computers at the central banks."

Corey was silent for a long while. Finally, he said, "OK, I can't deal with that right now. I need to get my stuff out of that house. I've got places to stay, and I'll call in sick for a couple of days and hope it all blows over."

"I haven't got any better ideas. At least none of us are on the lease, and so it's possible no one knows you're even involved." Rick stood up. "I'll walk over with you. I need to get my bike back. It's 3am. I guess it's about as safe as it's ever going to be." He raised a finger as Eve began to speak. "And we'll drop you off at your place. No one should have identified you either."

Eve looked like she had more to say, but after a moment, she just sat back, and her face lost all expression.

Rick looked at her closely. "Good, you're being sensible. Now let's get out of here."

CHAPTER 23

Rick's bike was still parked on E Street. The entire block across the street was a pile of construction dirt, rocks, and trash piled about ten feet above street level. Why this dump was right in the middle of Capitol Hill was a mystery only the DC City Council could explain. There was a ramp up from E Street that trucks used to dump snow during storms. They climbed the ramp and slowly walked east toward C Street.

There were no lights showing in the windows of their house and no one was on the street. Eve gave Rick a quick hug and walked back to the ramp, intending to circle around the block and back to her house. Corey and Rick waited until she was out of sight before descending a rough footpath down to the street.

"Looks OK," said Corey.

Rick looked at him. "You're thinking I made it all up."

Corey nodded. "That or your usual acceptable crazy has grown into really unacceptable serious crazy."

"Honestly, I wish you were right."

They crossed the street and walked slowly to the back door.

Suddenly, Rick threw his hand in front of Corey, stopping both of them.

"What?" Corey said.

"The window."

"What about it?" Corey said. "It looks the same as always."

"That's the problem." Rick shook his head. "That's where I was standing when I looked in and saw all the blood. The shooter was standing in the hall and damn near parted my hair with a bullet. That glass was smashed. Now it's fixed." He paused. "OK, or it was never broken and I really am as crazy as every other vet."

Corey headed for the back door. "Either way, there's nothing you can do about it. Let's go in."

The door was unlocked. Corey opened it slowly, and they both listened. The house was quiet. Without turning on the lights, they went through the kitchen and into the dining room. Even by the dim light from the streetlights outside, Rick could tell there were no bodies.

An arm came around his neck from behind and crushed his throat. Something hard poked into his back, and a heavily accented voice in his ear said, "Welcome home, cocksuckers."

Rick froze.

Corey was a step ahead. He whirled around with surprising speed, but the voice said, "No stupid shit, you son a bitch, or I blow a big fucking hole in your friend."

Corey put his empty hands out to the sides and stood still.

"Good, you not so stupid. Now, downstairs. Both of you. No lights and no stupid shit."

In the basement, the man behind Rick flipped the light switch with one hand and slammed his pistol into the back of Rick's head with the other. Rick fell to the floor with flares of bright light exploding in the back of his eyes. He wrapped his hands around his head and felt a familiar thick wetness under his fingers. It wasn't a serious injury, but damn, it hurt.

Without a word, their captor stepped over Rick and kicked Corey in the groin and then, when he folded over, flat-kicked him in the chest, knocking him back into one of the battered recliners.

He waved the gun between the two men and said, "Nobody moves."

Corey was still bent over, but he shot the gunman a bitter look and said, between clenched teeth, "You could have just asked, you bastard."

Rick looked up at the young Vietnamese. He was wearing a nylon shirt open over a sleeveless undershirt, jeans, and cowboy boots with pointed toes. His hair was swept back but carefully styled and gelled. The ragged tough look gave him the appearance of Elvis meets Bruce Lee. His face was covered with scars, round ones from acne, and longer, deeper ones, clearly from fighting and apparently fighting with knives. Rick thought he might have been more impressive if he'd had fewer scars on his face and left more on the people he'd fought, but all in all, this guy was definitely a hardcore Saigon street cowboy.

Without warning, one of his pointy boots drove deep into Rick's stomach. "This is for fucking my partner on train tracks," the man said as the kicks continued.

Rick curled up and tried to protect as many vital parts as possible. The muscles on his back and stomach absorbed a lot of the punishment, but a good number of kicks were getting through.

After what seemed a very long time, the man stepped back. Rick wasn't an expert in getting beat up, but he had the feeling it could have been worse. This guy had stopped for a reason.

"OK, where is camera?" the cowboy said. "Little fucking camera they gave you at that bastard's house." Another kick drove in for emphasis. "Where is camera?"

Rick realized he must mean the Bolex camera Pete Moten had given to him at the accountant's house, the one he had slipped into his jacket for the ride back to the bureau. Someone must have been watching the pickup.

When he caught enough breath to speak, he rasped, "It's at the bureau."

"What's *boo-row*?" Another kick. "Camera only, motherfucker."

"The motherfucking camera is at the bureau." Rick saw the boot go back and said quickly, "Downtown, the television office. The camera is downtown."

"Good. You go get it." Moving fast, the Vietnamese spun to Corey and slashed the pistol across his face. "You go get goddamn camera. You bring it here, or I'll kill boyfriend. I'll kill boyfriend real slow."

"OK, I'll get it." Rick rolled onto his stomach and started to get up.

This time he was stomped in the kidneys. "No goddamn tricks, motherfucker. Get fucking camera. Give me goddamn film."

"Goddamn film. Got it."

Another stomp. "No fucking jokes, cocksucker, or I kill you now."

"No fucking jokes. Got it."

The boot ripped right into the old wound in his right side. "I know you got shot by Cong. Right here, huh?" Another kick to the same place. "Huh?"

The pain was incredible. Rick felt like the room was fading in and out, a red haze blurring his eyes. "Uh, yeah, right there."

"And here."

His arm exploded.

"Cong almost blew your fucking arm off."

Rick could only writhe in agony.

The cowboy stepped back. "Go get goddamn camera. Give me motherfucking film."

"Goddamn camera. Motherfucking film. Got it."

"Now get out of here."

Rick got up to his hands and knees, tried without much success to blank the pain from his mind, and staggered the rest of the way to his feet. The cowboy pushed him toward the stairs.

"Go fast. You got motorcycle. Go fast."

Corey spoke up from the recliner. "Please hurry, will you? I think this guy means it – he'll kill us." He paused, then flicked his eyes to the gunman and added carefully, "Regardless."

"Stop talking, cocksucker." The cowboy spun around and threatened Corey with another blow.

Corey cowered behind raised hands, but Rick noticed that his eyes didn't look afraid. They looked calm and angry.

As he turned and walked slowly, carefully, up the stairs, Rick thought he should have paid more attention and gotten to know his housemates better. They kept surprising him.

The bike rumbled slowly through the predawn darkness, every pothole and stone sending a wave of pain through Rick's torso. He was going slowly, not only because going any faster was almost unimaginable but also so he could figure out what to do.

He had to get the Bolex. Clearly, this guy thought the film was still in the camera. He didn't know about the other can or that they'd already processed that film. There was no doubt in Rick's mind that Corey was right. They were both going to be killed as soon as he gave the camera back.

How did this low-grade moron know where he'd been wounded? He'd have to have read his military medical records to get that information, and he would bet anything that he hadn't gone through his records personally. That meant there was someone else involved – someone with government clearance. These hired guns weren't running things; they clearly weren't smart enough.

Therefore, whoever was directing the hunt for the film had enough clout to be able to order up classified government files and get them in a matter of days. Almost certainly, the same person who made sure the "A-roll" film had gotten lost. Twice.

Slowly, the steady vibration of the BMW began to loosen the knots in his body. All those hours of weights had kept the cowboy boots from doing any lasting damage to soft tissue and vital organs. It didn't mean that his whole body didn't hurt like hell, but he didn't think he was going to lock up or pass out – not for a while, anyway.

He was stopped for a couple of minutes on Connecticut Avenue as the Metro construction workers replaced the massive eight-foot-square iron plates that covered the access holes. He realized it must be nearly dawn if they were getting the street ready for traffic again. When the backhoe finally laid down the last plate and rumbled away, he drove on to the bureau, pulled into the narrow alley, and brought the bike into the rear courtyard. As he parked, he noticed Kyle's motorcycle was already there and idly wondered why he was working so early. Sam usually took the first shift because he had the most seniority and because there weren't that many runs at the beginning of the news day.

He found out what was going on as soon as he walked in. There were irritated-looking cameramen and producers milling around the halls. Apparently, some nutcase had jumped the gate at the White House and claimed he had dynamite strapped to his body and a dead-man switch in his hand. All the camera crews were willing to bet any amount of money that he was just wearing a bunch of highway flares and parts from an old radio, but the junior editor chosen to staff the Assignment Desk on a holiday weekend had decided to take it seriously and called everyone in early.

The President was already up at Camp David

preparing to celebrate Christmas Eve, and the consensus in the bureau was that, on the off chance that he wasn't faking, the bastard on the North Lawn should just go ahead and hit the switch so they could go back home. There wasn't a lot of sympathy for anyone who ruined a slow day when half the bureau should have been off.

No one was at the courier desk when Rick got there. Kyle must have been somewhere else in the bureau. Rick grabbed the desk and jerked it back.

He stared at empty space. The Bolex camera was gone. He looked under the desk and in all the drawers and even banged the coats hanging on the divider in case it was hung by its strap. Finally, he stood and stared at the space where he'd put it.

There was a smear of orange on the wall that had not been there when he had hidden the camera. He looked at it closely, touched it with his finger, and smelled it. Cheese.

More precisely, "Cheez".

He pushed the desk back and sat down to wait.

Kyle bopped down the hall a few minutes later, looking up in exaggerated surprise when he spotted Rick. "What are you doing here, dude?"

"Where is the camera?"

Kyle looked appropriately innocent and confused. "What camera?"

"The Bolex I had stashed behind the desk. I can see the Cheez Doodle smears from your fingers when you stole it. Where is it?"

"I have no idea, man." Kyle grabbed his coat. "I've got to go on a run."

Rick stood up, grunting with the pain, and slammed a hand down on Kyle's shoulder. His crushing grip stopped the smaller man and then pulled him close. Rick leaned down and said very slowly in his ear, "I know you stole the fucking Bolex. I need it, and I need it now."

"OK, OK. Don't get crazy." Kyle rubbed his shoulder after Rick released him. "I had to take it, man. I have to pay a lawyer and a probation officer and a counselor."

"I am truly sorry for all your troubles, but A, getting busted means you're dumber than even I thought was possible, and B, I still really need that camera."

Kyle finished putting on his coat, and, abruptly, turned and tried to run. He took two steps, and his feet went out from under him. Rick had grabbed him by the hood, and now he twisted his fist into the fabric, turning the heavy jacket into a makeshift noose.

"OK, stop, stop! It's in my locker," Kyle gasped. This time, Rick didn't release his grip until Kyle had opened the locker and handed him the camera.

"I'm sorry about the lawyer," Rick said.

"Don't forget about the probation officer and the counselor," Kyle whined.

Rick continued. "But, just to satisfy my curiosity, how did you get nailed for grand larceny?"

"The first time, it was so easy. No one was around, and I got such a cool pair of tires. The Rabbit rode like a dream." The younger man sighed. "I just thought it would ride so much better if I had all four tires, you know, a matched set. How could I know they'd be waiting for me?"

"You should have known they'd be waiting because someone had just stolen tires off one of their cars, you idiot."

"Yeah, apparently. Then they found the first set of tires, and that sort of made it a second offense." Kyle slumped into a chair. "The third and fourth tires kicked it over five hundred bucks, and that made it grand larceny." He brightened. "At least it's not guns or drugs. I still get to go to the White House, so I can keep my job."

"You never cease to amaze me." Rick started walking stiffly up the hall toward the cameramen's lounge.

"Hey, what's up with you?" Kyle said. "You're walking like you crashed the bike or something."

"Or something. Try and stay out of any more trouble."

As he turned the corner toward the lounge, an angry voice from behind said, "Hey! Biker boy!"

He turned, moving his shoulders and neck at once to keep the aching in his muscles to a minimum. One of the engineers, a big, blocky man who always wore a blue lab coat with "Lee" embroidered over the left breast, was coming up the hall, looking pissed. Rick gave him an inquiring look.

The engineer started shaking his finger in Rick's face as soon as he got close enough. "You and your fucking friends stop it!"

It wasn't hard to look innocent – Rick had no idea what he was talking about.

"Get your friends to get off the goddamn feed line. I don't have any time to deal with your silly games."

"I'd stop it if I had any idea what 'it' was," Rick said. "What feed?"

"Don't give me that crap. Someone is screwing with the feed from the West Front – the inaugural pool line."

Rick shrugged. "I have no clue what you're talking about."

The engineer's face turned red. "The hell you don't. Your fucking name is on it. Now cut it the fuck out before I get the goddamn Secret Service on your ass."

Rick shook his head. "My name? There is no way my name is on a feed I've never heard of."

"Come with me." The man whirled and banged open the doors to Telecine. "I'll show you."

Rick followed him into a room filled with equipment – some looked a bit like film projectors, but most looked like nothing he'd ever seen before. The man in the blue lab coat had already gone over to the left side, where the entire wall was covered with racks of electronic equipment and TV screens with test bars on them. The engineer pointed to a screen in the center.

"There. See it?"

At first, Rick only saw a thick line of black across the bottom of the screen, and then words appeared in blocky white letters over the black background:

Rick Putnam

Rick watched in amazement as the letters stayed up for a few seconds and then changed.

Call 4556 plus Zeke

As he stared, the line turned to black and then repeated.

Rick Putnam
Call 4556 plus Zeke

"Now get that crap off my feed line," the engineer said.

"What is it?" Rick said. He turned to the other man. "Look, Lee, I really don't know anything about this. Where is it coming from?"

"That's some sort of homemade closed captioning inserted into the vertical interval of the line coming down from the Inaugural Pool." Lee peered closely at Rick. "You really have no idea what that is, do you?"

Rick shook his head.

"OK, you can insert information into a TV signal when the phosphor refreshes…"

Rick kept shaking his head.

"OK, don't worry about how it's being done. All you need to know is some friend of yours is sticking a signal in my feed. It's not supposed to happen. It's coming straight from the truck to here. No one sticks anything in one of my signals. This is the most advanced computerized TV technology there is, and I don't need anyone screwing with it."

At the word "computerized", Rick slowly began to smile.

Lee looked at his face intently. "Yes, you do know who it is!" he said triumphantly. "Stop being so happy about it! Damn it, this is the official Presidential Pool line!"

Rick's smile grew broader.

"I'm not sure," Rick said. "But maybe I can get it stopped."

•••

When he got to the camera lounge, he looked around and found a black changing bag, stuffed it and the camera in his jacket, and went back to his bike. He watched the street for a minute for anyone who might be watching him, then took off fast, heading north. Once he was sure no one was on his tail, he made an illegal U-turn and headed south toward Motor Mouse.

The bikers lounging outside in the weak winter sun looked as if they hadn't moved for days. They made the usual jokes about his bike, but he ignored them. There really wasn't time to trade insults. He found Hector inside.

"*Feliz Navidad, Gordito.*"

"I hate that fucking name." The mechanic turned. "And what exactly is merry about this Christmas?"

"We're not in the war."

Hector looked at him for a moment. "Yeah, I suppose that's enough."

"Did you get what I asked for?"

"Yeah, although I don't know why."

"Because if we don't have each other's backs, no one else will."

"OK, OK, I know." Hector turned to his four-foot-tall mechanic's tool case. "Stop before you start whistling that fucking bagpipe song."

Rick hummed a couple of bars of "Garryowen".

"Damn, you are an irritating bastard." Hector unlocked a drawer and pulled out a paper bag. "Here."

Rick took the paper bag and looked inside. "Ready to go?"

"Ready to go."

Rick rolled up the bag. "What about the bike?"

"That German piece of shit not fast enough?"

"It's a lovely piece of precision machinery, but no, speed isn't one of its finest attributes."

Hector led the way to the back of the shop. "Don't you tell any of the guys outside that I even own this," he warned. He unlocked a heavy door and stepped out into an alley paved in old bricks. Next to a battered blue Dumpster, a heavy tarp covered something. Hector pulled up a side of the tarp just enough to reveal a bright green motorcycle with a low racing fairing and upswept pipes.

Rick whistled. "What is it?"

"Kawasaki H1 500cc triple. Race modified." Hector raised the tarp a bit higher so they could see the whole machine. "Fastest production motorcycle made, and this one is bored, balanced, and blueprinted. It'll hit two hundred miles per hour without even breathing hard."

"Damn. It doesn't look big enough."

"The Japanese don't know how to make things strong yet – the steel in the fucking springs still goes flat – but they sure know how to make them fast." Hector threw the tarp back over the machine. "I went down for Bike Week last year and saw them run at Daytona. They had to build a chicane with three more turns into the track just to keep the Kawasaki riders from lapping the pack."

Hector turned and put a finger right in Rick's face. "And don't you ever tell any of those morons outside that you even saw it. I've got a reputation. Now do you want it or not?"

"Hell yes, can you leave it outside?"

"Yep, here's the key."

Rick caught the small fob.

"It'll be right here." He threw Rick two more keys. "Double-chained to that Dumpster, just in case."

They went back inside the shop, a considerable amount of cash changed hands, and Rick headed out.

"Hey."

Rick stopped and looked back.

Hector held up a thumb. "Fuck 'em up, Zip. Stay alive."

Rick walked into the sunlight. "No sweat."

CHAPTER 24

Rick parked the BMW outside the group house. He pulled the camera and the black changing bag out of his jacket and went inside. As he came in the front door and through the living room, he could see the dining room and the stairs in the full glare of morning daylight. There wasn't a speck of blood anywhere. He bent down to look at the floor and saw where it had recently been polished.

"What the fuck are you looking at? Get downstairs!"

The cowboy was crouched at the top of the basement stairs, his pistol lined up on Rick's face. He backed down the stairs and waited cautiously as Rick followed.

Corey was still in the recliner. The blood had dried on his face, but there didn't appear to be any new injuries.

The Vietnamese grabbed for the Bolex, but Rick pulled it out of his reach. "Hey, do you want to ruin the film? If I don't get it in a can, you won't have shit, and your boss will kill you."

"How did you know I got a boss?"

"Lucky guess. Now can I get the film out of the camera for you or not?"

The cowboy thought a moment, then turned and fired at Corey. A hole appeared in the arm of the chair only inches from Corey's arm. Rick couldn't tell if it was terrific aim or he'd really just tried to kill Corey and missed.

"OK, give me the fucking film."

"No sweat."

Rick sat on the third step up from the basement and unfolded the film-changing bag. This was a lightproof fabric sack with a zipper opening running the length of one side and two sleeves with elastic ends attached to the other. Cameramen used them to load or unload a camera in broad daylight without ruining the film.

He unzipped the bag and put the camera in, re-zipped it, and slipped both hands up to his elbows into the sleeves. His eyes lost focus as his attention went to the items inside the bag.

The cowboy walked closer and looked at the bag. "What are you doing, motherfucker?"

"I said this once, but I'll repeat myself. I'm getting the film out of the camera and putting it in a can inside this bag so the light won't get to it," Rick said calmly, raising the bag on his arms to demonstrate. "If I don't, the film won't be any good, and your boss will kill you."

"We don't need to look at the fucking film. No good is OK." The gun came up and centered on Rick's forehead. "Joke's on you, motherfucker."

The bag puffed up as Rick fired the pistol hidden inside. He hit the cowboy in the right shoulder and spun him around. The man's gun clattered off into a corner of the basement.

Corey came up out of the recliner in a swift, smooth movement. He didn't exactly attack the other man; it was more like he flowed into him. The cowboy gave a cry of pain, seemed to throw himself headfirst into the stone wall of the basement, and crumpled to the floor.

Rick stood and pointed the bag at the gunman. He had a random thought that it might look a bit strange, but he sure wasn't going to bother taking the gun out. The cowboy didn't move.

Rick looked at Corey. "Very smooth – whatever that was."

"Aikido," Corey said. "Japanese monks invented it. You use the attacker's own violence against him."

"Seems to work."

"Well, I got tired of being beaten up as a kid because everyone thought I was gay, which I was, as it turned out, but back then, I just thought it was massively unfair. So, I played football, but that didn't fool anyone since I was the placekicker. After two guys held me down while another took out three of my teeth with a baseball bat, my dad even offered to go out and buy me a gun." He shrugged. "Yeah, like a pissed-off teenager with a grudge and a gun would have been a good idea. Anyway, I met this cool guy, and I started taking classes with him in the afternoons."

Corey squatted down and moved the cowboy's head back and forth gently, then checked the shoulder where Rick's bullet had hit. "This asshole looks OK. He hasn't any neck damage, and you appear to have drilled him through the meat and not the bone." He cleaned his hands on the unconscious gunman's pants and stood up.

"The truth was that this *sensei* – the teacher – was just incredibly cool and I had a mad crush on him. Sadly, he was married, and to a woman, worse luck, but the training paid off. Now I keep practicing because it calms me down and…"

Rick finished the sentence. "Keeps you looking good."

"Damn right." Corey looked over at the immobile cowboy. "Should we do something with this guy? Like maybe kill him?"

Rick pulled his hands out of the bag, leaving the pistol inside. "I've killed enough people. That's why I only bought a wimpy PK loaded with .22s. Let's just wrap him in duct tape and leave him here."

"Will he bleed to death?"

"Not unless he's a secret hemophiliac, and by the look of the scars on his face, I doubt that. Duct tape makes a good field dressing. It holds tight, and it's sterile. Anyway, the people he's working with are clearly professionals." He motioned to the stairs. "You should see the floors up there. They were covered in blood just a few hours ago, and now, I'm telling you, they haven't looked that good since I moved in. Not only are there no bloodstains, but the walls and that window have been totally cleaned, repaired, and repainted. These guys are covering their tracks; they won't leave him here."

He looked at the cowboy. "Of course, they may kill him just to tidy things up, but I can't take care of everyone."

"I'll gift wrap Saigon Sid, here." Rick pointed to the stairs. "You start getting all your stuff out. Let's make it look like we never lived here."

"Easy for you to say. You don't own anything."

"That's true enough." Rick walked into the other side of the basement and returned with a roll of duct tape from the workbench. "I'm trying to live like one of your Japanese monks."

"They don't approve of motorcycles."

"Damn. There goes another great idea."

Rick helped Corey haul the last box out of the house and carry it around to the alley. Corey was going to walk over to a friend's house and come back with a van. At first, he had started to use the house phone to call, but Rick jammed his finger on the button.

"This phone has got to be tapped."

"You've gone completely paranoid!" Corey said, and then paused. "What am I talking about? Three people are missing or dead – or missing *and* dead – and there's an unconscious Vietnamese hit man in the basement. Of course, the damned phones are tapped. I'll walk."

Rick smiled. "I'm not that sure about the three dead."

Corey shot him a look. "What?"

"I've got the feeling that the death of the Bionic Triplets may have been exaggerated. I can't prove it yet."

"Let me know, OK?" Corey headed off to get the van. "They weren't bad guys when they weren't driving me crazy."

Except for the weights, which were dumped on the sidewalk several houses away in the certain knowledge that someone would steal them, everything Rick owned fitted into a small duffel bag. He walked down to E Street and bungee-corded the bag onto the back of the BMW. After a moment's thought, he kicked the bike to life, drove up D Street, and parked next to the fence surrounding the Metro dig. Today, it was swarming with workers. Rick wondered what they thought had happened down there over the weekend.

He lit a cigarette and walked down the plywood boardwalk to Eve's town house. She opened the door before he even got there. She must have been watching, he thought.

Probably a good idea.

"Hey, Trooper. You look beat-up."

"Simple explanation for that." A smile turned into a grimace as the battered injuries in Rick's side gave him a quick pulse of pain. "Uh, I got beat up."

"You really have to stop doing that. It's a bad habit." Eve pointed to the Winston in his fingers. "Even worse than smoking."

Rick looked at the cigarette. "I might be able to stop smoking, but getting beat up seems to be out of my control."

"Well, so long as you aren't planning to quit either habit, how about giving me a cigarette?"

Rick flipped his cigarette onto the walkway and stubbed it out with his boot. He took two more from his pack, did the up-down trick on his jeans with the Zippo, and lit both cigarettes at once. Then he turned around, sat at the top of the town house's front steps, and offered one of the cigarettes over his shoulder.

Eve took it and sat down next to him. "What happened?"

"An idiot with a gun." He took a deep, almost bottomless drag on the cigarette. "He wanted the film."

"Where is he now?"

"Wrapped in duct tape in our basement. It turns out that Corey is a goddamn ninja assassin. I've never seen anyone move like that." He looked at her and shrugged. "Who knew?"

"I guess he just never had a good enough reason to beat you up, as hard as that might be to imagine."

"True, but if we'd ever argued over doing the dishes, it could have gotten real ugly."

"Stop being heroic. How did you get hurt?"

"The idiot with a gun used a pair of those damn pointy cowboy boots to persuade me to give him a camera." Rick thought for a second. "He knew just where to kick, too. Right where it says I got wounded in my military file."

"So, he was working for the government?"

"That or working for people with some pretty damn good government connections. I think the phone was tapped, too."

Eve looked up and down the empty boardwalks. "That's it; you're taking me with you from now on. If these guys are as good as you say, they've already spotted me."

She turned and ran a gentle finger down the marks on his face. "Plus, you need someone to take care of you. It doesn't look like you're all that good at it."

"That the only reason?"

She looked into his eyes, then looked straight ahead and concentrated on her cigarette. "No."

There was a pause. Rick stared at the side of her face, looking at the gentle curve of her cheeks and the strong and determined set of her mouth. She looked like the kind of person you could depend on, someone you wanted next to you on the firing line when the shit got serious.

The kiss started soft and restrained, but got more passionate as it went on.

It went on for a long time.

Finally, he gave a small gasp as she tightened her grip around his upper arm. She pulled back sharply and looked into his face. "Damn, I'm sorry."

"I'm not." He rubbed the arm. "I decided in that hospital in Japan that I wasn't going to let the crap that happened to me ruin the rest of my life. Or at least not when I was awake and in control." He rotated his shoulder. "Don't worry about it. I'm just going to have to get some new weights – couldn't fit them on the bike."

"Won't be room anymore, anyway. I'll be on there."

"I could try lifting you. Beats a set of weights every time."

The sun was washing the pastel colors of the town houses with a red-gold light flashing brightly off the windows. Eve stood up and headed inside the house, brushing off the seat of her jeans. "Time to saddle up, Trooper."

She shrugged into a denim jacket with a blanket lining, wound a scarf around her neck, and picked up a backpack from just inside the front door. "We need to find a place to stay tonight, and since it's Christmas Eve, I'll bet the inns are packed."

"And I need to make a phone call."

"A phone call?" Eve's eyebrows came together in question. "Didn't you just say that your phones were tapped?"

"That is a true fact. I've got to find somewhere else to call from." Rick laughed. "There's a technical problem at ABN I need to clear up."

"Are you going to explain what you're talking about?"

"Not until I'm sure, but I think it's all good."

They headed back to the BMW and slung her backpack on top of his duffel bag. He pulled a second helmet out of the courier bag and handed it to her.

She looked at it with a slight smile and then glanced up at his face. "Already had a helmet for me? You were certainly making some pretty big assumptions."

Rick snorted as he fastened his own helmet. "You were all packed and ready to go."

"Good point."

Rick pulled the bike upright and Eve slid into the rear seat. "Have you ever ridden a bike before?" he said.

"No. I've always been in vehicles that keep the rain off."

"Well, the first and only rule for the passenger is to hold tight to the driver. If you throw your weight around, we could get into serious trouble."

Her arms slid around his waist. "No problem."

"A little lower – right there is where the M79 grenade hit me."

She peered around his side. "Didn't our side use the M79?"

"Well, it got really confused during the fight." He kicked the bike to life. "I can't really blame the guys who hit me. At that point, the Cong were firing from behind a bulwark of dead GIs. I just happened to be a little less dead than the others."

"Well, please keep it that way."

The big bike pulled out and headed south down 3rd Street. "Working on it."

CHAPTER 25

The black Impala was driving south on Third Street just as Rick and Eve pulled away from the curb. There were two cars between them, and the driver thought that with any luck, the courier wouldn't notice him following them.

His face twisted slightly with irritation. The courier should have been dead – records destroyed, history altered, the past erased. It should have been easy. Just as easy as all the other lives, so many other souls erased from the world, in the years since that hot July day.

He is sweating everywhere, his fatigues dark with moisture. His crotch is still damp and stiff from when he peed himself when they were first hit by North Korean artillery. At least he's not the only one. Half the damn company shit their pants.

Who could blame them? They weren't frontline soldiers. It felt like only hours since they were pulled from occupation duty in Tokyo to police a bunch of crazy North Koreans.

"Police", my ass.

They were coming from all sides. There were no places to hide. Now, most of the officers are dead.

The Seventh Cavalry was supposed to hold this bridge. How can you fight when you can't tell who the hell is the enemy? They all look alike, and just last night a whole platoon had been wiped out by Commie soldiers dressed like damn peasants.

At least, that's what he'd heard.

Thank God the sergeant just moved through with new orders – shoot em all. Don't let anyone near – even women are fighters in this damn country.

A new group of refugees is heading toward the bridge; he hears the firing start on his left. He raises his rifle and aims. It's an old man with a white beard. He takes the rifle down and blinks, then aims again.

Still an old man.

He feels a cold, dead calm. The noise – women yelling, children screaming – all seems to fall away.

He feels nothing as he pulls the trigger and the old man falls.

He finds a new target – a woman – and fires.

Finds another target – another woman – and fires.

The cold inside him deepens as he restores the silence.

CHAPTER 26

Rick spotted the black Impala behind them as he made the turn onto Eighth Street and headed for the lesbian bar. He decided to keep on going. They'd just have to come back and get the film and the photoprints later. He kept an eye on the single side mirror that hadn't gotten smashed in that desperate dash through the woods. Damn, that seemed like ages ago. Eve shifted behind him; he could feel her take a breath and prepare to speak.

"Don't look at the bar," he called over his shoulder. "Someone is right behind us. I'm going to lose him."

He felt her arms tighten as she turned her head to the side and flattened herself against his back. Even in the current situation, he had to admit it felt damn good.

He passed the high walls and iron spikes of the barracks where the White House Marine guards were stationed, watching the yellow traffic light in front of the guard shack and the high blank walls that hid the Washington Naval Base. He slowed down, timing it so that he got there just as the light turned red. Kicking down a gear, he pulled the bike into a sharp left, scraping the pegs and hearing the horns and brakes of the cars he'd cut off.

Eve's grip tightened as he accelerated hard up M Street.

Behind him, he heard a steady horn blast and looked in the mirror to see that it was the Impala warning traffic as it fishtailed through the intersection. Other horns joined in a discordant chorus, but the Impala kept coming.

"OK, that didn't work," he said to Eve. "Now we're going to have to get extreme."

"You mean that wasn't extreme?" Her answer sounded muffled by his jacket.

He grinned and drove up through the gears.

By the time he hit the intersection where the entrance ramp to I-395 split off from M Street, he was going so fast that he knew he wasn't going to be able to stop. The light ahead was red. He looked for cars – nothing coming from the projects to the south, but the concrete supports of the highway blocked his view on the left side.

He hit the throttle and accelerated through the light, seeing a flash of a concrete mixer with an American flag painted on the barrel emerging from the darkness on his left. Then it was a wrenching dogleg left and right, and they were flying up the ramp onto the interstate.

At the top, he slowed to match the speed of traffic and started cutting quickly to the left, braking and accelerating to fit into tiny spaces between cars. He knew that only the bridge across the Anacostia was ahead, with its long sight lines. To the left, he spotted the unmarked exit ramp he knew was there.

He kept on juking through the cars – blaring horns and shouted curses marking his passage. At the last second, he slammed on the rear brake to lose momentum, but before the bike went into a skid, he came up off the brake, threw the bike to the left, and rocketed onto the ramp only inches from the orange sand barrels clumped around the concrete abutment.

He cut the throttle and slowed down as soon as they were on the ramp, knowing there was no way the Impala could have followed him. In fact, if the driver had waited at that light, he wouldn't even have reached the top of the entrance ramp in time to see them exit on the other side of four lanes of traffic.

"I think that worked," he said.

Her arms stayed locked around him. "You mean I can breathe now?"

"Yeah, and if you loosen up a bit, so could I."

He felt her sit back. "Who the hell taught you to drive, Trooper? Evel Knievel?"

"Hey, fast is the only way to ride a bike." He laughed, the adrenaline rush beginning to evolve into the giddiness that often followed a close call. "It takes your mind off your troubles."

"You must really have serious troubles."

"I'm not going to deny that."

"No, I guess you can't." She put her head around his shoulder so she could see ahead. "However, let's try and avoid any more therapy sessions for a while, OK?"

"OK." He slowed down to walking speed, finally stopping behind a line of cars waiting between traffic cones. On both sides were stands of evergreens and small bushes, the Anacostia River just visible through the trees on the right.

"Where are we?" Eve asked. "It looks like nowhere. I mean, we were just in the city. How did we end up in the middle of the woods?"

Rick pulled up to a man in an orange hat, a ragged insulated coat, and a money apron. "Tell you in a minute. Do you have ten bucks?"

"You really know how to show a girl a good time," she groused, as she dug into her jacket pocket. "Here."

He paid the attendant and they pulled ahead. The road changed from pavement into rutted mud, and then the narrow track between the trees opened into an enormous parking lot. Burgundy and gold colors were everywhere – on banners, on flags, on strands of bunting, and on every one of thousands of people walking, laughing, drinking, and eating.

"What in hell is this?" she said.

"See the stadium back there?" Rick pointed. "That's RFK, and this is a tailgate party. The Redskins are playing for the championship tonight."

"This is incredible. It's like a redneck Woodstock." Eve shook her head. "And how long are they going to keep that disgusting name?"

"You're kidding. Rename the Redskins? Probably never." Rick kept motoring slowly, weaving up and down the lanes of what was one vast celebration. "Anyway, I thought it was meant as a compliment."

"Redskin? That's what they called us when they murdered women and children in the Plains Wars. It's what the white kids called me at the boarding school where they sent me." She shook her head at the memory. "It would be just as bad to call them the Washington Niggers."

"To be honest, I've never thought about it, but I suppose you're right." Rick swept an arm at the racially mixed crowds. "But, after the riots, it's about the only thing that everyone in this city – black or white – agrees on. I mean, you don't see people getting together like this anywhere else."

"I guess that's a good thing," she agreed. "But can't they get together without having to have that Uncle Tom cartoon of an Indian warrior painted on their beer coolers?"

"OK, if you're not happy, I'm not happy. We're out of here. Hold on."

With that, Rick gunned the bike, popped it over the parking lot curb and up the grass slope toward the street beyond. They turned right on East Capitol and disappeared over the Anacostia River.

CHAPTER 27

Rick was sure he'd lost the Impala long before they even reached the stadium parking lot. But just in case, they'd run up through Fort Dupont Park, down Alabama Avenue where the corner boys selling drugs were some of the few people still working tonight, and finally down past the long wall that enclosed the massive brick wards of Saint Elizabeth's – the city's psychiatric hospital.

Crossing back over the Anacostia on South Capitol, he pulled into a filling station and began to fill the tank. The attendant, an elderly black man, just looked at him from his seat in the office, clearly warm and unwilling to miss any of the Redskins game on his tiny black-and-white TV.

Eve climbed off the back seat stiffly, walked around in a circle, stamping her feet and massaging her legs to restore the circulation.

Rick smiled. "Not used to riding?"

"Are there really shock absorbers on that thing?" She scowled at the BMW.

"Great ones. Strong enough to cross the Sahara."

"I'll bet anything that the Sahara has fewer potholes

than a DC street in a warm winter. I may never be able to walk again."

She took off her helmet and began to rub her fingers vigorously through her scalp. "Not to mention what it feels like to have a braid stuck under this thing."

"Think of it as extra cushioning if we go down."

She turned and glared at him with her hands on her hips. "Don't even joke about crashing this damn thing. There will be no 'going down'. Never, do you hear me?"

He grinned as he topped off the tank and replaced the pump handle. "Your wish is my command."

The attendant had finally hit a commercial break and slowly hobbled out to the pumps. Rick handed him a couple of dollars. "Keep the change. It's bad enough to have to work tonight. Do you have a pay phone?"

The man looked at him, then pointed around the side of the station and slowly headed back to the game without saying a word.

Rick waited until the door had closed and said softly, "And a Merry Christmas to you, too. OK, I need to make a call. I'll be right back."

One of the new anti-theft pay phones was mounted on the side wall of the station. Rick fished a dime out of his pocket – no banging these for a nickel – and dialed. The phone rang once and then someone picked up but didn't say anything.

"Hey, this is Rick Putnam," he said.

He recognized Steve's laugh. He didn't think he'd ever been so happy to hear someone's voice. Steve said, "So, you figured out the code. I guess swapping out 'Eps' for 'Zeke' wasn't all that hard, was it?"

"It took me a couple of minutes but 'Zeke' had too many letters." Rick grinned. "You need to get that signal off the pool feed, or you'll be responsible for the explosion of ABN's senior technician's head."

"Good, that means we get to play in the tunnels again. One of our favorite pastimes."

"Damn, I'm glad to hear from you," Rick said. "What the hell happened?"

"Well, I keep saying we didn't always have computers to play with, right?"

"Right."

"Luckily all of us were serious Dungeons and Dragons players in college – the real version, not the board game. Down in the steam tunnels and over the roofs and all that stuff."

"You mean like that kid who got lost out in Madison?"

"Yeah, except we don't get lost. Anyway, there's been a real game going on in DC for years, and being the champion team, we checked out the house as soon as we moved in. I'll bet you didn't even notice that manhole in the basement, did you?"

"A manhole?" Eve came around the corner and Rick leaned against the wall with a grin on his face and wrapped an arm around her. "No, I never noticed a manhole in the basement."

Eve looked at him quizzically and he smiled, mouthing the word, "Later."

Steve continued, "Yep, leads into the primary storm sewers and down to an outflow on the banks of the Anacostia. Luckily, it hasn't rained or we'd have been covered with shit. They really should replace those damn dual-use sewers."

"I completely agree. I have no idea what you're talking about, but I agree anyway." Rick's smile broadened. Then a thought drove it from his face. "But there was a lot of blood. Anyone get hurt?"

"That question goes to Mr Pickell here."

Eps came on the line. "Hey, Rick!"

Eve now was leaning against his chest with her head close enough to hear the voices on the phone. Rick enjoyed the warmth of her body against him.

"Hey, Eps."

"So, anyway, I grew up just slightly fascinated with things that go boom, you know?"

"You mean you used to set off firecrackers?"

"Firecrackers? Hell, no." Eps sounded insulted. "I don't think you'd call a plastic explosive made from rock salt with thirty percent of the explosive power of dynamite a 'firecracker',"

"Um. No, I wouldn't. But how did you make it so fast?"

"Oh, we didn't make it last night. I made up a batch a year ago – you never know when a little plastic explosive will come in handy. It's been in the refrigerator. You know that plastic tub with the label 'Mashed Beets'?"

Rick shook his head. "You mean I've been sleeping on top of a batch of unstable homebrew explosives for all this time?"

"Dude, you have no idea. A man has to have his toys. Plus, you don't really sleep all that much, so that's not a reasonable complaint," Eps continued.

"Anyway, after you left, we figured someone might come visiting, so we rigged a surprise in the hall."

"Wait a minute. That could have been me!" Rick tried to sound indignant, but couldn't quite pull it off.

"Nah, we had a bunch of mirrors set up and a string to a friction fuse. You were safe. When the guys with the guns came in, we gave them a chance, but they shot at us without even checking to see who we were."

Eps's voice was filled with pride. "I should say they shot at the mirrors we'd set on the stairs to the basement. After that, we figured we'd given them enough of an opportunity to act civilized, so we set off the focused explosives we'd mounted on the wall behind them and took off. We didn't really want to hurt anyone, so we didn't put anything in the mix – you know, no BBs or nails or anything."

"Hate to tell you, but someone bled all over the place."

"Really?" Eps talked away from the receiver. "Hey, guys, we may have a problem with the cleaning deposit on the house."

Rick couldn't help but laugh, and Eve smiled.

"I wouldn't worry about it. Corey and I were just there, and someone has cleaned it all up."

"Cool. Here's Steve."

Steve's dry voice came back on the line. "So, that's our story. You OK?"

"So far. Although people keep trying to change that. Where are you guys?"

"We're in one of our better hidey-holes. We've got a room at the Evangeline."

Rick's eyes widened. "The Evangeline? On 14th and K? That's a hotel for women only."

"Well, technically, yes, it is, but the night manager is one of the best Dungeon Masters in the city – lots of spare time on the night shift." Steve laughed. "It does mean we can't use the pool or the dining room – actually, it means we can't come out of our room at all except in the middle of the night. But otherwise, it's a very nice place."

"I'll just bet it is."

Steve's voice turned serious. "OK, we should cut this call off. We're bouncing through three exchanges, but better to be safe than sorry. We've all taken vacations from work, and we're just going to keep our heads low for a while. We're good at amusing ourselves, so that won't be a problem."

"You do that. This number going to work later?"

"Yeah, or you can call the desk at night and ask for Edna Ponds-Simons."

"E-P-S. Right."

"Keep your head down."

The phone went silent, and he hung up. For a moment, he just stood there, hugging Eve and taking deep breaths.

Then they headed back to the bike. He said, "Well, we'd better find a place to eat and somewhere to stay. I don't think we'd better go back to….Well, we'd better not go back to anywhere we've ever been, now that I think about it."

Eve smoothed down her braid and pulled on her helmet again. "I know a place we can stay so long as you don't mind a little breaking and entering."

"I don't know. I'm a clean-living, law-abiding citizen."

She gave him a look. "I've ridden with you, Trooper. You don't get traffic tickets for the kind of shit you pull on that machine. You get felony charges. Anyway, the place I'm thinking of is run by anarchists. The last thing they'd do is call the cops."

"My kind of people." Rick got on the bike and brought up the kickstand. "Lead the way, *kemo sabe*."

"First of all, that's a stupid phrase that either means 'sneaky Apache' or 'I don't know'. Second, it's culturally ignorant and insulting. And third…" She swung up on the backseat. "I'm completely lost after our beautiful tour of the ghetto, so you get to be the native guide."

"Sorry. Didn't mean to be insulting."

"Shut up and get me something to eat, and then head for 12th and K." She put her arms around his waist and tucked herself as close as possible to his back, shielded from the chill wind. "Let's go, *kemo sabe*."

People usually came to Washington from somewhere else and, on holidays, everyone headed back to what they thought of as their real homes. Downtown was just empty streets under gray skies, the rumbling of the BMW's exhaust the only sound. The usual crowd of hookers was working along 13th Street – their pimps would never let them take a holiday off, especially with all those suburban husbands driving in to watch the Redskins. They looked cold, smoking Kools and shivering in their skimpy outfits.

"Those poor women," Eve said, shaking her head. "What a life."

Rick glanced over, but returned his attention to the other cars, scanning methodically for anything suspicious. "This is nothing. Most days, there are hundreds out here."

"Three blocks from the White House. It's just wrong."

Rick smiled. "It'd be acceptable if they were further away?"

He grunted as her fist slammed into his side.

"OK, you've made your point, but please make it on the other side next time. That's a bit tender."

She punched him in the other side. "Better?"

He grunted again. "Much."

They swung into a parking lot at the corner of Vermont and L. The sign proclaimed it the Dee Cee Diner.

Rick said, "This is one of the few twenty-four/seven places around. Usually caters to the printers getting off work from the *Post*."

"Anything warm would work for me."

Parking the bike in the back behind a pickup truck, they left the helmets in the courier bag and headed inside the narrow green-and-white-striped diner.

Rick's glasses steamed up the moment they walked into the brightly lit interior. He pulled them off and squinted as he searched for two open seats.

"Down here, high pockets." Eve had swung into the empty booth right next to them. "We'd starve if I left everything to you."

"Probably," he agreed.

They gave the harried waitress an order for coffee and bacon, eggs, and toast. Breakfast was always the best bet at a diner. Rick took off his jacket.

"Unzip as much as you can," he advised, "or you'll get acclimated to the heat and freeze when we get back on the bike."

"Thanks for reminding me. I was trying to forget about getting back on that infernal device." She unzipped her denim jacket and pulled it down so it puddled around her on the vinyl seat. "Why not a car? Don't you ever get tired of being wet and cold?"

"Not really." Their coffee came, and he cupped his hands around the white mug. "I spent enough time in Vietnam being hot and miserable. Anyway, a bike means…" He thought for a second. "A bike is freedom. You can always leave, always park, always get through traffic, and always go where you want to go."

"Have you ever crashed?"

"Yeah, it wasn't so bad."

She stared at his face. "Not so bad? Are you nuts?"

"Bad accidents are always about cars." He grinned. "You only have to remember one thing if you drop a bike all by yourself, and you'll be fine."

"What's the secret?"

"Get off the bike."

"That's insane."

"Not really." He took another sip of coffee. "If you're rolling down a street at sixty miles per hour all by yourself, you'll lose some skin. If you've got a couple hundred pounds of motorcycle on top of you, you'll lose muscle."

"Wonderful. I can't wait."

Their breakfasts arrived, and they ate with the hunger of people who had been burning lots of calories just keeping warm.

When they finished and were enjoying cigarettes and a second cup of coffee, Rick spoke thoughtfully. "I think I may have worked out a way to get out of all this."

"Run like hell?"

He grinned. "Well, I did consider that option, but there are two problems with it."

She nodded. "These guys are government. There aren't too many places they can't find us, and now we know way too much for them to just let us get lost."

"Yeah, that was the first problem."

"And the second?"

Rick felt his jaw muscles clench with anger. "That bastard in the White House sold the lives of American soldiers to win a political campaign. I'm just not going to let that go. He's going down."

He crushed his cigarette out in the ashtray.

"That 'bastard' just took the White House in a historic landslide. Politically, he's bulletproof, and if you're thinking of taking more direct action…" Eve shook her head. "You can count me out. Custer liked suicide charges. My people preferred staying alive."

Rick shook his head. "I'm not going to walk up and frag the guy. It wouldn't be nearly enough payback for what he did. No, I want people to know what a sick, lying bastard he really is. I want him to be remembered as a traitor for hundreds of years." He did his up-down trick with the Zippo and lit another cigarette.

"That's sort of what happened to Custer," Eve said thoughtfully.

"Really?"

"Most of the other tribes who were there at the Battle of Greasy Grass talked and boasted about it afterward. The Northern Cheyenne got together and agreed to keep silent for one hundred summers." She looked at him closely. "That's not until 1976 – can you keep this secret?"

Rick nodded.

"Your white history books say that a bunch of crazy Indians just massacred Custer and his men for no reason at all." She had an intense inward look. "It's the other way around. The army was murdering us on the High Plains for years. One of the worst massacres was at a place called Sand Creek. They killed hundreds – women, children, and old men under a white flag – and then paraded through Denver holding up their hearts."

She took a deep breath. "That was Chivington's command. When Custer attacked three years later, he also expected to fight women and old men, but he didn't. His men fought warriors, but the warriors didn't kill him. They didn't kill Yellowhair."

"They didn't? But he died there, didn't he?"

"He was unclean – cursed because he'd dishonored himself when he broke his word not to attack." Her voice was low, almost a whisper. "None of the men would even touch him because they were afraid his spirit would make them sick as well. A Cheyenne woman knocked him off his horse, and another stabbed him to death."

She looked up. "The woman who knocked him down was my ancestor Buffalo Calf Trail Woman. He was an evil man and he died a coward's death. You whites may honor him, but you're really just remembering the lies they printed in the newspapers."

"You're saying I should be satisfied with getting him run out of office?" Rick was silent for a moment. "I'd like more. I don't want this President to have any glory in anyone's history books, even if it's just a mistake. And one more thing." He paused. "Remind me never to cross one of you sweet-looking Northern Cheyenne girls."

"Bastard." She reached across the table to punch him, but he pulled back, so she kicked him under the table. "Now, what's your big plan?"

"Well, I think that Watergate is going to prove bigger than anyone thinks." Rick took a drag on his cigarette. "But so long as it's just politics, it won't be enough. What we've got is dynamite, and it's going to have to be handled just as carefully. I'm not talking about newspaper reporters. None of them really understand how finance works, so they can't follow the money. It's going to have to be given to people who are familiar with the ways big money moves and have the power to dig the records out of the banks."

"The League of Super Accountants?"

"Sort of." Rick smiled. "I don't know if I mentioned it in all the quiet times we've had lately, but Corey works on the Banking Committee."

She looked doubtful. "Are you sure? He doesn't seem like the type to play rough."

"Because he's gay?" Rick laughed. "You didn't see him wipe out that shooter today. Anyway, I've heard all that crap about pansies and faggots, but trust me: the gay guys I knew in the army were as tough as anyone. And Dina…"

"Yeah, Dina would face down the FBI, the CIA, and the New York City police one at a time or all together." She made a beckoning motion with her fingers. "OK, it's all decided. Let me smoke another of your cigarettes and we'll head for a place to crash."

Rick handed her the pack and then did the trick with the Zippo.

She lit it and inhaled. "Why do you do that?"

"It was a dumb trick I learned in high school." He studied the battered steel case inscribed with "Seventh Cavalry" and "Ia Drang" for a long moment.

"And then, in the middle of the battle, after I'd already been wounded and had seen most of my friends killed, I did one of those little things I guess you just do in the middle of complete insanity. I wanted a smoke, so I pulled out my pack of cigarettes. Most of them already had blood on them – mine or someone else's – but one was still half clean, and I tore off the bloody part and…"

He made the move again, striking down with the lighter to flip the lid open and then back up to spin the wheel. He stared at the flame.

"And then I did my Zippo trick and the whole other side of the river just exploded. Gooks and all. The blast wave flattened me, but I held on to that damn cigarette. Grinning like a complete fool, I sat there and smoked and watched the flames."

He looked up at her. "It was an Arc Light raid. B-52s about a mile up dropping hundreds of bombs and just shredding the jungle and making the splinters bounce. I've never seen anything so beautiful before or since."

"That didn't have anything to do with your lighter."

"Probably not. Why take the chance? I've been doing this little trick ever since, and I'm still alive." He started to get up from the booth. "Now, you said we could find a place to sleep for the low price of committing a crime against people who don't believe in the rule of law. Let's get moving."

CHAPTER 28

Revolution Printers was on the fifth floor of a small office building on the corner of 11th and K. Rick had noticed the sign in the window months ago and idly wondered who they were. They pulled down the driveway and into the back alley. After Eve got off and they'd unwound their bags, he backed the BMW carefully into the small space between a dumpster and the brick alley wall. He put it up on the center stand and then got out by climbing onto the seat and over the top of the trash bin. Four empty cardboard boxes scrounged from the back door of a nearby liquor store served to shield the bike from anything but a determined search.

After he was done, he looked at it thoughtfully. "You know, I'm going to have to let Cosmopolitan Couriers know I've quit at some point. They'll probably make me give this back." He sighed and picked up his duffel. "Too bad. I've just begun to feel comfortable with the handling."

Eve shot him a look of disbelief. "You've spent hundreds of hours on that bike and you're just beginning to get comfortable?"

"Hey, it's like a marriage. Doesn't happen overnight."

Eve started toward the front of the office building. "Do yourself a favor, Trooper. Don't ever use that analogy with your wife – if you're ever lucky enough to have one. You or the motorcycle will be toast. Probably both."

As they walked down the driveway, Rick said innocently, "It's interesting; did you know that you have to steer a bike in the opposite direction from where you really want it to go?"

Eve looked to see if he was kidding. "That's not true."

"Actually, it is." He held his hands out as if they were on the handlebars. "It's all about centrifugal force and gyroscopes. Once you get going, the motorcycle just wants to stay upright and go straight ahead."

He pushed the left hand forward and the right hand back. "If you want to turn left, you actually push your left hand forward like you're turning to the right. The bike resists the change, leans to the left, and goes left. You push one way, and it goes the other."

"If you say 'just like a woman', I swear I'll kill you where you stand."

"Never crossed my mind." He put on his most innocent look. "However, the movement of a really responsive motorcycle carving turns on a winding road is a sensual pleasure."

Eve threw a hand up over her shoulder in a dismissive gesture.

He spotted her smile as she turned.

The streets were empty under the yellowish streetlights when they reached the front door. It was an older building, four stories of red brick at the bottom and a top floor of yellowish brick above a strip of concrete molding decorated with someone's idea of heraldic shields.

Eve didn't even check to see if the front door was locked. Instead, she began tapping the bricks, beginning at the edge of the doorframe. She didn't seem inclined to explain what she was doing, so Rick just held both their bags and watched.

When she had counted nine bricks to the right of the door, and five up from the sidewalk, she kept her finger on it as she bent down and picked out a long rusted nail from where it was lodged in a crack between building and sidewalk. Using the point of the nail, she pried out a large chunk of mortar from the top of the brick. Scraping the nail in the hole where the mortar had been, she extracted a key. She then replaced the chunk of mortar, pounding it back into place with her palm.

"The owners aren't all that concerned with material things," she said as she unlocked and opened the front door, "so they have a tendency to forget a lot of stuff. Getting paid, meeting deadlines, checking spelling, and house keys."

Inside was a dark, gloomy hall with walls layered in years of brown paint and the floors covered with battered linoleum that might have had a pattern on it at some point in the distant past. There were several doors on the first floor, but Eve headed up the wooden stairs.

"Who are these guys?" Rick asked as he followed.

"Well, the sign in the window pretty much says it

all. They're printers who believe in The Revolution."
Rick could hear the capital letters in her voice.

At the top of the fifth flight of stairs, Eve again used the key to open a door plastered from top to bottom with peeling posters, bumper stickers, and multicolored signs, some calling for marches against the war, others calling for marches to support women's rights, and at least one calling for a march in protest of another march.

Eve swept her arm across the colorful slogans. "Where do you think all those flyers and posters and big banners come from? The Protest Fairy?"

Inside, the lights were off and there was a smell of lubricating oil, various sharp chemicals, and library paste. In the dim glow from the dirty windows, Rick could see a bulky mass of machinery he assumed was the printer in the center of the room and, surrounding it, stacks of paper, boxes of ink, and a large pile of wooden strips he guessed were for holding up signs. Covering every inch of horizontal surface was a tide of printed paper – it looked like at least one copy of everything that had been printed here for the past decade.

He picked one up and angled it to the light. "Wow, the Beatles are going to play the Washington Coliseum on February 11th." He looked closer. "Oh, well, we're about eight years late."

"This place is a museum of countercultural history." Eve fingered a couple of large wall posters. "Here's the Mobilization to Stop the War from 1969, and this is the time they tried to levitate the Pentagon."

"How did that work out?"

"The Pentagon floated and the war ended. Where have you been?" She picked her way toward a large cabinet behind the printer, motioning Rick to follow. "I was here a lot during the Trail of Broken Treaties and again when the Movement occupied the Bureau of Indian Affairs. Someone had to get our side of the story out."

The cabinet was on rollers and she pushed it aside to reveal a set of stairs heading up. Rick looked up into the darkness. "Odd place to put stairs."

"Yeah, this building has been rebuilt so many times, I think they've lost track of exactly what's in here." Eve motioned for Rick to go up the stairs first and then pulled the cabinet back into place. A dim light bulb came on at the top of the stairs.

"From what I can see, the hallway was supposed to run all the way through, but at some point, they walled it off. I think Donna told me it was for a law firm, and all law firms want an interior stair."

Rick had done deliveries in any number of law firms. "Lawyers do love their stairs. I think it's because they make anyone who comes to see them walk as far as possible – humble them before the meeting."

There was a very sturdy-looking steel door at the top of the stairs. Eve unlocked it, reached in, and flipped on the lights. Then she went in, held the door open, and welcomed him in with a bow and a flourish.

The entire top floor was a single room – a totally open space except for some massive support beams and an enclosure that Rick assumed was the bathroom. Thick coats of paint covered the windows, but hanging lights illuminated hardwood floors and brick walls. A compact kitchen and counter occupied one corner, folding panels blocked off two sleeping areas on either end, and in the center of the space was an enormous U-shaped couch facing a fireplace. Wood was stacked neatly on a tiled hearth.

Rick took it all in. "Where the hell did this come from?"

"I said Donna and Shakib were revolutionaries against the rich. I didn't say they lived like the poor. As far as protest printing goes, they're the only game in town, and since they'll do work on credit and protest movements are always broke..." She shrugged. "Eventually, we all have to get our work done here."

Eve dropped her bag on the floor and headed to the kitchen area. "They decided they wanted a place where no one could find them. You might have noticed that the door behind you is made of steel. Close it, will you?"

Rick closed the surprisingly heavy door. When he turned the lock, he could hear bolts dropping into the floor. "You know, if I wasn't feeling so happy about the security up here, I'd say they were a bit paranoid."

Eve was rattling utensils in the kitchen area. "I'm having tea. Do you want anything?"

"Tea-sipping revolutionaries?" Rick dropped the bags, walked over, and sat at the counter. "That seems wrong somehow. However, I'm not a revolutionary, and I'd love some tea. Where are... Donna and what's-his-name?"

"Shakib. They've gone back to Lebanon for Christmas with his parents. He's a Maronite Christian, and they've combined revolution with personal profit

for centuries. They even have another house – a dump
right off the 14th Street riot corridor where they get
their mail and pay their taxes." She set out cups and
checked the refrigerator. "I don't trust this milk, so I
hope you don't want any."

"No, I'm fine. How did you find out about this place?"

"On November 5th, two of the young men holding
the Bureau of Indian Affairs got beat up by cops, and
everyone put on war paint and got ready to die. I
was up here when I heard about it, and Donna didn't
want me to go back through the police lines, so she
persuaded me to crash here." Eve laughed. "War paint
– it was lipstick, for God's sake."

"I've heard it's hard to buy good war paint in DC
these days."

"Ha. Ha. Ha. Make yourself useful and build a
fire." There were old posters stacked in a box next to
the fireplace. Rick crumpled a few and stuffed them
under the grate, laid the logs over that, and lit the
fire with his Zippo. They sat side by side on the couch
and watched the logs burn for a long time, not talking
much but relaxing in each other's company.

Finally, she stood up and said, "Let's go, Trooper."

"Separate beds?"

"Are you kidding?" She headed toward one of the
sleeping areas. "And listen to you refight the war all
night? No way."

He stood. "I can deal with it."

She spun around and put her hands on her hips. "I
know you can deal with it. You're strong and tough
and a very good man." Her eyes were suddenly filled
with angry tears. "But I've spent two days at your

side, damned near getting killed, and I want to go to sleep in your arms, and if you don't understand that, then you're not the man I think you are."

He grinned. "Wow, I'll bet you couldn't say that again if you tried."

She spun toward the bed. "Oh, the hell with you. Fight your damn war alone."

He followed her into the sleeping area and put his arms around her, burying his face in her neck and inhaling the warm scent of her hair. Then, without turning her around, he gently began to unbutton her shirt.

"No. No. No. I need a dust-off now!"

The voice in the receiver is telling him to stay calm. Telling him that help is coming.

"The sergeants are all dead. The lieutenant just put a bullet in his fucking brain, and shit, I can hear screaming again. They must have found someone else alive."

He whispers fiercely, "I've done enough. I've done my job. Now get me the fuck out of here!"

He tosses a purple smoke canister off into the tall grass.

"I've set the flare. Now get me out!"

Instead of the hard plastic of the radio, soft lips were on his mouth, stifling his cries. He wrenched his body from side to side, but strong arms held him tight and smooth legs wrapped around his waist. He calmed and began to wake, but the warm body on top of him kept on holding him, rocking in a steady beat.

Relief turned to something else. Something better, deeper, and stronger.

His hands slid down her back into the hollow at the base of her spine. Her arms and legs continued to hold him as she slid down and took him inside her.

Her body was a wonder, a marvel of new sensations. He couldn't stop running his hands along her sides, up her back, and over her breasts. He felt her long, unbraided hair falling across his body like running water.

The rocking turned to racing, and then a clenching of his entire body was met by an equal fierceness in hers. He fell asleep with her on top of him, her head against his chest.

For a couple of hours, he didn't dream at all.

Then he was in the jungle again.

CHAPTER 29

Christmas Day, 1972

He was fully dressed in his usual gray suit, leaning over with his forearms on his knees to keep the jacket from creasing against the straight-backed chair that, besides the narrow bed, was the only furniture in his YMCA room. The cold late afternoon sun coming in the open window brought the sound of church bells: long, jangling sequences that always seemed about to resolve into a tune, but never did. He concentrated on them, let them fill the spaces in his mind until it was almost like silence.

Save for the clangor of the bells, it was quiet outside, the usual sounds of traffic, work, and business missing. It was Christmas, and, from experience, he knew that in Washington, that meant empty streets and locked buildings. He was alone, but not lonely. He felt safe in the silence.

Thoughts and plans slowly circulated through his mind. The courier. It was too bad he was a vet; it gave him an edge – too many survival skills. He needed to get a handle on him and find some way to get rid of that damn bike. Slow him down. Bring him into a kill zone – lock it down and take him out.

Was the girl the handle? Who was she?

Idly, he wondered if the biker was a faggot like his buddy. He had come back for him – it could be love. Too bad Tung had screwed that up. That should have been the point at which everything was wiped clean. Well, Tung wasn't that badly hurt, and both twins were out trying hard to make it right. Cruising the streets in that stupid sports car and hoping to catch the guy by sheer luck.

Abruptly, he stood and stepped to the window. His room was high enough that he could see over the row houses all the way to the cathedral on the hill. He could even make out the scaffolding that still covered one side.

The bells had stopped, and he looked for a time at the city. Then he carefully closed the window, latched it firmly, and left.

He walked through the lobby, noting the young men preening and the older men watching. Outside the main door, he straightened his jacket and looked up and down the street. One light was on in the ornate stone wedding cake that was the Old Executive Office Building – someone holding down the holiday duty shift.

He walked across the street and up the steps to the restaurant. The illuminated sign was off, and a "Closed" placard was propped in the small window next to the door.

Nevertheless, the door opened as he came up the steps. Immaculately dressed and in flawless makeup, Mrs Jin welcomed him in. The lights in the front dining room were off, but he could see tableware and candles gleaming in the smaller room in the back.

These dinners had become a tradition over the years. The one small, warm piece of home and holiday in both of their lives. It was dangerous – might make them vulnerable – but neither of them was willing to shut the door on this last vestige of emotion.

She offered her cheek, and, careful not to actually touch, he brought his lips close and away. She closed the door behind him.

In jeans but no shirt, Rick was doing sit-ups when Eve awoke. She rolled over and watched the hypnotic repetition, the flex and pull of his muscles and the long, ridged scars crisscrossing his upper body like zippers. He knew instantly that she was watching, but he kept on going until he hit a hundred. Then he turned to face her and began to do slow, deep push-ups.

"You don't sleep much, do you?" she asked.

"Not anymore."

"Ever feel like talking about it?"

He looked down and concentrated on the floor as his shoulders bunched and swelled. After a few more push-ups, he looked up and said, "Talked about it, wrote it down, went to shrinks. Once I tried to write a country song about it."

"How did that work out?"

"Turned out my singing was a war crime."

She watched in silence again for a while. Then she said, "So, what are you going to do about it?"

"Keep working on it." He looked down again.

"There doesn't seem to be a quick and easy cure. Drugs and drinking don't work for me. I won't deny that I've gone off the beam – let anger or fear push me into some scary places. It'll probably happen again. Always have to work to get back to – maybe not normal, but…" Another pause. "Exercise helps; that and it keeps a lot of body parts working that the NVA did their best to turn into hamburger." Another pause. "Sleep is overrated." He looked up at her and smiled. "Although I will admit that some good things can happen in the process."

She returned his smile and then rolled onto her back, stretching her shoulders. "Should we be doing something? I mean, about the film and all."

"Christmas means empty streets and long sight lines."

She turned her head to him. "That's sad if that's all Christmas means."

"When you grow up with drunks, holidays are pretty much the worst time of year." With a puff, he finished his workout and rolled over onto his back. "Not that the rest of the time is all that great, but at least it isn't supposed to be magical and happy. Funny thing is how long you believe that everyone is as miserable as you are – that it's just the way things are supposed to be."

Rick stood up and began making a fire. "Do your people celebrate Christmas?"

"My people?" She sat up and pulled on his T-shirt, then headed for the kitchen area and started to make coffee. "A good number of the Northern Cheyenne - converted early on. It didn't keep the army from killing us, but now we get Christmas trees, Easter baskets, and all that. You'd be amazed what a normal American life I've led."

"No drums and dancing?"

Holding two steaming cups, she walked over to the sofa and sat. "No, we have that, too. When I was a kid, I loved the drum festivals – felt like I could dance all day. I guess the mixture should have been confusing, but somehow, it wasn't. It was just the way our family did things."

Rick dug out the Zippo from his pocket and set the flame to the posters under a new set of logs. Then he came back to the couch and took a cup from her. "Now, that sounds good. Tell me about your best Christmas ever."

Mrs Jin pushed the door from the kitchen with her back, swept into the private dining room, and placed the elegantly prepared duck on the small table. It was perfect – the skin crisp, the slices paper-thin, green onions and plum sauce on either side. She had done it all herself – the staff were enjoying their single day off. She only cooked one dinner a year and only for one man.

The room was perfect. The candles dim enough forthe aged velvet wallpaper to look brand-new, the flames dancing through the crystal glasses and reflecting off the polished silver. None of the usual cheap stainless steel utensils or thick functional glassware would be used tonight.

She watched with a well-hidden lurch of fear as he appraised the dinner, then relaxed as he looked up at her, and gave her a smile so slight that it would have gone unnoticed by anyone else.

"It's perfect. Please join me."

She bowed slightly and sat at the other side of the table. "I'm glad. I keep my promise for another year."

He raised a glass of wine and toasted her. "To another year." They drank, and then he said, "You know, you don't have to do this."

"I know." She took another tiny sip of wine, careful of her lipstick. "It's the doing of what I do not have to do, but which I want to do, that makes it worthwhile."

Her father drags her by the arm through the smoke. Soldiers are piling bodies under the bridge, but the shooting has stopped. She thinks that maybe they will get by unnoticed.

Then there is the soldier in green, and his rifle comes up and steadies on her face. Her father begins to beg – speaking the English he'd learned at the camp gates.

"Here, good girl. Good for you, GI. You take girl. I go." He shoves her forward and pulls her ragged shirt at the shoulders so it slips down and reveals her smooth, childish chest.

The soldier looks at her, and she expects the smile – that horrible smile that would mean another deal was made, another time of pain and fear about to begin.

There is no smile. There is nothing on his face at all.

Her father becomes desperate. He rips her shirt apart, pulls it off completely, and shoves her naked body toward the soldier. "Good girl. Good for you."

The soldier looks calmly into her eyes, and she thinks she can see just the shadow of a very different smile. He turns and shoots her father in the forehead.

She clamps her mouth shut to keep from screaming and stands rigid and shaking with her eyes wide open, fixed on his face. She hears dull thumps behind her and smoke begins to spread. Overhead, two jets scream past, rockets slamming into the others still crowding the road.

Then the soldier reaches out his hand and makes a gesture. It isn't the clutching, greedy grab that always means the beginning of a bad thing. It isn't a demand, just an offer.

She puts her hand up, and he takes it in his. Then he leads her off into the smoke, away from where her father lies. At one point, he stops and digs through his pack, finally finds an almost-new green T-shirt, and pulls it over her naked body.

It is a long walk, and, after a while, her leathery bare feet bleed, and she begins to limp. He picks her up, making sure that the big T-shirt still covers her entire body, and carries her.

Eventually, even terror can't win over exhaustion, and she sleeps.

It is night when he puts her down in front of the big doors and she comes awake. He pounds on the carved wood until the nuns open a crack and peer out. Without a word, he puts his hands on her shoulders and guides her forward. The nuns know better than to hug her, but they take her by the hand and lead her inside. He gives them money, then turns and walks away. She watches him until the doors close.

Mrs Jin – there had never been a "Mr Jin" – took another sip of wine and watched as he began to eat. It had taken many years to find him again, years where she had grown, learned, and begun to play in the dangerous games between nations. She'd kept the

T-shirt with his name stenciled across the chest, and finally, she stood in front of him in a Saigon restaurant, bowed low, and offered him Christmas dinner.

He had looked at her with the same quiet in his eyes – that look of inner silence.

"It's been a long time. I'd be delighted to share Christmas with you."

CHAPTER 30

Tuesday, December 26, 1972

In Kansas City, Harry Truman had died during the night. In a Washington already in post-Christmas slow motion, his passing was noted by government offices that simply didn't reopen and flags that flew at halfmast. The bombers started their raids again – giving Hanoi hell in the old man's memory.

Rick turned off the radio and said, "More guys are going to die. Those B-52s can't maneuver worth a damn."

Across the room, Eve was braiding her hair. "Then I guess it's time to get going, Trooper."

Rick was heading up to Capitol Hill to retrieve the evidence and contact Dina while Eve ran down some people in AIM to find if they had a safe way of getting out of the city. He figured that whoever was searching for them was used to seeing two on a bike. Splitting up might change the profile.

At the door, she came up and put her arms around him. "Stay alive, will ya?"

He pulled out the Zippo and showed it to her.

She stepped back and looked at it doubtfully. "You

know, as war magic goes, it's not exactly traditional. On the other hand, tobacco is a big part of our magic."

"There you go." He did the trick on his jeans and lit a Winston. She took the cigarette from his lips, took a drag, and, starting from his legs, blew the smoke over his entire body. Then she kissed him and put the cigarette back in his mouth.

"Good as I can do." She hugged him fiercely and then abruptly released him and headed to the kitchen. Rick watched her go. He couldn't quite take the ceremony seriously, but he didn't think it was a joke, so he just turned and headed down the stairs.

There was a phone booth on the corner of K Street. He noted the phone number and walked on until he found a second pay phone in front of a drugstore. He saw that it was the old model, so he dropped in a nickel and immediately pounded the coin return button with the palm of his hand. The nickel slipped across the levers inside and registered as a dime. The emergency tone in the receiver switched to a regular dial tone – another nickel saved from the clutches of Ma Bell.

He called Dina's apartment, asked for Paul Robeson, and went through the minus-one, plus-one routine she'd laid out. He hung up and walked back up to the first phone booth just as it rang.

"Don't you think this is just a bit too James Bond?" he said.

"Absolutely not," Dina answered. "Remember, I know what a phone tap sounds like, and I've got a tap on my home phone now. It's kicking the hell out of my love life. Speaking of love lives, where is Eve?

I just wanted you to meet her, not steal her away forever."

"I think it's more the other way around. She kidnapped me."

"Right. All you damn men are the same." Dina sighed dramatically. "Oh, well; in my heart, I knew she wasn't going to change and fall for me, so *mazel tov* to the two of you. Since you're a hopeless *goyim*, I'll also say 'good luck'. OK, back to work."

They agreed that Dina would locate Corey and arrange to meet as soon as Rick recovered the papers and the film. Rick hung up, walked back to the rear of the building, and extricated the BMW from its niche behind the Dumpster. He kicked it over, letting it warm up while he buckled his helmet. It was a bit colder than the past several days, but still above freezing. Riding would only be painful, not dangerous.

He pulled out of the parking lot and headed toward the Capitol, the dome almost invisible against a backdrop of cold gray clouds.

Parked on Eighth Street in the 240Z, Nguyen Vien and Tung Quan were watching the parade of gaily dressed men and women walk up and down the sidewalks. Vien was a mess, with his arm bandaged and splinted and his skin pale from the blood he'd lost in the explosion. Quan had a small bandage on the bullet wound in his shoulder, but otherwise he had recovered – at least physically.

Emotionally, his failure had blossomed into an almost uncontrollable rage fueled by the contempt he thought that the courier had shown by letting him live. He wanted the motorcyclist dead and, preferably, only after a long period of significant pain.

First, they had to find him. The last time they saw the courier was here on 8th Street, so they were going to sit here until they spotted him again. They smoked cigarettes and made crude comments about all the women passing by.

A block behind them, Mrs Jin was sitting in the front window of a Chinese restaurant watching them – and the rest of the street. The owner of the restaurant owed her money, so there had been no trouble getting the right seat, and no questions about why she was blocking their best table without ordering anything but a pot of tea.

At the moment, she was wondering if she should have kept the two Vietnamese men on the job. They had done badly – shamed her in front of the man she wanted most to impress. However, it was difficult to find good people in Washington. Certainly, there were many killers, but the young black men were bad about taking orders and terrible about keeping quiet afterward. No, it was better to give Vien and Quan a chance to redeem themselves.

She scanned the street again, watching the young men in leather and denim meet and mingle. She wondered how they could be so free right here in the nation's capital, especially when the White House had practically declared open war on men who loved men. Just last month, she had been paid to follow a newspaper reporter for days with orders to prove he was homosexual. She knew that the search was fruitless on the first evening when she saw how his wife and children greeted him. That didn't stop her from completing the job – political money was just as good as anyone else's, she thought.

Rick parked on G Street just south of the gay bar and left his helmet and heavy gloves locked to the bike. He walked up 8th Street, trying to watch everything and everyone around him.

It was early enough that the bar was still locked. He knocked on the thick green paint of the door and waited, then knocked again. Finally, he heard the lock click, and the door opened; the owner gave him a suspicious glare and let him in.

"I need to go get something we left upstairs," Rick explained.

The owner shrugged his shoulders without saying anything and went back to stacking beer in the big coolers behind the bar. Rick took that as permission and made his way to the upstairs apartment. The can of film and the printouts were behind the dirty tub where he'd left them. He untucked the back of his shirt, loosened his belt, and stuffed the photos flat against his back. Then he tightened the belt over them and tucked the shirt back in. With the leather jacket, it was hard to tell he was carrying anything.

Before he left, he looked out the window. He spotted the 240Z immediately and then saw that one of the Vietnamese men was already heading toward the bar. For a moment, he felt regret that he hadn't taken care of this one earlier. Then he shook his head.

No more killing.

On the other hand, the man in the street had his hand in his jacket pocket. Clearly, he didn't have the same feelings of restraint. It was time to leave.

First, he put the papers and the film back behind the tub. He wasn't going to take any chances with them flying out at high speed – he'd seen a courier lose a multivolume legal brief when he hit a pothole coming down Pennsylvania Avenue. Extremely sensitive and quite expensive documents had fluttered down like a heavy snow.

In his motorcycle boots, he made a lot of noise coming down the back stairs, and the owner had straightened up from the cooler and was giving him an annoyed stare by the time he came into the bar.

"Don't open the front door," Rick said. "A guy with a gun is looking for me. Is there another way out of here?"

The owner looked disgusted. "Did you really have to drag your goddamn troubles to my place? Dina really owes me a big one." Then he pointed back over Rick's shoulder. "There's a door all the way back through the storeroom. There's an alarm on the door that'll go off and alert the cops, but frankly, I think that's probably a good idea right now." He started to bend down. "I'm going to just lie quietly on the floor until the police show up. Just don't steal anything on your way out."

"Thanks a lot." Rick spun around and headed down the short hall. "I owe you."

"Damn right you do."

A fist began to hammer on the door.

As soon as Rick opened the back door, a loud, clanging bell went off overhead. He was in another narrow alley crowded with trash barrels and piles of old boxes.

He jogged over to his bike, kicked it to life, and took off without bothering to put on his helmet or gloves. He turned south on Eighth Street and passed the Marine Corps barracks, which always triggered the same question in his mind. How did the short-haired, wide-shouldered White House Marine guards get along with the "Great Gay Way" just a block north? Not well, he suspected.

At the south end of 8th, he turned right on M Street. Then he pulled over to the side and took the time to put on his helmet. Being stopped by the DC police could really be dangerous today.

Suddenly, he heard the heavy, almost flatulent sound of the Datsun's engine making a double-clutch downshift as it swung onto M Street only yards behind him.

Time to dance.

CHAPTER 31

The BMW *thunked* up through the gears, but Rick knew the sports car could take him in a straight-line speed contest. That being the case, he should probably avoid engaging in one. He came off the throttle just a bit and threw what he hoped looked like a frantic glance over his shoulder.

They were closing fast. Perfect.

Abruptly, Rick hit the rear brake, kicking it into a screeching slide to the left. Then hard pressure on the front brake really brought his speed down, the Earles forks pushing the handlebars up. At the last second, he released both brakes, dropped the front down, swept into an easy half- right turn, and accelerated up New Jersey Avenue.

He could hear the Datsun's brakes slam on, but the tires stopped squealing almost immediately. They'd realized they couldn't make the turn and were going to take the next right and cut around the block. With that thought, he took a fast left and blew right past them going the other direction just as they came around the corner.

Another shriek of tires. That driver isn't bad, he

thought as he watched in the side mirror. There's not a lot of room for a bootlegger turn with all those cars parked on both sides. There was a crash of metal on metal behind him and the wailing of a car alarm.

OK, the driver wasn't all that good.

The sports car slowly gained on him as he whipped to the right – weaving through a gas station and surprising a couple of drivers at the pumps – then north into the spaghetti of ramps where South Capitol Street merged with the Southwest Freeway. There wasn't much traffic, but you could always count on at least some tourists to be driving around in a daze.

Rick spotted the blue-and-gold license plate of a Pennsylvania driver in front of him and shot past on the right as the driver slowed in confusion at an unmarked split at the top of the ramp. He knew the poor guy was going to slow there, because it had taken Rick months to master those stupid ramps.

Heading down and into the eight-lane tunnel under the Mall, he met still less traffic, because the road didn't go anywhere. Sam Watkins said that someone had the bright idea of routing I-95, and the massive river of traffic flowing up and down the East Coast, and squeezing it straight through the middle of DC. The protests over the plan had resulted in the cancellation of the rest of the road, leaving only a tunnel to nowhere.

The Datsun must have worked out the ramps: Rick could hear the engine echoing off the tiled tunnel walls. He swerved across three lanes and onto the exit marked "US Capitol". He could hear the Datsun gaining on him as he tore up the ramp.

He made an illegal right turn coming out of the tunnel, hauled the big bike right again onto E Street, and right again at the end of the bridge over the highway. Three DC cops were sitting, smoking, on their Vespas, outside the Pension Building, and one of them gave him a small wave as he thundered past. The cop knew the scooter could never catch up even if he tried.

A hard left and Rick was in Chinatown. Since these brightly colored restaurants were open, it was one of the few places in the city where the streets were filled with pedestrians. He thumbed the horn button, but there were just too many people. Behind him, he could hear the Datsun getting closer, moving faster in the clear space he left behind.

Then his only remaining side mirror exploded.

He shot a look back and saw the passenger's head and shoulders poking up through a sunroof and taking aim again. They clearly weren't worried about collateral damage.

He began to swerve to throw off the man's aim, but that only forced him to slow down. He slammed into a right turn, the bike so low that the crash bars in the front were grinding sparks from the pavement. A block ahead, he could see the temporary board barriers that marked a Metro dig. He frantically checked on both sides, but they were blocking the entire street.

Standing on the pegs, he peered ahead and into the dig, hoping it wasn't deep – just a short drop onto soft dirt where he could still drive.

No luck – he couldn't even see the bottom.

Straight ahead, Rick saw a gap in one of the barriers.

Stretching across the dig was an I-beam that braced the timbered walls against the pressure of the surrounding earth. Only a foot wide and looking smaller by the second, it offered a slim chance of escape.

At his speed, there wasn't time to think. Without slowing, Rick shot through the gap and sped across the narrow beam, his knees braced against the tank, every muscle straining to stay still. His eyes were locked on the far side, trying to ignore the front tire as it tracked along the beam.

He could feel when the front wheel began to creep to the left. Any attempt to correct the drift might make it worse and he could not stop. Glancing down past the beam, he could see that the curving sides of a subway station were being built far below, fingers of concrete and reinforcing steel reaching up for him. It looked like an enormous bed of nails.

There was no way he'd survive a fall.

Ahead, there was another temporary wooden barrier, an eight-inch-square balk of timber across the bottom holding a rough fence made up of two-by-fours. On the other side, there had been just enough space between timbers to cut through to the I-beam. This time, the fence was set dead center, and there was no way around.

At the last second, he pulled hard on the front brake, loading up the front shocks and putting all the bike's weight over the front wheel. Then, just as he hit the heavy timber and he could feel the bike begin to rotate forward, he jumped.

There was a slow, quiet moment as he flew over the handlebars, his boots just scraping the top rail of the barrier. Then he smashed into the pavement, skidding for yards before he could force his body sideways and turn his momentum into a thrashing roll, his helmet banging. Rolling was no fun, but it was a lot less damaging than scraping along the asphalt.

It seemed to take an inordinate amount of time to stop, and when he finally did, he lay on his back for a moment to take inventory. While every damn inch of his body hurt, nothing seemed to have stopped working. Anyway, he thought, a fair amount of his body was already throbbing – how much worse could it get?

He rolled over, pushed up to his knees, and looked back. The only evidence of the collision was that the heavy wooden barrier had been pushed a couple of inches forward and skewed it a bit to the side. There was no sign of the big BMW.

With a groan, he levered himself to his feet, fighting to keep his balance, then stumbled back to the I-beam. Below him, the beautiful black machine lay impaled on rebar and bent almost in half.

People had gathered and stood watching him, asking if he was OK, did he need an ambulance, and probably wondering if he had just been showing off. He took off his helmet, thanked them for their concern, said he was just fine, and limped off.

The leather jacket, gloves, and boots had done their job – held against the abrasion, but everywhere his jeans had touched the pavement, the tough cloth had simply vaporized. Blood flowed from several shallow gouges on his legs, spreading a crimson stain into the fabric. He knew that although only his legs hurt like hell now, it would be inevitably worse when all the abused muscles in his body began to stiffen.

He had to find a place to hide or a place to fight – it didn't look like there were any other choices. Heading west, he passed shuttered shop windows and an open wig shop – thinking for a moment of buying one of the red, white, and blue Afro wigs as a disguise. He dismissed that idea as crazy and wondered if it meant he was going into shock.

Behind and to his right, he heard the distinctive snarl of the 240Z. From the sound, his pursuers had found another way across the Metro construction and were closing in. He had to get somewhere safe – and fast. There was only one place to go.

A handful of bikers were lounging around Motor Mouse as he staggered up. The beefy one who had insulted his front forks the first time stood up. "Man, you look like shit. That German piece of junk fall apart under you?"

"Nah, I decided you were right, and so I dropped it straight into a Metro dig," Rick responded. "Looks like a shiny black pretzel now."

"Too fucking bad. Looks like you picked up a bad case of road rash as well."

"Really?" Rick looked down at his shredded and bloodstained jeans. "Hadn't noticed," he said casually. "Hector inside?"

"You kidding? Bars aren't open yet. Where else would he be?"

Stumbling in out of the winter sun, Rick couldn't see anything in the dark garage. "Hey, *Gordito*," he called.

"Goddamn it! I hate that fucking name!" Hector roared. He spun around with an enormous crescent wrench raised, and then saw how cut-up Rick was. He dropped the wrench into the top tray of his tool chest and approached, wiping his hands on a rag. "Zippo, you keep coming back like a dead-broke bar girl, and now you look like you just tried to screw one of the bears in the zoo."

"What can I tell you? She was one goddamn cute bear." Rick slumped down on a stack of tires. "I'm here to pick up the rice burner." He paused as he heard the screech of brakes outside. "But I seem to have a little problem. These two Saigon street thugs keep trying to kill me."

"Understandable."

"Yeah, screw you too. That's them outside."

Hector shot a quick glance at the door and shouted, "Hey, Smits, Hawk. Tell those two zipperheads we aren't open and they aren't welcome."

Rick could hear the scrapes outside as the bikers stood up from their plastic chairs.

"What the hell do they want with you?" Hector hit a doorbell button on the wall over his workbench, and Rick could hear a buzzer go off upstairs.

"I've got something they want." Rick turned to head outside. "They've already tried to kill me and even some of my friends to get it."

"What the hell have you got? You started selling smack all of a sudden?"

"Nothing that profitable," Rick said as he limped back into the sunlight. "Apparently, it's the reason all of us were stuck in the shit over in Nam for so long. The reason a lot of good guys died." He stood up slowly and walked to the garage door. The two Vietnamese were out of their car, facing off against the bikers.

Both Vietnamese had guns out, but one looked like he was about to fall over. The other cowboy saw Rick in the shadows and waved his pistol at the bikers. "Get the fuck out of the way. We just want that guy."

The bikers looked at Rick, then back at the men with guns, and began to move to the side. "Hey, we don't even know him. He's all yours."

There was the very definite sound of a shotgun racking, and Hector walked out and stood next to Rick – the shotgun cradled in his arms. A voice in the window above them said, "Guns!" and the bikers both spun around, caught pistols as they dropped from the second floor, and turned back to face the men by the sports car. Rick spotted a movement over his head and looked up to see two hunting rifles emerge from the windows and center on the two men in the street.

"You want Zippo here?" Hector said. "I don't like him, but I'll be fucked if anyone who didn't get killed by gook assholes over there is going to get killed by a couple of gook assholes outside my shop. Now, if you want to argue about this, just pull those triggers, and we'll see whose arguments hold up. Otherwise, get the fuck out of here before the cops show up."

The two Vietnamese looked at each other. Then the battered one almost fell into the passenger seat. The driver shouted at Rick, "This isn't over, asshole."

He got in, and the Datsun took off – tires smoking in a full burnout.

Rick nodded to Hector. "Thanks."

"Shut the hell up. You just dropped us in a pile of crap." The mechanic turned to go back inside. "Now my guys have to watch out for these morons coming around hoping for better odds."

"Maybe not. That Kawasaki still there?"

"I told you it would be."

The sports car came up to the street corner on the left and pulled to the curb, clearly prepared to wait.

"If you don't mind, I think I'll hang around until it gets dark." Rick walked inside with Hector. "You got any bandages? Maybe an extra pair of jeans? I seem to have ripped these somehow."

"Sure, I'll trade." Hector rummaged in the back of the shop, and then threw a first aid kit to Rick. "Are you going to tell me what the hell is going on?"

"You sure you want to know?" Rick asked. "People who know about this have a way of getting killed."

"The Skins aren't playing. I've got nothing else to listen to."

CHAPTER 32

It was early evening when Rick stopped the bright-green Kawasaki directly in front of the Datsun and blew the horn. As the two men jerked alert, he gave them the finger and took off, the rear wheel smoking and whipping. The sports car coughed to life and followed.

The Kawasaki was one fast machine. In the first block, Rick realized that the acceleration was sliding him back on the bench seat and forcing his hand to rotate the throttle – making the engine go even faster. He loosened the grip of his right hand, the speed dropped, and he jerked forward.

He spun the throttle again, and the front wheel immediately began to lift off the pavement. Finally settling the bike into a steady pace, Rick realized how drastically different it was to control this explosive crotch rocket. He was going to have to relearn the reflexes formed through thousands of miles on the BMW.

On the other hand, the soft rubber tires stuck to the road like Velcro, and he was almost drunk on the raw power in the triple cylinder engine. He'd have to take it slow in the beginning, but this dance was going to be a hell of a lot of fun before it was over. The gloomy twilight was darkening, and the sodium yellow of the anti-crime streetlights was everywhere. Rick turned and twisted through downtown, making sure he stayed just far enough ahead of the 240Z to keep them coming.

The Kawasaki's engine shrieked as he sliced the wide curve around Dupont Circle and blipped up two gears to beat all the lights along P Street. The transmission was so smooth he sometimes couldn't tell when it had completed a shift through his heavy boots – an altogether different feeling from the BMW's heavy mechanical *ka-chunk*.

He went left along P Street Beach, then crossed Rock Creek Parkway at M Street and danced through all four lanes of the dense traffic crawling through Georgetown. He crouched low over the tank and pushed into turns aggressively, searching for the limits and the potential of the race-tuned machine.

At the right turn to Wisconsin, he looked back. The Datsun was still there. It was a few cars back, so Rick deliberately missed a shift as he came out of the turn. The engine howled as the tachometer needle flew high into the red zone. He banged down all the way to first gear and almost stopped before he recovered. The sports car was just making the turn, and Rick knew that the inevitable fever of a close race would begin to wear away at the driver's sense of limits. He wanted him to be right on the ragged edge of control.

He goaded the other driver by making too many glances behind him and slid just a bit off the apex as he cut the corner onto P Street. He knew that the long straight stretch studded with stop signs in front of him was dangerous, so he carefully stayed just out of reach – jerking to a near stop and screaming away when the Datsun's bumper was almost touching his rear wheel.

Then he took the ramp down to the Rock Creek Parkway and opened it up. Behind him, he could hear the Datsun's tires complaining, but the car was keeping pace on the sweeping turns.

He went airborne briefly on the reverse-cambered turn onto Beach Drive and ripped through the tunnel and past the zoo at well over a hundred miles per hour. After that, the turns got sharper and he downshifted aggressively, slowing with the engine rather than the brakes as he fell into the turns and pulled out with a bit more power each time.

He blew right through the red light at Fletcher's Mill and pressed hard into the chicane turns that followed as his feel for the machine improved and he settled into a rhythm. When he slammed on the brakes and slid his rear to the right to make the sharp left turn at Beach Drive, he could hear the tires of the sports car screaming as the driver fought to keep from launching right into the water of Rock Creek below them.

He had just brought the bike upright from the ninety-degree left when he pushed it down into a hard right onto Ridge Road and up into the park. There were no streetlights here, and only his single headlight lit the long, hard uphill spiral.

He knew the tough green racer now, and he finally put everything into the dance. The tires gripped and squirmed on the rough asphalt as he increased speed on the uphill climb. He was approaching his limits, and as he heard the car behind him lose rear traction and take the car into a badly controlled powerslide, he knew the other driver was well beyond his.

At the top of the hill, he picked up even more speed, the trees whipping past in the cone of his headlight as he cut the apex of each curve with a perfection he hadn't shown before. He knew every inch of these dark roads from far too many sleepless nights, and he felt the calm of the dance slip over him.

Finally, he reached where he had been heading all along – the left-hand turn just at the peak of the hill. There was nothing but pitch-black trees on the right, and the wooden fence of the riding center blocked the view around the curve to the left. He remembered the pounding fear the first time he'd gone in to this turn at top speed and found the curve tightening. He had almost put the BMW in the woods that night.

Not tonight. As they roared into the turn, the red 240z was only yards behind the green motorcycle. Rick pushed the powerful bike into the turn well above eighty miles per hour, the tires at the limit of adhesion, the pegs grinding on the road, left knee thrust out for balance.

Right at the end of the fence, he pushed just a bit harder – putting all the strength of his muscular arms into twisting the handlebars against the turn. For a moment, he thought he was going to slip out, but the tires held, and he bent inside the road's curve, hit the low curb, and flew over the hard, dead grass of the meadow on the left.

Rick fought his reflexes and didn't touch either brake, instead using the throttle to drive the rear wheel spinning down into the dirt and grass. He found that tiny bit of traction he needed, leaned almost off the bike on his left side, and shot past a four-foot-high white granite stone by less than an inch.

Behind him, he heard a wail of tires and a massive impact of metal on stone.

He fought the bike to a stop, holding to a straight line across the bumpy ground. The trees on the other side of the small meadow came close, but he turned in a wide circle and looked back.

As he'd hoped, in the dark, the driver of the Datsun had been following his taillight and not the road and the heavy car had tracked right behind him as he went up over the curb – almost, but not quite, matching the bike's decreasing arc.

A row of foot-thick white boulders had been placed to keep cars from driving or parking on the grassy meadow. There wouldn't even have been time for the driver's muscles to react before the Datsun wrapped around the rock and spun violently off to the right.

As he approached, he saw that the rock had punched deep into the center of the hood, driving the engine back between the driver and the passenger. Stopping next to the front window, he looked in. Both men certainly appeared to be alive – alive and screaming in pain.

He heard sirens in the near distance. Time to leave.

Heading back the way he came, he saw the blue-and-red flashes light up the dark woods in front of him, and he switched off the motorcycle to douse the lights and carefully coasted off the road and between some trees. He turned his face away to prevent a flash of pale skin as the police cruiser went by. When he heard it stop at the horse paddock, he pushed himself backward onto the road and then coasted without lights down the curving road, steering by the reflected glow that always lit the darkest Washington night.

Dropping into the long final turn, he turned the switch, bump-started the engine, and drove calmly into the wealthy neighborhoods of upper Northwest DC, keeping the engine to a low purr, obeying all the speed limits, and carefully putting his foot down at all the stop signs.

CHAPTER 33

Wednesday, December 27, 1972
Rick jerked awake in the usual tangle of sweat and terror. For a moment, he just lay on his back and stared at the ceiling, taking the long road back from the tall grass and the blood-soaked mud. Then he turned his head and looked into clear brown eyes.

How did he get this lucky?

"Good morning."

"Hate to break this to you, Trooper. It's not morning," Eve said.

He laughed and stretched. "Well, it's about as close as I ever get."

"Are you ever going to win that battle?"

"Don't know." Rick rolled over and pulled her in close. "All I can do is ride it out in the dark and try to stay sane in the sunlight. I am not going to give the bastards the pleasure of seeing me ruin the rest of my life, but man, it's not easy. Let's change the subject."

"I will in a second. Which particular 'bastards'? The US Army or the North Vietnamese?"

"Both."

"OK, what's the plan for today?"

He sighed theatrically. "I was hoping for a bit less of a serious turn in the conversation."

She kissed him lightly on the forehead. "All in good time, friend."

"OK, first I'm going to have to take a long bath, do a workout, and take another bath."

"Are you putting cleanliness next to godliness or right over there next to obsession?"

"There's a bit of that, but mostly, heat followed by exercise followed by more heat means I should be able to walk again."

She ran her hand down his stomach. "Yeah, walking is important, I guess."

"If you don't cut that out, this conversation is going nowhere." He tightened his grip on her back and trapped her hand between them. She began to wiggle her fingers.

"Final warning, Little Deer."

"Yeah, I know, she liked Running Bare. Ha. Ha." Eve looked at him closely and then took a deep breath. "My real name is *Esevona'keso*. It means 'Buffalo Calf', and before you say something stupid, it's very important in our traditions."

Rick was silent for a minute. "She was the one who killed Custer?"

"Among other things. She also fought in a battle earlier the same year and charged the cavalry alone to rescue her wounded brother, Chief Comes in Sight. In your histories, that's called the Battle of the Rosebud. In ours, it's the Fight Where the

Girl Saved Her Brother."

"So, you're a warrior?"

"Hardly. If anything, I'm a healer." Eve smiled. "You're looking at the second-best Jingle Dress Dancer at Lame Deer High."

"Maybe that would work better than the baths and the workout."

"We'll never know. I left my dress at home. I didn't think I'd be doing a lot of dancing in Washington."

"Maybe I should look up the girl who beat you for first place." She pinched him hard. He squirmed away and said, "What else is there I don't know about you?"

She moved close against him, and he could feel her smooth, athletic muscles. "Well, I was captain of the girls' lacrosse team."

"Another tribal ritual?"

"Maybe for the Iroquois up in New York, but we got it from Baltimore. The reservation doctor was our coach. He'd made varsity at Johns Hopkins." She snuggled back against his chest. "Enough cultural bonding. Let's hear some more about your life."

"I don't know what there is to say." He kissed her on the top of her head. "I had a childhood so bad that I ran away to join the Army, and then…" He trailed off and then started again. "Then there were a long couple of days in the Ia Drang Valley where I lost a lot of friends, a good deal of blood, and maybe a part of my soul." He shook his head. "God, that just sounds like a load of crap. Self-pitying and dumb."

Eve levered herself up on her elbows and put

both hands on his face, staring intently into his eyes. "Listen. I believe in all that 'crap', even after highly trained professors have been trying to knock it out of me for four years at Dartmouth and three years of Georgetown Law. You have terrible wounds. They're written on your body and carved into your soul. I'd like to help you heal."

He stared back. "I don't know if it's something that can heal – at least not forever. All the guys I know fall down at some point."

She kissed him on the chest. "Didn't say I'd heal it, just said I'd like to help." She relaxed back down onto his chest. "On the other hand, we do have some powerful healers back in Montana, and the land itself has sacred powers."

He wrapped his arms around her. "I'd like to see that. Couldn't be worse than a VA shrink, anyway."

"OK, back to the plan for today. Just baths and workouts, or are we going to war?"

He laughed, then turned serious. "I guess we're going to war. Or, better yet, figure out how to use these documents to stop one particular war."

"And screw the President?"

"That too." He rolled out of bed and headed for the bathroom. "I'm really not a pacifist, and I've got a need to see some justice done."

It was gray and cold, so Rick kept the speed down as they cruised up to Capitol Hill. As he always did, he thought about the classic problem of motorcycle thermodynamics. Should you drive slowly so it wouldn't be as cold but you'd spend more time getting where you were going, or speed up and suffer through the increased wind blast for a shorter period? Or should he just get a bike with a full fairing and a windshield?

Nah, sitting behind a slab of plastic would spoil the dance.

Eve pulled herself a bit closer to his back. "This is not a rational form of transportation. I ask you again, why not a nice warm car?"

"Hey, watch what you say. Motorcycles are a very important part of my personal belief system."

"So, you believe in freezing to death?"

Rick ducked down behind the Kawasaki's small windshield, and Eve shrieked as the full force of the wind hit her.

Rick sat up again. "See, that's why you should never make fun of someone's religion."

"I will get my revenge, you know." Her hands disappeared under his jacket. "I am a master at the ancient Cheyenne torture of cold feet in bed."

"Threats, always threats." He stopped and began to park. "OK, no more jokes. We're here."

They walked up 8th Street to the Townhouse, and, again, Rick's glasses immediately fogged over. While he pulled them off, wiped them down, and waited for them to heat up enough to stop condensing, he didn't see the middle-aged woman from the Seoul Palace get up from a corner table and turn her back to walk toward the restrooms.

Eve tugged him over to the table where Dina and Corey were sitting. They pulled off their jackets and gratefully clutched two waiting mugs of coffee.

Dina looked at them intently. "There's something different about you two."

Eve nodded and smiled.

The older woman said, "Congratulations, you make a good team. Now, let's move on to unimportant matters like the hopefully short and painful future of the schmuck in the White House."

"The papers and film are still over at the other bar." Rick sipped at his coffee. "I got rudely interrupted by my friends from Saigon."

"Those bastards again?" Corey looked around the room. "What's it take to discourage them?"

"Don't worry."

Corey turned his eyes to Rick. "Why not?"

"You are a respected member of the congressional staff. Do you really want to know?"

After a pause, Corey said, "No, not really."

Dina broke in. "That's wonderful, if slightly scary, news, but I doubt they were working alone. Let's block out a plan, go get the evidence, and scatter."

She turned to Corey. "You get to lead the prosecution team."

"Are you kidding?" The lawyer bristled. "Have you forgotten that I'm gay? The President and his staff are already accusing everyone and his brother of being a faggot. One wrong step and my career is history."

Dina smiled. "Sweetie, you really are preaching to the choir, you know. How long do you think I'd last if anyone knew about my girlfriends? But there is one big difference. I'm a Democrat."

"So?"

"So, you know damn well that half the Republican

congressional staff spends their nights up in the bushes around the Iwo Jima Memorial or dancing their cute little butts off at Lost and Found and Grand Central." She shook her head. "I'll never figure out why all you boys get hot for guys with deeply conservative family values."

"It's the dress code," Corey deadpanned. "But that puts me more at risk. My only hope is to stay deep in the closet and hope to not get caught."

"Not if you've got Rick's evidence. Someone from the White House comes after you, and it's mutual assured destruction." She tapped her finger on the table for emphasis. "Spread the stuff around. Give a bit of the information to every gay staffer on the Hill so no one can be sure they've snagged all of it."

Rick spoke up. "Hey, it's not just about keeping you guys safe and warm in your day jobs. I want the war stopped and that rat bastard ruined. Not just out of the White House – ruined forever."

"His name should be a synonym for betrayal," Eve added. "The only way he gets remembered is as the worst President ever."

"Remind me never to go to war against a woman," Corey said. "OK, I'm in. There are a lot of gays who fought in that jungle – they just had to keep their mouths shut and their legs crossed – and they'll be just as pissed as you when they find out the truth. We'll do it right."

Eve asked, "Do it right?"

"Yeah, no half-assed leaks to the *Post*." He nodded to Dina. "You're right. A lot of top Republican staffers are gay, and they've got a lot of influence over the GOP caucus."

Corey took a small leather notebook from his coat pocket and began to make notes. "Even without subpoena power, we should have enough juice to get the bombing stopped immediately, and then I'll take it to friends on both Banking Committees and we'll put the accountants to work. It may take a while, but we'll take him down. It probably won't be public like that circus Sam Ervin is kicking off, but one day, the real powers in this town will sit down in the Oval Office and tell him exactly what will happen if he doesn't quit."

"I don't think anyone is here, but I've got a key," Dina said as they reached the door to the lesbian hangout. "Let's hurry up, get the evidence, and get out of here. We need to split up."

She opened the green door and headed straight for the back hallway and up the stairs. Rick closed the door, but realized it didn't have a thumb lock – he would need the key to lock it up. With a shrug, he followed Eve and Corey up to the small apartment.

The prints and the film were still behind the grimy bathtub, and Rick pulled them out and handed them to Dina, who took them over near the doorway, where she scanned them quickly under the bare light bulb.

"OK, this is the real thing." She turned to hand the papers to Corey. "Up to you now."

"No. It will be up to me." A hand with a straight razor reached across Dina's neck and a middle-aged

Asian woman grabbed her by the other shoulder and pulled her back a step. "Now, hand those papers to me, or she will die."

Rick looked at her closely. "Wait a minute. I know you. You're Mrs Jin from the Seoul Palace."

She hissed in anger.

Corey put the printouts and film on the cot next to him and stood up. "Rick, you really should think before you open your mouth."

"You think I won't kill this bitch?" The Korean woman tightened her grip, and a thin line of blood appeared on Dina's neck.

Corey looked relaxed as he took a step toward her. "No, the problem is that I do think you'll kill her. I think that now we know who you are, you'll kill all of us."

The razor slashed across Dina's throat, and she gurgled and fell, her hands up in a futile attempt to stop the gush of blood. Mrs Jin took a quick step toward Corey, but then cried out and fell as Eve flew in from the side and tackled her at the knees.

Again, Rick had a hard time seeing what Corey actually did, but in seconds, the razor rattled against the far wall and Corey had one hand gripping the woman by the thumb and the other on her neck. They stood frozen for a moment, and then she shuddered and went limp.

Corey stepped back. "Eve, you can let go now. She's unconscious."

Rick shot over to Dina and crouched at her side. One look at her pale face told him that she'd already almost bled out. God knew he'd seen enough of that to know. Eve fell to her knees on the other side and put her hands on the slowing pulse of blood coming from her throat.

"Is there anything we can do?" she asked.

Rick shook his head.

Eve bent down and hugged the big woman desperately, then gave her a kiss on the lips. "I'm so sorry, Dina. I couldn't be the woman you wanted, but you were a true friend."

Dina's eyes flicked to Eve's face and then Rick's. She looked intently at him for a second, and then her eyes glazed over and she was gone. Rick knew that she'd asked and been answered in that quick exchange. He closed her eyes and then pulled Eve to her feet.

"We've got to get out of here."

Corey looked at the Korean woman crumpled on the floor. "What do we do with her?"

"Is she going to die?" Rick asked Corey.

The slim man shook his head.

"Then we'll leave her here. I'll call the cops. Nobody touch that razor. If we're lucky, she'll get arrested for murder."

Corey picked up the film and the printouts and started for the door. He paused and crouched down by Dina's body. "I wish I could have known you longer, girlfriend. I think we would have had some good times. Just for that, I'll ruin that crooked bastard for you. That's a promise." He disappeared down the stairs.

Rick gently pushed Eve back and looked at her. "Come on. We'll wash off that blood and get out of here. It's over."

Eve's face crumpled, but there were no tears. She

said, "No, it's not over." She let Rick lead her to the sink. "It'll never be over."

"No, it never is. But you have to keep going anyway."

CHAPTER 34

Rick hung up the pay phone outside a small corner store with high windows of glass brick and turned back to the bike.

Eve, still sitting on the back of the motorcycle, examined his face. "What's wrong?"

"Somehow, when the desk captain refers to the location of the crime as 'a lezzie bar', I don't get the feeling that checking out a report of a fight will be a high priority." He swung back onto the Kawasaki. "I hope that woman doesn't wake up and take off before DC's Finest manage to fit a visit into their busy schedule."

Eve put her arms around him and pressed her face into his back. Rick could feel her quiet sobs through his jacket.

He kicked the bike to life. "OK, we need to get off the streets and figure out a way to get out of town."

Eve said in a voice straining to be normal, "I've got a way."

Rick pulled away from the curb. "A quick flight to Belize?"

That got a brief laugh that seemed to catch in her throat. She sighed, "God, this sucks. No more jokes, OK?"

"OK, but it won't help."

"It can't hurt." She wiped her eyes on the back of his jacket. "I went to see some of my people. They've agreed to help. We just need to get to them."

"What people?"

"My people. That's all you need to know. I've got to keep them safe."

"Fair enough." He pulled into traffic. "I've got to drop something off at Motor Mouse, and then we'll grab our stuff from the printers."

"Motor Mouse?"

"My people. That's all you need to know."

She punched him in the back.

He smiled.

Once again, the quiet filled the Impala. It was parked inconspicuously a block away from Motor Mouse with an excellent view of the grimy garage doors. The Vietnamese were gone – he'd gotten them on a military medevac flight deadheading back to Da Nang to pick up another load of wounded. They would take a long time to recover, but after their repeated failures, they were fortunate to be alive at all. He had refrained from disposing of them more permanently because he thought they might be useful in the future and, more importantly, because too many people in the DC Police Department and other, less public, agencies were already quite curious about them.

He'd cut off the driver's morphine while the nurse was out of the room and cross-examined him at some length. Between moans, he had identified this dubious-looking courier company as perhaps the one place where he might be able to pick up the trail. When Mrs Jin had called him at the YMCA with the news of her involvement with the murder of a congressional staffer, he'd told her to disappear for her own safety and that they would see each other again.

They always did.

Now, he was on another solo mission, and, if anything, it was a relief. Other people just complicated things – made it hard to concentrate.

The key thing that needed attention was that damn film, and Mrs Jin wasn't completely certain that the courier even had it any longer. There were other people involved now. If that was true, he couldn't resolve the situation with a single clean kill.

Well, that was the way it was.

He settled back and let his mind clear.

The plastic chairs sat empty in front of Motor Mouse when Rick pulled up. Idly, he wondered if the usual occupants had jobs they needed to go to or families who wanted to see them. It was hard to think of outlaw bikers as having a life outside of the club. The big doors were almost closed, but he could see a gleam of light inside, so Hector must still be there.

Eve looked at the grimy town house and the small crowd of hookers huddled on the corner next door. "Classy place."

"It grows on you. Sort of like mold." Rick pulled off his helmet and grinned as he scratched his hair. "Luckily, we won't be here long. Come on in and meet a friend."

Inside, Hector was watching a lathe grind down

a brake drum, the metal-on-metal howl filling the small space. Rick walked up and tapped him on the shoulder.

Hector spun around with a tire iron raised to strike and then angrily threw it across the room when he saw who it was. Grimly, he turned back to the lathe and spent several minutes methodically finishing the smoothing and checking the work with a micrometer.

Finally, he switched off the machine and said without turning around. "So, Zip, you finished your business?"

"I think so."

"Who's the girlfriend?"

"Let me introduce you. Eve, this is *Gordito*. *Gordito*, Eve."

The mechanic turned and said, slowly, "That is not my name."

"It's OK. Eve isn't my real name, so we're even." She stuck out her hand. "And with luck, we'll never speak again, so it won't be a problem."

After a short pause, the mechanic shook her hand, and looked at Rick. "Zip, you don't deserve to be this lucky."

Rick took out a Winston and lit the Zippo with his usual up-down motion. "I think you're right."

"That trick still working?"

"Better than ever." Rick inhaled the smoke deep into his lungs. "It's been like the war the last few days. People dying all around me, and I'm still here."

Hector turned back to the brake drum and smacked a hammer against the release lever until it loosened. "So, what do you want from me?"

Rick took the pistol out of his jacket. "Just returning this. We've got to travel, and this will inevitably cause problems."

"Funny, most people think it solves problems."

"Yeah, well, most people are wrong. You want it back or what?"

"Should I worry about the cops looking for it?"

Rick considered for a moment. "I doubt it. I put one into someone's shoulder, but he's not the type to file a complaint. Anyway, he's definitely got other things on his mind right now."

"OK." Hector turned, took the gun, put it away in one of the drawers of his toolbox, slammed the drawer closed, and locked it. "Anything else?"

"Nope, just wanted to say thanks and *adios*."

Rick stuck out his hand, but Hector ignored it. "Zip, you were probably the sorriest damn soldier I've ever met, and what's worse was that I made the mistake of saving your butt back there and it almost got me killed." The mechanic turned away and picked up a rag to wipe his hands. "You were a useless fuck in the Cav. You're a useless fuck now. Please just go away and stop dumping your problems into my life."

Rick smiled. "Love you too, Gor–"

"That is not my name!" the mechanic shouted.

"Whatever you say." Rick and Eve walked to the small door next to the roll-up garage entrance.

As soon as Eve opened the door, she seemed to disappear, as she was yanked off her feet and a large pistol appeared in her place.

"Freeze!"

Rick froze.

"OK, here's how this is going to work," said the quiet, solid man holding the gun. "I want the film and anything else you got from the bookkeeper. Do you have it?"

"Not anymore."

"No problem. You're going to stand here quietly until your girl and I get into that car over there and leave. Then you've got two hours to go and gather up every frame of that film and every page of evidence from wherever you put it or whoever you gave it to and bring it up to the vacant building on the northwest corner of 14th and Irving."

Eve suddenly jerked as she tried to pull away from his hand on her arm. The man tightened his grip and rested the gun against the back of her head.

"Young lady, this is a forty-five-caliber automatic. It will leave pieces of your pretty face two blocks away and still have plenty of power to kill your boyfriend. Please don't do that again."

Rick looked into her eyes, seeing anger but no fear. "Please, just do what he says."

The man pushed the gun under his coat but still pointed it at Eve. He began to walk backward toward his car. "Very sensible. Remember, two hours."

Rick didn't take his eyes off Eve. "No problem."

He watched, motionless, as the man shoved Eve into the passenger seat and the Impala pulled away.

Behind Rick, there was the sound of the breech cracking as Hector safetied his shotgun. "Sorry, man, I didn't have a shot."

"I know." Rick watched until the Impala turned the corner and disappeared. "It's not your fight, man."

"I know." The mechanic propped the shotgun by the door and turned back to his tool chest.

Rick pulled out a cigarette and paused to look at his lighter before scraping it up and down his jeans. It lit.

"Still works, huh?" Hector looked over. "Light one for me. I think I'll need all the good luck I can find tonight."

The newsroom was as it always was.

Somehow, Rick thought something should be different since so many things had happened to him in the past few days. However, the purposeful chaos of the newsroom hadn't changed at all.

As he walked in, the senior producer was on the phone to New York. He raised his eyebrows in mute question. Rick shrugged. Don Moretti dashed by with a red plastic can of film, and Rick followed him into the tiny edit room.

Moretti immediately started putting the processed film on the edit blocks, his hands moving with precise speed even as he looked at Rick. "What's been going on, fella?" he asked. "You weren't here the past few days. They brought some Neanderthal with a speed-freak death wish in to replace you. We couldn't even get him into the White House. I think the problem was that he couldn't spell his name."

"I've been busy." Rick lit a cigarette. "Personal stuff."

"Hell, you know that's not allowed in this business." Moretti began to screen the film on the tiny viewer, spinning the reels as he searched for a shot. "Give me that cigarette and tell me what I can do you for."

Rick put the Winston between the editor's lips and lit another. "I need to make a phone call, and then I need a can of 'B-Roll'."

"'B''B-Roll'?" Moretti looked up sharply. "You mean like tight shots of a line of pencils writing on pads, or shots of the Capitol? You starting your own news business?"

"Hardly. I just need a can of blank film – small size, silver color with the tape still on it."

"What for?"

"It would really be hard to explain. Can we just consider it a favor?"

Moretti spotted the segment he was looking for, whipped the viewer up, and pulled the film off the synch block and onto the splicer. He pulled another strip of film from the bin at his side and laid in a tape splice. Then he racked up a smaller reel and began furiously winding the film on it.

"OK, you get this into Telecine in the next" – he looked at the clock – "thirty-two seconds, and I'll make a fake can for you."

The film ran out and spun on the reel, the end snapping on the table. Moretti popped the reel off the hand crank and shoved it at Rick, who fast-walked down the hall and through the double doors.

A bored-looking engineer looked up from the game of solitaire on his desk. "That Moretti's?"

"Yep."

"Good, the director is starting to have kittens." The engineer seemed to remember something. "Hey, Lee said thanks for getting the crap off his line."

"Always happy to help out the engineering side."

By the time Rick returned to the edit room, Moretti was spinning some junk film on a small plastic core. Rick turned to the phone, dialed a number, and asked for Edna Ponds-Simons.

"He's got Eve," he said without preamble, "and I've got to go and get her. Any ideas?" He listened and then asked, "You carry that around with you? Wait, of course you do. Can you meet me outside in about five minutes?" He hung up the phone.

Moretti had a silver can filled and taped. "What should I mark it?"

"Hadley B-roll."

There was a pause. "Hadley? You're bullshitting me. You know he's dead, right?"

"Him and a lot of other people." Rick took a deep breath. "Don, I can't tell you what's going on, but please believe me, I really need what you've got in your hand."

After a second, the editor scratched the title on the label and held out the can. "Here you go. Hope you know what you're doing."

"You and me both." Rick took the can and walked quickly down the hall to the door that led to the courtyard where he'd left the Kawasaki. Just as he pulled open the door, Paul Smithson, the bureau chief, stepped into the small alley from the door on the other side.

Without even thinking, Rick grabbed the older man by the elbow and pushed him hard to the right, spun him around the corner, and pinned him against the brick wall with his right forearm hard across the older man's throat.

Smithson put his hand up to the back of his head. "What the hell do you–"

"Shut the fuck up." Rick spoke in a cold, almost emotionless voice – straining to keep the rage from taking over. "You took the Hadley film, didn't you? You took it and you had that girl fired. Right?"

Smithson paused for a second and then nodded – all the bluster had gone out of him.

"Well, you fucked up." Rick pushed again and Smithson's head bounced off the brick wall.

"See this? This is what they wanted." Rick held the silver film can inches from Smithson's face.

He wanted to scream at the old bastard, but with considerable effort, he kept his voice low so no one passing between the buildings could hear.

"That son of a bitch in the White House. You know, the guy you used to work for?"

Rick gently tapped the film can against Smithson's temple.

"What's in here is going to take him down. All those bastards in the West Wing are going to be arrested, and then the fucking criminals in the Committee are going to be walked out in handcuffs…"

Rick's right arm was shaking from the effort it took not to crush the older man's throat.

"And finally, when he's lost every friend and ally he's ever had, the President is going to pay for what he did. Americans – soldiers and marines and pilots and sailors – real Americans who believed your bullshit have been dying. Dying because that greedy fuck made a political deal with the South Vietnamese and took fucking money for your fucking campaign."

Rick thrust the older man away and Smithson stumbled a couple of steps down the alley. He turned and began to speak.

"Son, you've got it–"

"Old man" – Rick's voice was just above a whisper but it cut through like a knife – "just shut the fuck up and pray. Because I'm going to meet right now with a very quiet guy with a very large gun. He's got a friend of mine and…"

Rick's voice didn't break.

It simply stopped.

He forced the next words out through clenched teeth. "If I come back alone…"

Another pause.

"Don't. Be. Here."

Rick stepped back and went to get his bike. Smithson walked quickly the other way and lost himself in the evening crowds on Connecticut Avenue.

CHAPTER 35

As he drove to the rendezvous, Rick noticed how both sides of 14th Street still showed the marks of the '68 riots – scorched exteriors, rubble-filled lots, and an eerie emptiness. He remembered watching the television as the 82nd Airborne locked down the city to enforce an absolute curfew. There had been machine guns deployed right in the middle of these intersections. In some ways, the people had never come back. The streets that had been the centers of black life had been the worst damaged. Even the desperate spray-painting of "Soul Brother" on stores and small businesses hadn't saved them.

Sam had said that during those rage-filled days, even when he didn't wear a helmet so everyone could see he was black, he still had to blast through here at top speed, hanging over the side of his bike. He claimed he came under sniper fire, but Rick thought it was far more likely that he was just embellishing the story a little.

Today, the sound of the Kawasaki's engine bounced back off the empty row houses as Rick cruised well below the speed limit. For a moment, he saw the humor in it. After all the crazed driving he'd done in this city, now he was terrified he'd be stopped and miss this meeting.

For the hundredth time, he checked that he had the can of film. Yes, it was right there in his inside jacket pocket.

The building on the northwest corner of the intersection with Irving looked like it had been a car dealership before the riots. Now it was two stories of flaking paint, scarred cinder-block walls, and shattered glass in an expanse of rubble-strewn asphalt with weeds growing through the cracks. A ribbon of blue paint that once had been a cheerful decoration ran around the walls at the level of the second floor, looking black under the streetlights.

It looked as if someone still held out hope for renewal. There was a flimsy construction fence around the lot – chain-link strung between poles held upright by cinder blocks filled with concrete. On the other hand, the fence was old and rusted. Any chance of rebuilding had probably been destroyed by the ruthless economics of inner-city mortgages.

The fence wasn't buried in the ground, so Rick shoved it aside, pulled the bike in, parked it, and closed the fence behind him. The Kawasaki had a built-in lock that kept the front forks from turning, and he considered whether he should leave it unlocked in case he wanted a fast getaway. Then he decided that if everything went wrong, he wasn't likely to be coming out at all, and if it went right, he wouldn't be in a hurry. He locked the forks.

He walked slowly toward the smashed dealership, trying and failing to make out any details in the deep shadows inside. It looked as if the new cars had been parked on both the first and second floors – there must be a vehicle ramp to the second floor somewhere. There were enormous gaping holes facing 14th Street on both floors where once shining new cars had been showcased behind plate glass.

He stepped through one of the windows, careful to avoid the remaining shards of glass and the twisted metal left by scavengers. Inside, he stood for a few minutes, waiting for his eyes to adjust to the dim light coming in from the streetlights outside.

"Up here."

The voice came from high in the back of the dark building. That's where the car ramp must be, he thought.

Walking carefully, shuffling his feet to brush aside the wire snares, glass knives, and jagged steel daggers that covered the floor, and moving slowly enough to pick out and avoid the smashed metal desks strewn about, he made his way to the rear. As expected, a car ramp swept in a wide curve to the second floor, taking up the entire width of the building. It began on his right and ended in the shadows above him to the left.

He slowly walked up the ramp. Just as his feet felt where the floor leveled out on the second level, he heard, "Stop right there."

It was the quiet man who had taken Eve. He was standing against the wall to his left – completely hidden in deep shadow, and it wasn't until he stepped forward and was outlined by the light coming in through the broken windows that Rick could pick him out.

With a smooth motion, the agent drew Eve from darkness behind him. She seemed to have her hands tied behind her back, and the man was holding her casually by the upper arm. In his right hand, the .45 was in a relaxed grip, pointing somewhere between both of them. Rick thought he was making it clear that he could shoot either of them in an instant.

Rick found it oddly difficult to talk. His throat felt dry and tight. He coughed and then asked Eve, "You OK?"

"I've been better," she replied.

"Please stop talking. We have business to conduct," her captor said without much emotion in his voice. He waved the pistol at Rick. "Have you got the film? Give it to me and you two can leave."

Rick walked a few steps, moving off the ramp and toward the front of the building, but carefully not getting any closer to the agent. Then he stopped, turned, and put his back against the right wall. He still couldn't clearly see Eve and her captor in the dim light but knew he was also invisible in the deep shadow. In his head, he knew exactly where they were standing – for once, his memory was useful instead of merely painful.

Rick took a deep breath and blew it out in a tired sigh. "No, I really don't think I can do that. I think that you'll have to kill both of us whether we give you the film or not. You can't afford to leave us alive with what we might know."

Then he slowly pivoted until he faced the front of the building with his right side toward where he knew the agent must be – this presented the smallest target to his opponent. As quietly as he could, he reached into his jacket and pulled out the film. Transferring it to his left hand, he reached into his pocket again.

"The fact is that we actually don't know anything except that a bunch of assholes have been trying to kill us, but I don't think you can afford to take my word on that." He held the film up with his left arm straight so it was far from his body. He twisted it in his hand so it glinted in the dim light.

"Now, here is the damned film. It's never even been developed. I've got no idea what's on it and don't care."

He was sure he could feel the man's trigger finger tighten.

"Before you do something stupid, consider the chance that I might be lying. Imagine how dumb you'll feel if you kill us both and that's not the right film and you have no idea where the real one is."

There was a pause, and then the voice came from the shadows. "I could simply take the chance."

"You could."

There was another pause. Then the man spoke again. "OK, we'll make a deal. You throw that film over to me, and she'll walk to you."

Rick tossed the can high and edge-on to the floor so that it clattered and rolled noisily before settling near to where he knew the man and Eve were standing.

Eve walked carefully until she stood next to Rick against the wall.

The voice came again from the deep shadows. "It looks right."

"Now you're about to make a big mistake," Rick said calmly. "You're about to shoot us."

"Where's the mistake?"

"You can't see me, but I've got a pistol aimed right between your eyes. I can't see you either, but I have a perfect memory. Usually it's just a curse because it keeps replaying the damn war, but right now, I know exactly where you are."

There was a pause. "The question is whether I believe you."

"Yes, it is."

He pulled his right hand out of his jeans. The down-up motion was almost too fast to see, and without stopping the upward motion, he underhanded the Zippo in a high arc toward the opposite wall. At the same time, he shouted, "Now!" squeezed his eyes shut, and drove sideways into Eve, knocking her to the floor and thrusting his hand over her eyes.

Orange flame blossomed into a painfully bright blaze of brilliant white as the magnesium shavings Eps had packed into the lighter's wind guard ignited. Even with his eyes closed, it hurt, but Rick knew the other man would be blinded completely. He heard a gunshot, and a big bullet *thwacked* into the concrete just over his head.

He opened his eyes to see a jet of flame reaching out from the ramp to the agent, followed instantly by a second as the double thundercrack of a shotgun reverberated in the concrete room. The magnesium burned out at that instant and darkness returned, but Rick still had an image on his retinas – the agent arched backward with his head pinned to the wall and his face transformed into a scarlet mask.

The silence that followed was broken by the sound of a shotgun's breech breaking, shells ejecting, new shells going in, and the weapon being readied again.

Hector walked slowly up the dark ramp with the shotgun locked against his shoulder and aimed into the darkness of the opposite wall. Rick could just make him out as he carefully walked closer, poked with his toe, and then crouched down over the body.

In a calm voice, Hector said, "This thing does make a mess. Damn near blew his head off."

He picked something up off the floor, stood up, and walked over to where Rick and Eve were lying. "Good thing you told me to look away. That wasn't no ordinary lighter, Zip."

"I've been telling you that for years."

Hector held up small silver square. The Zippo. "Do you want it back?"

"I guess not." Rick stayed where he was. "You can keep it. It's got to be damn near empty by now."

Hector went to the wall over their heads and put his finger in the large hole. "Man, those forty-fives really do some damage."

He turned toward them, and in the light from the front window, Rick could see him toss the lighter up and down in his palm.

"I don't think I want it. Last thing I want to be reminded of is you and the goddamn Seventh Cavalry. Anyway, I think I'm going to quit smoking. It's bad for my health."

"OK." Rick gestured with his hand. "Toss it over. I'll give it to Eve."

"The hell you will," she said. "And would you please stop chatting and get off me? I think you broke a rib, Trooper."

Rick could see as Hector looked at her and his teeth flashed in a smile.

Then the smile froze and Hector's eyes jerked wildly. A line appeared across his neck, and blood, black in the dim light, burst out. Rick and Eve were drenched in seconds. As they watched, Hector slowly fell to his knees and then toppled forward onto Rick.

Standing where Hector had been was Mrs Jin – razor in her hand and the glitter of tears on her face.

"I loved him." She gestured back to where the agent's body lay. "He killed my father. For that, I loved him."

She bent down over Hector's body with the razor held out in front, reaching for Rick.

"I loved him," she repeated softly.

The Cong machine gunner is right next to him, firing over the pile of bodies. Inches above him, Corporal Pickens's dead eyes flicker in the light of the muzzle blast. He must be quiet.

Can't breathe.

Can't move.

•••

Then he *did* move.

His right hand shot up and clutched the woman's throat. His arm locked to keep her away. She flailed with the razor, but he pulled his face under Hector's body, and the tough leather of his jacket protected his arm.

In all his dreams, he had been helpless, unable to change one instant of the inevitable progression of events in the blood-soaked mud under the tall grass.

But this was no dream. This was real, and he could fight.

He could win.

The pitiless determination that drove him to year after year of weights and endless days of squeezing that goddamn pink ball poured into his grip. The frantic fear of the past days of pursuit and his anger at his friends being hunted raised him from the deep well of years spent battling darkness and despair. Now, the woman lying at his side gave him a fragile hope that he could heal his invisible wounds. He had come too far and suffered too much to lose now.

Slowly, steadily, his fingers began to close. He could feel the muscles and cartilage of the woman's neck being crushed in his grip. She pulled back, twisting violently.

An expert at survival in a last desperate effort to survive.

His hand never weakened. His fingers drove deep, stopping her breath, clamping off her blood, ripping the life from her body. He never closed his eyes, forcing himself to watch as she fought her final battle in a lifetime of struggle.

For an instant, Rick thought he could see her face soften in the dim light.

Like a child woken from nightmare by the loving touch of a parent.

Then she was gone.

He held her long after she stopped moving.

CHAPTER 36

New Year's Day, 1973
The wind was brutally cold.

It swept across the flat land and the hard-packed snow. There were no clouds, but the sun looked weak and small in the immense blue sky.

Rick could see where the land rose to the mountains in the far distance. It would take some time to get used to this much sheer unbroken space.

He had time.

"Like what you see, Trooper?"

He felt her arms come around him where he stood in the door of the small cabin. Eve leaned into him, and he felt as if a bubble of joy had just enclosed them.

He wrapped his arms across hers.

"Starting a new year in a big new place. Works for me."

She looked around his shoulder. "It's nice and quiet now. When it warms up, I'll have to deal with relatives." She snuggled into him. "I can't decide what's worse – being chased by the CIA, the FBI, and the Bureau of Indian Affairs, or the tribal elders. I know that federal agents don't come deep into the reservation these days, but they should have laws to keep my aunts away."

"It's a good place to hide, and I'll buy a bike so we can leave when it gets warmer." He thought for a moment. "But I do see one problem."

"What?"

"I'll have to start obeying the speed limit." He reached back and pulled out his wallet, removing one of two driver's licenses. "I'm afraid that Rick Putnam passed away back in DC – at least for a while."

She let him go and they went back into the cabin, where a fire was burning in a small iron woodstove.

"Can you get used to some guy named Jack?"

"Cheyenne men change their names several times as they go through life."

"What about women?"

"No, once we settle on something, we don't ever change."

"You're telling me," he said playfully.

She swung a fist at him, but he caught it, wrapped her up in his arms, and they fell onto the couch. After a short period of struggle, ending when both of them groaned from still-unhealed injuries, he asked, "What would my Cheyenne name be?"

"First of all, you don't get to have a Cheyenne name. It's not a joke."

"Fair enough."

"But if you did, it could be…" She paused. "It could be *Hevovitastamiutsto*."

He pronounced it carefully, trying to mimic all the tones and pauses. "What's it mean?"

She slipped her hand inside his shirt and rested it

on his chest. "Whirlwind. For the way you sleep."

"It's a little better now. At least I'm not waking up alone."

"No, you've already woken me up by then." She grinned, then clearly thought of something. "Did you hear the radio?"

"Nope. Got sort of lost in the landscape."

"They've stopped the bombing of Hanoi. The peace talks are back on and all the remaining American troops are coming out." Eve gave him a squeeze. "Corey came through."

"Damn." He shook his head. "We paid a high price. Hope it was worth it."

"You don't get to choose those who go into battle beside you," she said. "That's something only they decide. Your duty is to make their sacrifice mean something."

Rick nodded. The two of them sat in each other's arms and looked into the fire as the small cabin slowly filled with a comfortable silence.

ACKNOWLEDGMENTS

Authors usually seem to have dozens of people to thank when they get a book published. The way this worked out, I didn't have that many people working with me but that makes the efforts of those listed here all that more crucial to getting *Courier* finished.

Dean Krystek was the only agent who deigned to read the manuscript, he was also the primary editor, a relentless cheerleader, and a professional who was so dedicated to this project that he continued putting it in front of publishers for three years. The same day that I was going to give up and self-publish *Courier*, he emailed to say that this British publisher was "going to take it with him on vacation."

Which brings me to the redoubtable Emlyn Rees of Exhibit A Books, who came back from vacation and sent me a note saying he "genuinely loved this novel." There is no way to describe what that meant to me – but it's framed and hanging on my office wall where I can see it while I write. Emlyn, and his successor, Bryon Quertermous, have been deft and subtle editors who have improved the book without making it theirs, not mine. I know there are wonderful artists and editors over in England somewhere who have made me look better than I have any right to expect but, sadly, I really don't know who they are so they'll just have to accept my generalized thanks – sort of like the rushed end of an Oscar acceptance speech.

I'd like to thank Donald Critchfield, John Herrick, John Rivello, and Ellen Clifford who read the various drafts and let me know when I was heading off a cliff. Finally, I have to acknowledge the dispatcher at Metropolitan Motorcycle Messengers who realized that I had no idea where I was going and sent me to ABC News in 1973 to carry their film around. I have to mention all the incredible producers, correspondents, and technicians at ABC News who gave me the best of professional and personal role models and a career that most people can only dream of.

Author of
WOUNDED PREY

SEAN LYNCH

THE FOURTH MOTIVE

A Farrell and Kearns thriller

Introducing Wm. Shakespeare: Detective.

"The great master who knew everything."
Charles Dickens

> "The smells and sounds of Cambodia are vividly brought to life. Maier is a bold and brave hero."
> Crime Fiction Lover

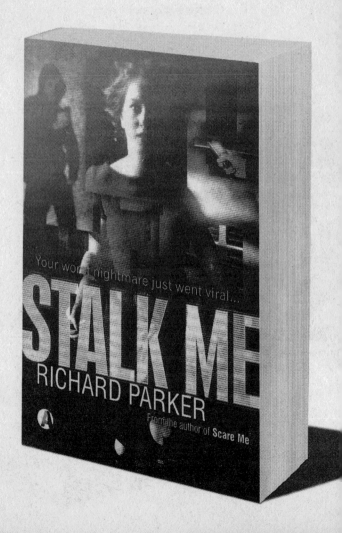

"The action is non-stop, and the blood flies off the page."
Linwood Barclay

PRAY THE COPS FIND YOU FIRST...

THE BALLAD OF MILA

MATTEO STRUKUL

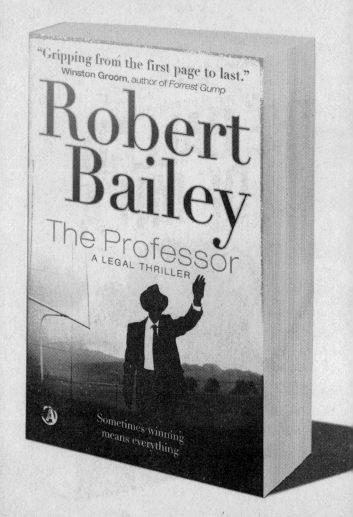